Whistling Artist

Whistling Pines book 7

Dean L. Hovey

Print ISBNs
Amazon Print 9780228623793
LSI Print 9780228623809
B&N Print 9780228623816

Copyright 2022 by Dean Hovey
Cover art by Designs by Christine

This book is a work of fiction, a product of the author's imagination. Any resemblance to actual events, people, or places is coincidental and unintended. Some Two Harbors businesses are used fictionally.

Dedication

To Linda and Bob Smith

Acknowledgement

As always, there is a group of people who deserve credit for helping mold my manuscripts. Brian Johnson is my Two Harbors muse, filling my head with plots, locations, and characters. Without his persistent nudging, the Whistling Pines series wouldn't exist. I turn to Brian when the characters stop speaking to me. I tell him I'm stuck, and he responds with pages of zany ideas that somehow fit into the plot and get my creative juices flowing.

Julie, who tolerates my hours hovering over the keyboard, reads the first draft of each book, offering opinions and correcting medical situations and terminology.

Deanna Wilson willingly reads isolated chapters and out of context fragments of the first draft while correcting errors and urging me on. She's also my police and horse consultant. Margaret Pearson Nelson offered her library resource assistance to add tech detail to the contributions of my fictional librarian in this book. Mike Westfall, Clem MacIlravie, and Fran Brozo read early drafts, offered opinions that steered me to this final version. Anne Flagge and Natalie Lund proofread and removed my myriad typos and grammatical errors.

Many thanks to Jude Pittman of BWL for her editorial help and support.

"Art is not what you see, but what you make others see."
– E. Degas

Prologue

July 17, 1975

Deborah Evenson was putting the final touches on the background of a nearly complete painting when she heard footsteps behind her. Assuming it was her model returning to the studio, she didn't look away from the canvas.

"What the hell?" A male voice exclaimed. "That's Nikki."

With a touch of frustration, Deborah replied, "I know it's Nikki. I've been working on this painting for months."

The man snatched the palette knife from Evenson's hand. "You have no right to paint her nude."

Turning toward the man and picking up a rag, Evenson wiped the paint from her hands. "She's an adult. Her posing for a painting is none of your concern."

"Where's Nikki?"

"Get over it! She's a grown woman."

"Where. Is. Nikki?"

Letting out an exasperated sigh, Evenson replied. "She was going to wash her car."

The man stormed out of the studio.

"Hey! Leave the palette knife!"

Heated voices brought the artist to the window. Nikki, who had a short fuse, waved her hands and swore at the man. In return, he pointed the palette knife at her and swore back. He was still yelling when Nikki got in the car and started the engine. Jumping into the passenger seat, he tried to turn off the engine and remove the keys. The engine raced and the horn blared as Evenson ran out of the house.

With blood dripping from his hands, the man opened the passenger door and stood. "I assume there are a shovel and tarp in the garage." When Evenson failed to move, he yelled. "Don't just stand there, fetch them."

Chapter 1

May 13, 2022

I had no idea who Deborah Evenson was or why her painting hung in Whistling Pines Senior Residence. Her painting dominated the west wall of the residents' lounge, opposite the fireplace. I'd looked at it during my tenure as recreation director, each time noticing some minute detail that had previously escaped me. I watched as Bingle, the Whistling Pines maintenance man, unhooked the huge painting from the mounting bracket and slid it down the ladder.

Howard Johnson, the resident standing alongside me, watched the removal process. "I hate to see it go, but it was technically on loan from the Crowder-Evenson trust."

"How long has it been here?"

"It was apparently loaned to us in the late 1970s, shortly after Whistling Pines was built. I think the Evenson painting and the moose head over the reception desk showed up around the same time."

A crowd of Whistling Pines residents gathered around the painting as it leaned against the wall. Joining them, Howard and I got our first close look at the piece of art, previously hung high on a wall. From my usual vantage point, and depending on the sunlight, I'd either see a landscape with smoke rising from the chimney of a cottage or the silhouette of a tigress. Now, closer to the painting, a whole new set of detail was evident.

Standing only a foot from the painting, the tigress was lost in the detail of the landscape. I was in awe of the artist's ability to change the scene by drawing my eye to different details. "What looked like smoke rising from the cottage's chimney is a swarm of butterflies swirling into the sky."

Howard nodded. "In the years before her death, Deborah Evenson adopted the Salvador Dalí style. He was known for his paintings of melting clocks. She was noted for creating complicated paintings that changed when viewed from different perspectives."

What appeared to be the cottage when the painting was high on the wall, now appeared to be a burial crypt when viewed from a foot away. The blades of grass around the cottage/crypt were thousands of tiny people reaching toward the swirling butterflies. The orange sun, in the upper right corner, was an accumulation of tiny yellow, orange, and red crosses. I looked at the six-foot high painting again and saw hundreds of tiny details that had escaped me when I'd viewed the painting from afar.

I felt a sharp pain in my right foot, and a shoulder jabbed me in the ribs. "Quit hogging the view," Hulda Packer, the resident responsible for most of the misinformation circulating in the Whistling Pines rumor mill, said as she rolled her walker across my foot. I stepped back and let her push through the people gathered in front of me. Stopping with her nose nearly touching the painting, she hesitated. I assumed she was taking in the enormity of the highly detailed and delicate painting until she spun her walker, rolling it over my foot again. "It's a mess. I can't make out anything."

Howard smiled at me after Hulda passed, "Everyone's a critic."

I chuckled. "There's a great Benjamin Franklin quote about critics. 'Any fool can criticize, condemn and complain and most fools do.'"

Ginny Johnson followed behind Hulda and leaned close as she passed. "Hulda has a hard time identifying the pictures in our paint-by-numbers classes. She was sure Abraham Lincoln was an elephant in a top hat."

After Ginny passed, Howard and I moved closer to the painting. "Evenson's art was wasted here," he commented. "This is a museum piece."

"Where is it going?" I asked.

"The Tweed Museum at the university in Duluth, is hosting an Evenson show. They're pulling out the pieces they have in storage. They've also borrowed Evenson art from private collections and the Minneapolis Museum of Modern Art."

"The Tweed Museum had pieces that weren't on display?"

Howard led me toward the dining room where the late breakfast crowd was eating. "Deborah Evenson was an art student at UMD in the 1960s. They have a large collection of her early works from that period. I understand that many of them were rough, while she developed her sense of style. After graduation, she built a studio on a hillside overlooking Two Harbors. That's where she refined her style and created paintings like that one."

Stopping by the dining room door, I frowned. "Most recent college graduates don't have the money to rent a studio, much less build one."

Howard's smile told me I was missing something important. "Deborah Evenson had a benefactor who built the studio and supported her until she gained notoriety."

"Aah."

"Have you heard of Charles Crowder?"

"The Crowder name is familiar, but I don't know why."

Howard leaned back, preparing to teach. "Reread your Minnesota history. Charles Crowder was an astute Chicago railroad magnate. Coming late to the iron ore rush, he saw the patchwork of mines and mining leases. Realizing that the iron ore probably ran in veins rather than pockets, he bought up the mineral rights between the patchwork of mines. He then made a killing when the high-grade ore pockets were mined out and the mining companies realized how foolish they'd been to focus on individual mines instead of the bigger picture.

The Crowders became very rich by leasing their mining claims. In addition to buying large houses and setting up trusts for future generations of the family, Charles established the Crowder Foundation. It's one of the largest charities in the U.S., directing virtually all of its endowments to the arts."

"Like Carnegie, Vanderbilt, Hill, and Rockefeller. They made millions and millions early in their lives, then spent their later years establishing libraries, charities, and universities."

Howard smiled, hinting at my naivete. "They made their fortunes off the labor of the people they abused. Then, sensing their approaching mortality, tried to redeem themselves to their maker before standing before the pearly gates."

"And Deborah Evenson was a beneficiary of a Crowder endowment."

Howard's eyes sparkled. "Charles Crowder was Deborah Evenson's...I suppose sugar daddy might be the wrong phrase to describe their relationship. I heard that Charles spent a lot of time in Deborah's studio, making sure she had anything she needed or wanted. I'm sure he felt as if he was her patron. Personally, I think he held the purse strings with iron fingers, extracting from her as much as he gave."

"He was her patron," I said. "I suppose she was like most artists, needing a financial backer so she didn't have to wait tables."

Blanche Martin was standing near the dining room door within earshot of us while awaiting her usual tablemates. She turned to us, looking disgusted. "Charlie Crowder was in his eighties when Debbie and I were in college. He gave her money and gifts. But he also spent a lot of nights in the studio he built for her. I can assure you that he wasn't posing for a portrait…if you get my drift."

Digesting Blanche's comments, I looked at Howard. "Is that how you saw it?"

"Old Charlie got something in return for whatever he gave anyone. He donated to politicians and got preferential treatment of his business interests. He donated to build a shelter for the homeless but made sure it was located far from his hotel. I'm sure he exacted some payment from Deborah Evenson in return for his patronage."

"You think she was his mistress."

Howard raised his eyebrows. "It doesn't matter what I think. The *town* thought that's what she was. I don't know otherwise."

Howard took a step toward the dining room, but I stopped him. "Who would know?"

"She was a recluse who didn't socialize with anyone in town. I doubt she confided in anyone. Why would she put her life's work at risk by casting aspersions on the person who was enabling her?"

"*Who indeed,*" I said to myself as Howard walked away.

Chapter 2

The removal of the Evenson painting stirred dozens of discussions. Most of them were rumor-filled musings about Crowder and his relationship to Deborah Evenson. I listened, avoiding engagement in a topic that was beyond my knowledge.

I caught Jenny, who was my wife and the Whistling Pines Nursing Director, in her office. Hoping to tap into her local experience, I asked, "What do you know about Deborah Evenson?"

Jenny looked up from the computer. "I'm not a patron of the arts, so my knowledge is limited. She was a darling of the local communities when I was growing up. She judged art competitions at area high schools and spoke to school children and adults about drawing, painting, and the process of creating an artistic work."

"Did you ever hear her speak?"

"She came to my ninth-grade art class. She was absolutely beautiful both physically and in personality. She had endless patience and offered pointers rather than criticism. Everyone was inspired by her." Jenny peeked over my shoulder. "I'd say the boys were inspired by her physical presence more than her art. It's safe to say every boy had a crush on her."

"Ahh, she was attractive."

Jenny smiled. "Deborah Evenson exuded sensuality. She wore tight-fitting jeans and sweaters with plunging necklines."

Ignoring the vibration of my cell phone, I asked, "What do you know about her relationship with Charles Crowder?"

"I don't know anything except unfounded rumors," Jenny replied, reaching for her ringing phone. "Hi, Nancy." She listened to the Whistling Pines executive director. "He's sitting here. Let me put you on speaker."

"Why haven't you responded to any of my calls or texts, Peter?"

"I assumed my incoming phone calls were either my mother, Jenny's mother, or telemarketers. I don't answer any of them during work hours."

After a sigh, Nancy said, "Come down to my office with Jenny. I've got a favor to ask."

Jenny disconnected the call with a frown. "Why would Nancy want to see us together?"

I stood and looked at my cell phone, noting six text messages from Nancy and several phone calls. "I don't have a clue, but she's called me repeatedly."

Nancy met us in the hallway and closed the door after we walked into her office. "Do you have plans for this evening?"

Jenny and I looked at each other. Jenny shrugged. "Nothing special. We usually watch television after doing the supper dishes."

"Good. Find a sitter for the night and dig out your fanciest clothes. You're going to the opening of the Evenson Art Exhibit."

Jenny shifted uncomfortably. "This is kind of short notice for a sitter."

Nancy reached across her desk and dialed the assistant director while we waited. "Wendy, you're babysitting Peter and Jenny's children tonight." My mouth must've fallen open because Nancy smiled. "I'm paying you overtime," she told Wendy.

After listening for a moment, Nancy hung up and smiled. "Any other issues?"

"What's going on?" Jenny asked.

"Because we contribute to the Tweed Museum, Whistling Pines was given two tickets for the Evenson show opening. My husband has a customer meeting, which puts you two next in line as the best Whistling Pines ambassadors."

"We're hardly art aficionados," I protested.

"All you have to do is show up, sip wine, sample appetizers, and make general comments about how impressive the exhibit is." Nancy stood, signaling the end of the conversation. "You're free to leave work now if you need time to put up your hair and get dressed."

"I've got charts," Jenny protested.

"They'll still be here in the morning."

* * *

15

With Amy fed and asleep, Wendy and Jeremy ate hamburgers, then set up the Monopoly game. Jenny put on makeup, then chose a simple black dress and a strand of pearls. I wore my all-purpose wedding and funeral suit. Holding the kitchen door for her, I pecked Jenny's cheek. "You look beautiful."

"I feel like I'm going to be over my head."

We waved goodnight to Wendy and Jeremy as dice rattled on the dining room table. "I own that railroad," Wendy said. Jeremy grumbled as he counted out money for the rent.

I closed Jenny's door and got into the car. "I'd be much more comfortable going to a music recital, or even a funeral."

"Hmm, I wonder if your mother will be there?"

I froze. "Why did you even mention that?"

"I'm just curious. Isn't this the kind of thing she goes to?"

I got in the car, started the engine, and blew out a breath. "I suppose this is probably the type of event my mother likes to attend."

"We haven't seen her in weeks," Jenny said as I drove toward town.

"You say that like it's a bad thing."

"She's your mother..."

"And I'm pleased we live thirty miles away so she can't drop in on us."

* * *

The Tweed Museum of Art is buried in the University of Minnesota-Duluth campus behind the student union. We found a metered parking spot and followed a well-dressed couple past Kirby Hall and through a maze of hallways to the Tweed Museum entrance.

Jenny pulled me close as we waited in a short line. "I loved UMD. Walking these hallways brings back fond memories."

The woman in front of us turned and smiled. "The architects paid wonderful homage to Duluth. All the academic buildings are connected with hallways or tunnels, so students never have to step outside during our daunting winter weather. It can be -30 with a raging blizzard and everyone is in shirtsleeves as they go from class to class."

"I loved going to school here," Jenny said, smiling at the woman who was my mother's age.

The gentleman, dressed in a tuxedo, turned and nodded. "Our grandson is an engineering student. We're pleased that he chose UMD, although I wish he was as interested in his studies as he is in the cute art student who consumes his free time."

The woman weighed her words. With a sly smile asked, "How is that different from our days here, dear?"

"I think that's the point I was making, dear," he replied.

Our conversation ended when the line moved ahead. A young woman holding a clipboard, probably a working student, smiled at me. "Your names, please."

"Peter and Jenny Rogers," I said.

Running her finger down the list, she nodded and put a check next to our names. "Ah, you're the Whistling Pines representatives. Audrey Rogers asked if you'd arrived yet."

A chance meeting with my mother was unlikely, so I glanced at Jenny who said, "I told her we'd be at the opening of the Evenson exhibit."

With a gentle squeeze of my arm, Jenny signaled me to play nice. I nodded. "Ah, my mother is here."

"She was with the curator earlier. They were discussing Ms. Evenson's later works, displayed on the back wall."

Jenny held my arm like we were entering the grand ballroom. Murmured conversations surrounded us as people stood in front of paintings, sipping wine. A male student in a white shirt and dark pants approached us with a silver tray. "White wine or cider?"

I was about to sip my cider when I heard Mother's distinctive laugh. I looked at Jenny, who smiled. "Follow the sound of your mother's bangles."

My mother was speaking to three couples while hanging onto the arm of a man wearing a lavender suit. I glanced at Jenny. "I'm betting Mom's escort is a politician."

"I'll take that bet. No local politician would be caught dead in a purple suit. They all wear a *full Norwegian*."

"What's a full Norwegian?"

"It's a dark blue suit with a red tie. It was the only outfit I ever saw Vice President Walter Mondale wear."

Mother sensed our approach and turned. Her smile was genuine and broad. She hugged Jenny and winked at me. "I'm so pleased you're here." She touched the elbow of her companion who turned, revealing his white silk shirt and yellow ascot. "Jenny and Peter are my daughter-in-law and son. This is Ewell Blankenship, the museum curator."

Shaking hands, Ewell smiled politely. "Audrey is one of our most generous patrons. She was very pleased when she saw your names on the guest list."

"We were offered the opportunity to attend the event at the last moment," I said.

Mother held Jenny's hand like they were long lost friends. "I'm amazed you could find a sitter for the children on short notice."

"One of our co-workers offered to watch the kids," Jenny replied. "Jeremy and Wendy were playing Monopoly when we left."

Ewell laughed. "Oh my, I haven't thought about Monopoly in thirty years." He drew a breath, then nodded to the nearby wall. "I know you recognize Evenson's *Cabin in the Glade.* It's been on display at Whistling Pines for decades."

Mother nodded. "It's so nice to be able to display it with the companion piece, *Cottage on the Cliff.*"

I looked at the familiar painting. Then, my eyes followed Mother's gaze to an adjacent wall where

19

a painting the same size, with a similar color scheme, was hung.

I looked back and forth at the two pieces, then turned to Ewell. "They're backwards."

"What?" he asked, cocking his head.

"Visualize them reversed," I said. "The cabin picture should be displayed to the left of the cottage picture. Look at the colors."

A small group of patrons had gathered, waiting to speak with the curator. Having overheard my comment, the dozen people all stared at the two large paintings.

A woman with a diamond necklace dangling into her cleavage pointed to the cottage painting. "That young man is correct. I think these were painted as a diptych."

"What's a diptych?" Jenny whispered.

Leaning close to her ear, I replied, "A diptych is a pair of paintings created to show a single scene. They're always displayed together."

The curator stepped forward and asked the patrons to step back from the paintings so they could be viewed unobstructed from across a broader space. Crossing his arms and cocking his head, he considered the two paintings. "I think Peter's correct."

The curator turned and disappeared into the crowd. Mother stared at the pictures, then looked at me. "I didn't know you had an artistic eye."

"I'm not artistic, but the arrangement of those two paintings seems wrong."

After looping her arm around mine, Jenny looked at Mother. "Peter's artistry isn't limited to music. He's a right-brain person—able to see patterns in music, color, and art. That's how he plays music by ear."

It became a rare occasion when my mother looked at me like she actually saw me as an adult, not the child she remembered. "Of course! That makes so much sense."

With four male students in tow, the curator returned. They rearranged paintings so the cottage and cabin pictures were alongside each other on the same wall. Ewell stood back and drew a breath. "My God, they *are* a diptych!"

Jenny's hand tightened on my arm, and I looked at her. "Peter, they're breathtaking. They were impressive apart, but together, they're incredible!"

Hearing Jenny's comments, the curator cocked his head, then drew a breath. "There was a stipulation in Ms. Evenson's will that these two paintings couldn't be shown together until after her death. I wonder why she wouldn't want them displayed like this?"

A crowd started to gather, and I felt their bodies crushing in on me. Seeing a path through the throng, I took Jenny's hand and led her to an area displaying Evenson's earlier works.

"Why did you pull me out of the crowd?" Jenny asked.

"It felt too much like being jammed into an overcrowded Humvee. I couldn't breathe."

Framed by the diptych, the curator was expounding on the themes Deborah Evenson had explored in that pair of paintings. We listened for a few minutes, then Jenny turned to me. I expected her to comment on the art. Instead, she smiled and said, "Don't you think Ewell Blankenship looks like an iris?"

"What?" I asked, positioning myself so I could see the curator in his lavender suit.

"The purple splits at his chest and his silk shirt draws my eye to the yellow ascot. He looks like an iris in full bloom."

Laughing, I turned away and led her to the exit. "I'm not sure the curator was going for an iris look when he chose that outfit. But I can't argue with your take on his appearance."

"We're leaving?" Jenny asked. "Wendy doesn't expect us home until ten o'clock."

"We've made our appearance, representing Whistling Pines. Let's take advantage of a couple hours alone and do something special."

Squeezing my hand as we walked toward the student union, Jenny's pace sped up. "Let's go to a movie. It's been ages since we saw a movie with romance or even strong language. I'm tired of SpongeBob and Mystery Rangers. Let's go to a romcom, buy popcorn, and pretend we're on a date."

"We could have a quiet dinner and eat warm food without cutting up the children's meals."

"I'd rather go to a movie."

Chapter 3

I was less than sparkling the morning after our date night. The movie we'd seen was a sappy, funny, and heartwarming romantic comedy. Jenny held my hand throughout the evening and the quiet time without Jeremy and Amy brought back memories of how we'd fallen in love.

With a cup of coffee in hand, I walked through the Whistling Pines dining room during the breakfast rush. I greeted people and listened to discussions of bodily functions, grandchildren, the quality of the food, and pros and cons of the current political situation, both in Minnesota and Washington D.C. There were differences of political opinion, but the talk was civil. To any casual observer, it would appear I was wasting time. In fact, I was "taking the temperature" of the facility.

Howard Johnson, the self-appointed Whistling Pines mayor, waved and pulled out the empty chair at his table. His tablemates, two octogenarians, smiled as I sat. "How was the movie?"

Anyone living in a large city would've been surprised by the question, wondering how someone in a senior residence would've known that I'd been to a movie with my wife the previous evening. In the small town of Two Harbors, there were few secrets. The daily routine for the senior citizens of Whistling Pines was…dull, and news of anything outside the norm, spread quickly.

"I'd rate the movie three and a half stars out of five," I said, taking the empty chair. "The ending was too predictable."

Howard and his tablemates nodded. "I suppose the girl kissed the frog and he turned into a prince."

"That's old school. The girl found a lonely computer programmer on the internet and after weeks of texting they finally met for coffee. He was handsome, witty, and swept her off her feet."

Lee Westfall shook his head. "That's pure fiction. Everyone knows that computer programmers are introverted nerds who can barely communicate."

Chuckling, Howard nodded. "My son told me that an extrovert programmer is one who stares at your shoes when he speaks to you."

Chuck Dahlgren frowned. "I don't get the joke."

"Most programmers are so reserved that they stare at their own shoes when they speak. An extrovert stares at your shoes," Howard explained.

Waving off the explanation, Chuck shook his head. "I still don't get it."

Lee leaned forward and whispered, "I heard you went to the art gallery last night. Were there any racy paintings?" Lee raised his eyebrows suggestively.

"It was an exhibit of Deborah Evenson's work. Like the painting from our lounge, Evenson's paintings tended to be complicated, multi-level images that changed with your viewpoint. I didn't see any nude images in any of them."

Sipping his coffee, Chuck shook his head. "I don't get that kind of painting. I like to look at a piece of art and know what I'm seeing. Those Picasso things were strange. I mean, there's a face here, a hand there, a boob in a triangle on the edge. They look like they were painted by a third-grade student."

"We discovered that the painting that had been displayed here was created as half of a pair," I said. "When the two were displayed side by side, they looked different than each by itself."

Howard brightened. "They were a diptych."

"I'm amazed that you know that word. It's not part of most people's vocabulary."

"I know a lot of things, Peter. Most of them are so deeply buried in my brain I can't bring them out. Diptych jumped to the front of my brain when you mentioned the two pictures that were meant to be displayed as a pair." Howard paused. "I wonder why was one of the paintings hung here without the other?"

"The museum curator said there was a clause in Deborah Evenson's will that said the diptych wasn't to be displayed together until after her death."

Lee cocked his head. "Was there something that embarrassed her when the two paintings were together?"

"Not that I saw," I said. "The half taken from our lounge showed a cottage in the woods. The half that's been displayed in the UMD art department showed a cabin on a windswept Lake Superior shoreline. They looked nice together, but I didn't see anything that made me think they shouldn't have been displayed together, as they'd been painted."

Howard stroked his chin, deep in thought. "Debbie Evenson was a bit of an enigma. She was immensely talented and was generous with her time. I believe she went to every art class in the region, inspiring the students and offering tips on painting." Howard paused. "On the other hand, she lived alone in her studio in the hills above Two Harbors. She had a male patron. It's rumored that he stayed with her when he was in town. As I recall, she was close to one of the UMD art professors who brought students to Evenson's studio to both learn from and to model for her."

Lee snorted. "As if anyone would recognize any of the models she painted. Her pictures were such a mess of things, they reminded me of…a collage."

Karla Telker was sitting with her back to me. I heard her chair slide back, then she whispered in my ear. "Don't believe everything those old codgers tell you. Debbie came to my classroom every year. She was a dear woman who exuded talent and inspiration."

Chuck coughed. "My son was in one of your art classes and Debbie inspired him. She was the only thing he talked about for three days. He was more inspired by her sweater than her art."

"Debbie was very attractive," Karla agreed. "I think that was one of her challenges. She struggled to get people to look past her appearance to see what she was creating."

Chuck rubbed his bulbous nose, a spider web of red capillaries. "It would've been easier to look past her appearance if she'd worn bulky sweatshirts and baggy pants."

Karla drew a deep breath and glared. "Chuck, you are the poster child of the 'Me-Too movement.'"

"Me-Too? Are we talking about drinking? If we are, then I'm all in, me too."

Wendy's distinctive laugh came from one table over. "See! That's what we women endure." Her words were sharp, but she had a broad grin.

Clenching his eyes shut, Howard shook his head. "The Me-Too movement addresses the sexual abuse of women, Chuck. It started with Hollywood starlets speaking out about exploitation by male producers and directors, then spread as women spoke up about similar abuses across many industries."

Lee nodded. "The Hollywood casting couch."

Karla slid her chair next to me. "That's used as an example of the blatant acceptance of powerful men abusing their positions of power."

Dolores, my former neighbor and the benefactor who gave Jenny and me the deed to her house as a wedding present, was sitting at the table with Karla. "Deborah Evenson gave many gifts to Two Harbors. Some of the residents, like Chuck, were oblivious to them."

"Thank you, Dolores," Karla said, nodding. "The community benefited from many of Evenson's gifts."

Hulda Packer, one of our most vocal and confused residents, stopped at the dining room door. "Peter, get your butt over here. It's time for the painting club."

I glanced at the others, who were all smiling. "I guess I'd better fire up the van and drive the students to their art class."

Lee placed his hand on my arm as I stood. "Are they improving? I saw a couple of Hulda's paint-by-numbers pictures and...I guess I didn't know that Abe Lincoln had an elephant trunk nose."

Dolores leaned close. "That wasn't Abraham Lincoln. It was Jimmy Durante."

"I don't think so. Durante used to wear a bowler hat. The elephant was wearing a top hat."

I left the discussion and went to my office to get the keys for the van. Kathy Christensen fell in step beside me. "I'm somewhat concerned about our art class."

"What concerns you?"

Kathy is slim with a huge personality. "We agreed that it's time for the art class to move on from bowls of fruit." She paused and said, "Hulda suggested we hire a human model."

I set my coffee cup on the desk and retrieved the key ring from a peg behind the door while I chose my words. "It's a big jump from peaches and oranges to drawing a human body."

"Especially if you're drawing nudes."

Freezing mid-step, I turned to Kathy. "You're joking."

"Hulda told Melissa, our instructor, that she thought we should hire a nude model. Nearly everyone agreed to chip in to pay the modeling fee."

I took Kathy's elbow and steered her down the hallway, toward the lobby. I pictured the people in the van. The dozen art students were all women. "Let me guess. Hulda wants a male model."

Kathy's grin unsettled me.

"You're kidding me, right?"

"Nope. Hulda and Melissa were talking about getting one of the male UMD art students to model for us. Melissa knows one of the professors. I guess people routinely post modeling openings on an art department bulletin board."

"Are you pro or anti nude modeling?" I asked.

Most of us are Scandinavians and…well…we don't even hug our relatives, much less look at naked bodies."

"I sense a but coming," I said as we passed through the front door.

"Melissa assured us that the modeling would be tasteful and…well…artistic."

"I'll talk to Melissa," I said before jogging past the line of art students to the van.

* * *

Melissa's art studio was in a space that had once been a shoe store. The windows overlooking the street were filled with easels displaying paintings for sale. While most were Melissa's work, others were consignments from her best students. None of the Whistling Pines artists had their work for sale.

After helping the ladies exit the van, I followed them into the studio that had once been a storeroom. Melissa had converted the space, using lots of overhead fixtures that provided oblique lighting. A dozen easels were arranged around a platform. Melissa covered a table with a checkered tablecloth. On top of the tablecloth were a bottle of chianti wine in a wicker wrapper, a wedge of Parmesan cheese, and a cut glass cylinder filled with spaghetti noodles. My first thought was that the display was a big jump from a bowl of fruit. None of the students seemed concerned by the complexity of the subject matter as they migrated near the back of the room to pick up their supplies.

I approached Kathy, who was arranging a blank sheet of paper on her easel. "How do you feel about drawing the wine, cheese, and spaghetti?"

Cocking her head, Kathy considered the display. "This really won't be any more challenging than trying to shade the fruit and the shadows cast behind it."

"But the cut glass cylinder casts lots of shadows. Drawing the woven chianti basket will be difficult."

I got *the look,* letting me know I was missing something. Kathy glanced at the rear wall where the ladies were lining up. "They're picking up supplies," I said.

"They're filling their wine glasses, Peter. This class has very little to do with drawing and everything to do with sipping wine and listening to Melissa. She regales us with stories about painting on the West Bank during the `60's while being seduced by cute French men who sipped wine in quaint sidewalk cafés."

I followed Kathy to the wine line. Melissa was dispensing wine from the plastic tap on the side of a box. She laughed as the women spoke, and I realized that Melissa had a head start on the drinking. After bypassing the line, I put my hand on Melissa's shoulder. "Don't over serve my residents. I don't want to clean up vomit after our return van trip."

Melissa tipped her head back and roared, as if I'd told her the funniest joke she'd ever heard. "Peter, wine and art go together like flowers and sunshine."

"I heard a rumor that the class is ready to move to more challenging projects."

"We've had discussions about using a human model. Are you interested?"

"In starting the class?"

Melissa laughed again. "As the model!"

She stepped back, slowly examining me from head to foot. I'd never felt like someone had visually undressed me, but Melissa's inspection made me feel like I should cover my crotch with my hands. Flashing back to the Me-Too discussion at breakfast, I had a better appreciation of how women feel when being ogled.

"Um, no. My job description doesn't include modeling."

"I pay $200 per session."

"No."

"You wouldn't be totally naked. I'd drape a sheet tastefully across your thigh so none of your male attributes would be visible to the students." She paused, then smiled, "Or wouldn't you need anything larger than a handkerchief to cover yourself?"

"My male attributes are quite happy inside my tighty-whities," I said.

Melissa's sly smile made me squirm. "Hmm, I mistook you for a boxer guy."

With words escaping me, I stepped back, nearly tumbling over Hulda Packer, who'd overheard my conversation with Melissa.

In typical Hulda fashion, she'd heard half the conversation and then misconstrued the rest. She looked at me, then wrinkled her nose. "I'd rather have a real beefcake model. Peter's kind of skinny for my tastes."

I fled for the door before anyone else weighed in on my modeling credentials or underwear choice.

Chapter 4

I chose to spend the 90 minutes in my office making signs for the weekly movie. Inspired by the art class, I reviewed movie options and chose *Gauguin the Savage*, a story about the painter's struggles to find himself, eventually travelling to Tahiti, the site of his most memorable paintings.

I'd just started printing the signs when I heard someone step into my tiny office. "How do you tune a Jedi tuba?"

Brian Johnson, the tuba player from the Two Harbors band, sat in my guest chair. Brian had inserted himself into my life after I'd rendered first aid to a band member who'd been poisoned during a concert. His presence was always announced with a joke. I turned and said, "I don't know. How do you tune a Jedi tuba?"

"You use the fourth."

I let out a groan, which made Brian laugh. "Do you get it? A Jedi uses the force, and a tuba player uses the fourth?"

"Yes, I got it. Do you have a special reason to visit," I asked, "or did you just stop by to tell me your sick joke?"

Brian's grin turned to a pout. "You don't have to be insulting."

I waved off his comment, knowing his years of telling sick tuba jokes had left him with a thick skin. "What's up?"

"I heard you were investigating Deborah Evenson's death."

Brian's comment caught me off guard. "I thought her death was natural."

"The obituary was a summation of her life and accomplishments. It didn't list her cause of death."

"I'm not an expert on obituaries, but I rarely see what caused the person's death. There's often a note requesting donations to a charity related to the decedent's death, like the American Cancer Society, or Breast Cancer Awareness, but I don't recall any obituary actually identifying the cause of death."

Brian nodded. "Especially murders. There might be a newspaper article about the murder investigation, but they never say that a tuba player was drowned in beer. Nope. Never."

Feeling my chain being yanked, I closed my eyes. "Is all this leading to a punchline?"

"No, no, no. I was just saying…"

"Saying that no one has ever reported a tuba player being drowned in beer."

Sitting up straighter, Brian continued, his eyes sparkling. "Did you hear about the two tuba players who walked past a bar?"

"Um, no I didn't hear about them."

Brian stood, still smiling. "That's because two tuba players have never walked past a bar without walking in."

"Goodbye, Brian."

"See you later, Doc."

Karla Telker stepped aside to let Brian exit my former broom closet turned office. "I overheard Brian's comments about Deborah Evenson's death. My son was one of the EMTs dispatched to Deborah's house when she fell. She had a broken hip that was repaired in Duluth. She developed pneumonia and succumbed to that."

"Thank you for that clarification."

Karla nodded. "There were a dozen crazy stories flying around the dining room and I thought you should know the truth so you can help throw water on the flaming rumors."

"I hope you did that when you heard them."

Pausing, with a smile, Karla shook her head. "I didn't."

"Why not?"

"People have fun enhancing the rumors. It's rather like when we played *telephone* as children. Someone would whisper a phrase, then it was repeated around a circle until it came back to the beginning. The words and message were always twisted and misheard, rendering the original message little more than a noun in a long sentence of modified verbs and adjectives."

"But…"

Karla put up her hand. "It's not my job to ruin the fun. I rather enjoy hearing the changing story through the course of a day."

"Hulda overhearing the story guarantees that it will be twisted and confused."

"Yes, especially now that she's trying to save money by not replacing the batteries in her hearing aids."

"I suppose you expect me to communicate the correct story."

"That's your job, isn't it?" With that question, Karla was gone.

I was halfway to the residents' lounge when I spotted Jenny walking toward me. I stepped into the alcove outside the hair salon and waited for her. "What's up?" I asked.

"How much do you know about Deborah Evenson?"

"I'd hardly heard of her before yesterday."

"What have you learned since yesterday?"

"She was a very creative artist, who shared her talent freely, until she died of pneumonia after hip surgery."

Jenny's brow was furrowed, and she glanced around to see if anyone could overhear us. "There's more."

"More? Would you care to elaborate?" I asked.

"Depending on who you believe, she was either a generous mentor who helped dozens of young artists hone their skills, or she was a predator taking advantage of young artists and models."

"Which was she?" I asked.

"I don't know. I only saw the supportive mentoring side of her. There are rumors about the stream of young people lured to her studio to model for her, then plied with alcohol before being taken advantage of in their weakened state."

I nodded to a pair of residents who walked past while composing my reply. "People look for sinister motives in things that happen in private settings."

Jenny lowered her voice. "I know. Two Harbors is a small town and Deborah Evenson was an outsider who lived remotely. She had contacts in the art community and there's little question that she mentored several UMD art students every year. People saw college students entering and leaving her secluded property with no idea who they were or why they were there."

"And people assume the worst because it makes the best stories." I checked the hallway for eavesdroppers. "Brian Johnson hinted that there were questions about Evenson's death. Shortly after that, Karla Telker told the true story about Evenson's hospital death from natural causes."

"I've heard rumors from her committing suicide to being murdered. On top of that, I was told that she'd killed her art professor after her college graduation."

"If she'd killed her professor, she'd be in prison. I'd discount that as pure rumor."

Jenny put her hand on my arm. "Call Kerry and ask about the professor. After that, you should take a walk through the dining room. You need to throw water on some rumors."

As Jenny walked away, I dug my cell phone from my pocket and punched in Kerry's direct number. "How can I help my favorite guitar player?"

"Hello to you, Chief. I'm doing fine. Thanks for asking."

"I don't feel the need to indulge in foreplay with you."

"Social graces are foreplay to you Army-type guys?"

"It's more a cop than an Army thing. In the words of Sergeant Joe Friday, 'Just the facts, ma'am.'" Then he paused. "You're right, it is an Army thing. No officer engages in small talk."

"Jenny heard a rumor that Deborah Evenson killed her college art professor. Can you check on that?"

"I seriously doubt…"

"Yeah, me too. But I need to quash that rumor, and facts are the most effective rumor killer."

"Hang on. Do you think that crime occurred here in Two Harbors or in Duluth?"

I heard computer keys clicking in slow deliberate keystrokes as Kerry entered data with his unscarred hand. The fingers of his other hand were covered with pink scar tissue and didn't flex much.

"Like most rumors, there are very few facts accompanying the basic information. Let's assume the art professor died after Evenson moved to Two Harbors."

"Well, Evenson was never arrested for anything. She had a few speeding tickets, but aside from those, she had no criminal record."

"Is there some way to see if there was an unsolved murder?"

"If the murder was back in the '70s, it'd be an open case in a dusty file cabinet. It might be faster to ask your residents or search newspaper archives. Why don't you call the library?"

"*Me*?"

"Yeah, just call the librarian…"

"Why am I calling the librarian? I'm not a cop."

"It's not a police case, Peter. You're trying to put a stopper into the rumor mill leaks."

I sighed. "Fine."

I made the call. Margaret Jensen, Two Harbors' new librarian, promised to look for a newspaper article about the murder of a UMD art professor. After the call, I walked to the dining room with my coffee cup. The room was empty except for two men playing cribbage and Wendy, who was working on a crossword puzzle in the back corner. After drawing coffee from the urn, I walked to Wendy's table and sat down. Officially the assistant director of Whistling Pines, Wendy filled in wherever she was needed. Because her job was unstructured, I sometimes found her working on a crossword in the dining room.

Wendy set her pencil aside and looked around. "I heard Deborah Evenson invited young men to her studio to do more than model. She was quite a…"

Cutting off what I feared would be an explicit word, I said, "I think the politically correct term is, 'tart.'"

Wendy shrugged. "That works."

39

"Deborah Evenson is today's topic of discussion?" I asked.

"A lot of the residents remember her although no one seems to have known her. That doesn't stop most of them from repeating rumors about her reclusive lifestyle. Most however, assume she was doing something illegal or immoral in her studio."

"Like what?"

"The usual array of immoral acts attributed to reclusive single women. Sex. Drugs. Alcohol."

After helping Wendy with two crossword clues, I walked to Dolores' apartment. She invited me in and turned down the game show playing on the television. "It's nice to have a moment to chat. Please tell me that the rabbits haven't destroyed my hollyhocks."

"We haven't had time to do much gardening with the new baby and Jeremy's school and Cub Scout commitments."

"Of course," she said. "I just think back and miss the time I spent weeding and nurturing the flowers. I found weeding very cathartic."

My thoughts on weeding flowerbeds ran more toward torture, but I held my tongue. "What do you know about Deborah Evenson?"

"She built a studio up the hill from town. Aside from that, she kept to herself."

"Did you know her personally?"

"Not at all. She travelled in artistic circles and my interests were more associated with my church and the Republican party."

"I see. The artistic circles and Republican circles didn't intersect?"

Dolores scoffed. "Artistic people, like your mother, tend to view the world as a place that can be improved with other people's money. Republicans view the world as a place where people can pull themselves up by their bootstraps, where money should be kept by the people who earned it instead of being doled out to people suckling at the government teat."

Ignoring Dolores' political incorrectness, I changed the topic. "I heard that Deborah Evenson's art professor disappeared."

Dolores stared out the window before answering. "I think it was about 1974. Her professor moved into the studio with Evenson, which set the rumors flying. The professor had been living with Evenson for a couple years. Then one day she was gone."

"Gone, as in moved away?"

"No one seemed to know. I don't like to indulge in rumors, but the predominant theory was that the professor developed artistic differences with Evenson and moved on."

"It's rare for tenured professors to leave their faculty positions."

"I'm not sure if the professor was tenured, and I'm not convinced she left willingly."

"What do you mean?"

"Deborah Evenson had a benefactor." Dolores paused, searching her memory. "He was a railroad man from Chicago. Yes, Charles Crowder was his name. I think he had a soft spot for Evenson, and he wasn't interested in supporting both Deborah and her live-in professor."

"Do you think Crowder threw the professor out?"

"I think it's more likely that he gave her a one-way ticket to Paris, then shipped her clothes afterward."

"What else do you know about Charles Crowder?"

"I met Charles and Edith Crowder at a few fundraisers. He always wore a suit, and Edith wore designer dresses. They knew how to socialize and made generous donations to local charities."

"Did they live in Two Harbors?"

"Heavens no! They lived in the cultural center of the Midwest, Chicago."

"Chicago is the cultural center of the Midwest?"

After staring at me for a moment while trying to decide if I was uninformed or impertinent, Dolores composed herself. "After Mrs. O'Leary's cow burned down most of the city, Chicagoans worked hard to build a city of culture intended to rival New York. They built performing arts theaters to rival Broadway, the Lyric and Lithuanian opera houses, the Joffrey Ballet, numerous art galleries in the West Loop and River North districts, the Museum of Science and Industry, the Field Museum of Natural History, Adler Planetarium, Shedd Aquarium, and the Lincoln Park Zoo. Charles or

Edith were on the boards of half of those institutions, and they worked hard to bring exhibits and theater troupes to town."

"I'm confused. If they were such great patrons of Chicago art, why were they in Two Harbors?"

Dolores reveled in her knowledge. "Charles made his money building railroads and leasing mineral rights. He followed in the footsteps of the rail barons of the 1800s like J. J. Hill. He found areas that were unable to deliver goods from remote areas to the industrial and shipping hubs of the U.S. While building rail lines to the iron ore mines, he bought promising tracts of timber and lower grade iron ore in northern Minnesota. His rail lines terminated at Two Harbors and Duluth, which brought him to the region. He and Edith helped the local shipping and mining barons develop art and higher educational centers of northeastern Minnesota."

"They discovered Deborah Evenson?"

"I don't know if they discovered Deborah, but Charles gave some of her paintings to museums in Chicago and New York. Evenson's name became known internationally within a few years, and her works were sold by New York art auctions."

"That's a big jump for a young woman freshly graduated from UMD."

"Charles took her under his wing. He built her Two Harbors studio and provided for her until she could sustain herself through art sales."

"What did Crowder get out of it?"

Dolores had been speaking dreamily until I'd asked the last question. She stiffened and replied, "I don't participate in rumor mongering."

"I'm sure there were rumors about improprieties between Deborah Evenson and Charles Crowder."

Dolores drew a breath and looked out her window. "Before Deborah's studio was built, Charles kept a suite in a Duluth hotel. Once the studio was built, he gave up the suite and stayed at Evenson's studio when he came to Two Harbors."

"I'm surprised Crowder's wife put up with that arrangement."

"As I recall, Edith Crowder passed away in the late 1960s, shortly before the Evenson studio was constructed."

"It sounds like there may have been a May/December romance between Deborah and Charles."

"I attended an Evenson event in Duluth about 1970. Charles left me with the impression he thought of Deborah as his protégé or daughter, rather than his lover." Dolores paused and looked from the window to me. "I can't say the same for Deborah's professor. She and Deborah were close. Too close."

"Do you recall the professor's name?"

Dolores leaned her head back, trying to dredge up the name. "Annika! Deborah referred to her as Dr. Annika. I think her surname was Banks. Yes. As I recall, Professor Banks had a touch of gray in her hair, so she was probably forty-five or fifty years old. It was somewhat pathetic. Dr. Banks hung on Deborah, who was a recent college graduate, like ivy."

"I've heard two versions of the professor's departure. One is she moved away; The other is she was murdered."

"I recall discussion about Dr. Banks' disappearance, but I don't have any knowledge of what happened to her." Dolores paused. "I'm aware of a few women who had relationships with other women. Those were often tempestuous and ended badly."

I smiled, "As do many heterosexual relationships."

Dolores' eyes lit up. "Touché."

Chapter 5

I was luxuriating in the shower with hot water pounding on my back when the bathroom door opened. "You've got a phone call," Jenny said.

"Turning off the water, then reaching for a towel, I asked, "Who'd call at this hour of the morning?"

"Ewell Blankenship."

"Did he say what he wanted?" I asked as I dried off and pulled on underwear.

Jenny handed me the cell phone, "He said he wants to speak with you."

"Peter, can you come to the museum as soon as possible?"

"I have to work this morning. I could drive to Duluth after work if you had something pressing."

"There's a morning phenomenon you need to see."

Sitting on the bed with Jenny watching, I said, "You need *me* to see some morning phenomenon?"

"Yes," the curator said.

"Um…why me, and why this morning?"

"You were the person who suggested the two Evenson paintings were a diptych, and you obviously have an eye for nuanced details. I think you'd be the perfect person to view this."

"I'm confused," I said. "Why do I need to see it this morning? Did the paintings get damaged overnight?"

"No, the paintings are fine. It's just that…the janitor noticed something this morning when the sunlight shone obliquely across the diptych. There's something that's not visible under the usual lighting."

"I'm still confused."

"Deborah Evenson put something into the texture of the painting. There's an image that's only visible as a shadow in subdued lighting."

"What's the image?"

"I'd prefer to have your view of it rather than describing what I've seen."

"I'll talk to my boss and ask if I can come in late today."

"Please come quickly. The sunlight is changing."

Jenny watched me as I ended the call. "The curator wants you to drive to Duluth now?"

"Apparently, there's another image in the Evenson diptych that's only visible in the morning light." I pulled on a polo shirt and added, "Tell Nancy I'll be there after I've been to the museum."

"I'm not sure I can explain why you'll be late."

"She wants us to be Whistling Pines ambassadors. Tell her the Tweed Museum needed my consultation."

"Do you think she'll believe that?"

Tying my shoelaces, I shrugged. "I guess we'll find out after I see whatever it is that the museum curator finds so exciting."

* * *

The traffic between Two Harbors and Duluth sped along Highway 61 until it became London Road east of Duluth, and slowed to 30 mph. Although the cars continued to drive well over the speed limit, the traffic became erratic as people slowed to turn.

Familiar with the east end of Duluth, I turned up the hill well before the signs directing people to UMD and The College of St. Scholastica. I enjoyed driving through the comfortable old residential neighborhoods as I climbed up the hill leading away from Lake Superior.

The visitors parking lot across from the student union was nearly empty. Although it irritated me, I paid a parking meter for an hour, knowing that the campus police delighted in ticketing cars parked at expired meters or in no parking zones. Winding through the hallways past the campus bookstore, I approached the museum entrance. The Tweed Museum lights were off, and I expected to find the doors locked, but the door opened. I walked through the Evenson exhibit and found the museum curator in conversation with a female student dressed in jeans, athletic shoes, and a worn t-shirt.

"Peter!" Blankenship exclaimed as I approached them in the darkened room. "I was afraid you were going to miss Sadie's discovery. The rising sun is diminishing the shadows." Blankenship gestured for me to walk toward the wall where the diptych was mounted. The young woman followed. "Sadie, explain what you saw."

"Um, I was sweeping the floor in here. I hadn't seen the two Evenson paintings together, so I was kind of excited about getting to view them without the crowd. As I was going to turn on the lights, I stopped at the switch and looked toward the windows and saw this." She said, gesturing toward the diptych.

Blankenship stepped back, letting the young woman revel in her discovery. "At first, I focused on the colors and images in the painting. Then I focused on the surface of the canvas and the shadows."

As I grasped the shadowy image, my expression must've changed because Blankenship spoke. "It brought to mind Picasso's *Guernica*." Seeing my blank look, he went on. "Guernica was a Spanish City bombed by the Germans during the Spanish Civil War. Picasso captured the pain and tumult of the residents in an abstract painting."

I moved from side to side, hoping to find a spot where the shadows were more distinct. Instead of sharpening the image, I saw more hazy details in the shadows. I looked at Sadie and asked, "Was the image sharper earlier, before I arrived?"

"Not really. I mean, I saw the person sprawled on the ground right away, but as the sun rose,

49

more detail came into view. I mean, I didn't see the devil at first."

"The devil?"

"If you get down on your knees, you get a different perspective," Sadie suggested.

Squatting down, I studied the image and could indeed see a shadowy figure poised over the person lying on her back. "The person above does appear to have tiny horns, doesn't he?"

Sadie sat on the floor with her legs crossed. "I think the devil is about to stab the woman on the ground with his pointed tail. His horse is rearing up in the background."

Blankenship wiped an area of the floor with a handkerchief, then knelt beside us. "It's incredible. I'll have to work with the engineering staff to erect blinds and indirect lighting, so this detail is visible to our evening visitors."

"Are you an art student, Sadie?" I asked.

"I'm a women's studies major, but this…it's inspiring. I might change my major to art."

I took out my cell phone and tried to capture the shadow images without success.

The curator watched my feeble photography attempt. "One of the art professors is a professional photographer. I'll ask him to come over after we erect some lighting. I suspect he'll have better equipment than your cell phone. He uses multiple pictures of the same image with different focuses, then overlays the images to create a single photo with the illusion of depth."

I stood and stretched. "Can you explain how Evenson created the shadow images, Dr. Blankenship?"

The curator led us to the paintings. As expected, the shadow images disappeared as soon as we moved in front of the paintings. "Sadie and I were studying the brushstrokes and texture before you arrived. I..." he let out a sigh and shook his head. Crossing his arms, Blankenship considered the paintings. "I think the artist laid down the texture with a palette knife. She must've spent days or weeks making subtle ridges, then walking to the side where she examined them with oblique lighting. Once she'd created the texture she wanted, I think she painted over it, creating the diptych with the cabin/cottage scenes."

"What do you suppose the tiny Bibles that look like smoke and the cross mean?" Sadie asked.

Blankenship spread his arms, gesturing to the entirety of the two paintings. "Sadie, I think an analysis of these paintings could be the subject of a doctoral dissertation. There are literally dozens of images and themes."

Sadie looked at me. "Are you an art guy?"

"I'm a musician."

"Why did Dr. Blankenship call you to see the dead body?"

From the mouths of babes, I thought. "Half of the diptych was displayed at the place I work, and I noticed that the two paintings appeared to belong together."

"It's really odd," Sadie said. "I mean, you can't see the entire dead body or the devil until you have them together."

I looked toward the curator. "I suppose that's why Deborah Evenson didn't want those two paintings displayed together until after her death. She concealed something she didn't want to face."

"Perhaps the images are meant to be as sinister as they appear."

"I just read *Down Girl* by Kate Manne. She discussed how our male-dominated culture demeans women and keeps them underpaid and subjugated. I wonder if the artist was depicting her own experience with misogyny?"

Sadie's comment threw my thoughts back to my discussion with Dolores. *Had Charles Crowder used his power to control Deborah Evenson? Was he the devil who was stabbing her with his tail while she lay helplessly on the ground?*

"Thank you both," I said. "I'd like to see the painting again after you've constructed the oblique lighting."

Blankenship nodded and smiled. "I'll call the building engineer immediately. Then I'll contact our photography expert. Perhaps we'll have more to talk about in a day or two."

I offered my hand to Sadie. "It took someone special to recognize those shadows as an image meant to be seen in the paintings. Thank you."

Sadie blushed. "I couldn't believe what I was seeing. I ran to Dr. Blankenship's office as soon as I saw the devil image."

"You did well." I turned to Blankenship. "You should buy her a pizza." Sadie's eyes lit up.

"That's a great idea, Peter."

Chapter 6

Seeing the art class lined up under the portico, I hustled to move the van from its parking spot in the back of the lot, to the line of ladies awaiting their transport to the art studio. I helped Hulda up the steps and stowed her walker behind the driver's seat as the other art students climbed aboard. The group was always chatty, but their conversation seemed louder and more excited than usual. Maybe this was due to the two new students who'd joined since the news of wine being served in class had spread through the residents.

I parked in front of the art studio and Melissa, the art teacher, met us on the sidewalk. She sidled up to me as I helped the ladies down the van's steps. "Are you coming into the studio today?"

"I hadn't planned to," I said as I helped Hulda Packer down the steps.

"Today was the day we were going to start drawing nudes and my model is a no show. Will you fill in?"

"No."

"I'll pay you $300."

After unfolding Hulda's walker and pointing her toward the studio, I turned to Melissa. "I'm not going to model for the class."

"I bet you'd model if I offered you a million dollars."

"For a million dollars, I'd consider it." I said with a laugh.

"Good! So, you're willing to compromise your morals for a million dollars. Now we just have to negotiate the price."

"I was kidding about the million dollars. I'm not going to be your male model." I paused as I had a thought. "Why don't you pose for the class?"

Melissa, who was about seventy, sighed. "I think the students would benefit more from drawing a well-toned body than someone like me, whose body has been ravaged by two pregnancies, age, and gravity."

Hulda, who'd been toddling toward the studio door, paused. "Wendy would pose for us."

With a momentary vision of Wendy's partially exposed tattoos and her expressed willingness to go on the naturist cruise, I blurted out, "No!"

Surprised by my emphatic outburst, Hulda glared at me. "Wendy is cute and not shy. I think she'd be a perfect model."

"Wendy is the assistant director of Whistling Pines, and it would be highly inappropriate for her to pose nude for your art class."

"Peter, you are such a prude." Hulda spun her walker around and walked in the door.

Melissa and I watched Hulda walk away. "Wendy is cute. Would you be opposed to her posing in a swimsuit?"

"Is this a negotiation like whether I'd pose for something less than a million dollars? You're going to start with Wendy in a swimsuit while working toward pasties and a G-string?"

Melissa's smile was unsettling as she turned and walked into the studio without answering my question.

"Please don't contact Wendy," I called after her, knowing I had no leverage to stop Wendy from doing whatever she chose.

Driving back to Whistling Pines, I tried to banish the vision of Wendy posing for the art class from my mind. Back in the office, I dropped into my chair and turned on the computer, planning to check emails and delete the daily pile of advertisements and spam.

"A tuba player walks into a bar."

I turned in my office chair as Brian walked in and sat down.

"It cost him $300 to repair the dent," Brian said with a grin.

"I can tell my son that joke," I said, rolling my chair away from the desk.

Kerry Stone, the Two Harbors Police Chief, stepped into my office. He paused at the door, waiting for Brian to respond.

"Do you want a joke for your son, Chief?" Brian paused, considering his mental list of tuba jokes. "What do you call a musical instrument on your bathroom counter?"

Kerry shrugged.

"A tuba toothpaste."

Picking up a pen, I wrote down the jokes, then put the slip of paper in my wallet.

"You couldn't remember those jokes until you got home?" Brian asked.

"I could remember the jokes, but I might not remember to tell them to Jeremy."

Brian glanced at Kerry. "I suppose you're here to talk about the dead woman depicted in the painting."

"Just because Peter thinks there is an image of a dying person in a painting, doesn't mean there's a dead person. He told me there are also a cabin, cottage, and crypt in the painting and none of them exist."

Raising his eyebrows, Brian smirked. "Would you like me to show you the cabin and cottage? I've seen them and I suspect the crypt is in a Duluth cemetery."

Kerry's pleading eyes looked at me. "I'm not opening a murder investigation based on an image hidden in a painting."

"Brian, do you know when the diptych was painted?"

"Hey! I'm a tuba player. I've got pages of jokes, but no information about art or dead bodies." He looked at me. "You've got a building full of resources, ask them."

"That would be opening a can of worms," I replied. "I'll get too much information and most of it will be fiction or rumors."

Waving his hand, Kerry stepped away. "Call me when you get through with the sorting."

Brian's eyes sparkled as I did a slow burn. "Looks like you've got a murder investigation, Doc."

"You do recall that I prefer Peter to being called 'Doc.'"

"Doc is an honorific, acknowledging your time as a combat Navy corpsman."

I moved past the issue, knowing I'd be Doc in Brian's mind regardless of what I said. "I've got a job, a wife, and two kids. I don't have time to track down a murder that may or may not have happened."

Standing, Brian continued smiling. "If you need my help, don't call."

"You mean, don't hesitate to call."

Brian stepped to the office door. "No, I meant what I said. Don't call me. I've got a gig next weekend and I'm locking myself in the tubararium to practice."

"Do you really have a soundproof practice space you call the tubararium?"

"The tubararium is the only way to keep the neighbors from complaining about the noise."

* * *

With my mind awash with thoughts about the image in the painting and the prospect of throwing the question out to the Whistling Pines residents, I sat staring at the blank computer screen.

The phone jarred me from my daydream. "Are you coming to pick up the art class any time soon?" Melissa asked.

The cell phone clock showed that I was already fifteen minutes late for the pickup, and I was a ten-minute drive from the art studio. "Sorry. I'm on my way."

I grabbed the keys and ran out the back door to avoid engaging in an unwanted conversation before I got the van. Pushing the speed limit, I arrived at the art studio half an hour late. I parked the van at the curb and rushed inside to retrieve my passengers. Perplexed because they weren't lined up in the outer display room, I walked into the studio.

The students were intently drawing as Melissa circled among them offering encouragement and suggestions. The back of a head covered with long brown hair was visible to me above the nearest easel. The model was facing away from me, with her head tipped down. I glanced at the nearest drawing and saw a rough outline of a woman's naked back, right down to her butt sitting atop a stool. I was about to turn and sneak out when Melissa called out my name. "Peter, wait. We're nearly done."

"Um, I'm here to pick up the students," I mumbled.

Hearing my voice, everyone turned my way, including the model. Sherry Vogel, buck naked except for the sheet draped over her left thigh, smiled at me. "Hi, Peter," she said, apparently unembarrassed by my presence despite my view of her naked torso.

It took a second for me to connect the naked woman sitting in front of me with the neatly dressed person I'd seen playing an alto saxophone in the Two Harbors band. "Um, hi Sherry. I didn't know you were a model."

Rising from the stool and pulling the sheet around her waist, Sherry continued to smile. "It helps pay for my art supplies at school. Paint and canvas are expensive."

I recalled a book title, *What Do You Say to a Naked Man?* The answer being *nothing.* Tongue-tied, I stood with my mouth open and unable to speak.

Sherry, less uncomfortable with the situation than I was, asked, "Are you playing with the band again this summer? I was thinking about going back to the clarinet and I could use a couple lessons."

"Sure," I said, my mind racing as I focused on maintaining eye contact with Sherry, rather than glancing at the naked breasts of the young woman I'd heard was a minister's daughter. "Give me a call and we can pick a time to work on your clarinet skills."

"I really appreciate it," Sherry said, wrapping the sheet around her waist, before stepping down from the platform, and walking through a door that appeared to be a changing room or toilet.

Feeling a hand on my arm, I looked down at Kathy Christensen, who was smiling. "You can stop staring at the door. Sherry's gone to change."

"I…um…"

"…was unprepared to see the minister's daughter naked?" Kathy suggested.

"Yeah."

Melissa nudged my elbow, and we walked outside. "My model showed up."

"I saw that."

"Don't you think everything was tasteful and artistic?"

"Does her father know…?"

Melissa took a sip from her coffee mug. "I assume he doesn't. The Svenska Gotters aren't very open-minded about things like public nudity."

"What are Svenska Gotters?"

"They're a religious group who bought an old Baptist church outside town. I heard they're fundamentalist Swedes who emigrated to Finland because they felt Sweden was too liberal. Finding the Finns narrow-minded and intolerant of outsiders, they moved to Two Harbors. I heard their beliefs fall somewhere between the Baptists and Amish. They have two saunas outside the church: one for men and one for women. After the sauna, they run down to Lake Superior and immerse themselves in the frigid water."

With an air of superiority, Hulda stepped over. "They're Swedish Lutherans who splintered off from the Finnish Orthodox Church. They believe anything that's fun or feels good is a sin."

Shaking her head, Karla overheard the conversation. "There is no Finnish Orthodox Church."

Hulda waved her off. "They follow the Finnish Vatican. Someone told me all their children were born by holy intercession because none of them ever had sex."

"I think the term is, 'immaculate conception.'" I quickly remembered the futility in correcting Hulda's comments.

"There's nothing immaculate about getting pregnant without sex. I mean, what's the point if no one enjoys it?"

Karla's eyes rolled so far back I thought she was checking her scalp for dandruff.

"The SGs, as they call themselves, have beliefs somewhat right of center. I had coffee with one of the women who said they felt the Baptists didn't go far enough in condemning alcohol and gambling. Other than that, they're a normal protestant sect. Well, except for the saunas and dipping themselves in Lake Superior."

Sherry swept out of the changing room wearing an oversized t-shirt, shorts, and sandals. She nodded as she passed, either not hearing or ignoring the conversation about her father's church.

Karla stopped me on her way to the van. "You handled Sherry's nudity very well, Peter. I didn't see you break eye contact the whole time you spoke to her. That was very courteous and professional."

"Yeah, I'm known for my courteousness and professionalism."

Karla walked away and Melissa leaned close. "Sherry's naked body is one of those things you can't unsee."

"Yup. It's etched there alongside my mother pulling up her hospital gown to show me her gallbladder surgery stitches."

"If you became a student, you'd become accustomed to viewing the naked female body as a sculpted piece of art, not a sex object."

"I sincerely doubt that," I said as I helped Hulda up the van's steps.

Kathy waited patiently for Hulda to ascend the steps. She leaned close. "I suppose it'd be difficult for a sailor, like you, to see a naked woman as something other than a sex object."

"I don't think it's fair to stereotype Navy personnel as…" I stopped my protest when I realized Kathy was smiling at having effectively gotten my goat.

Stopping on the top step, Hulda looked past me to Melissa. "That skinny little girl was cute, but I really want to see some beefcake."

I turned my head to see Melissa's response. She was grinning and nodding. I made a mental note not to walk into the art studio unannounced. I didn't want to see naked models, male or female.

Sherry swept past the women waiting to get onto the van. "Peter, I'll call you about clarinet lessons later this week."

I nodded, my thoughts immediately going back to the image of Sherry's naked body perched on a stool in the art studio. That image was replaced by one of Sherry wearing a white shirt and black shorts, playing an alto saxophone on the bandstand stage.

I felt Melissa's hand on my arm and was brought back from my daydreaming. As if reading my mind, she said, "Don't worry, Peter. Sherry won't show up naked for her clarinet lesson."

* * *

Discussions among the art students on the return trip to Whistling Pines were loud and emphatic. I caught snippets of conversations that varied from a critique of Melissa's boxed wine to the model's youth, to general disappointment that Melissa hadn't provided a male model. I attributed the boisterous, uninhibited conversation to the wine.

Karla Telker hung back as I helped the last ladies down the van's steps. She watched me unfold Hulda's walker. Together, we watched Hulda totter away. "I wonder if Pastor Vogel knows his daughter is paying her way through college as a nude model?"

"Are you going to tell him?"

"It's not my place to rat out the SG pastor's daughter." Karla paused, "I think you should tell him."

Putting up my hands in protest, I took a step back. "No way. I've never met the man and I'm not a Svenska Gotter. Two Harbors is a small town without secrets. If he doesn't already know, I'll bet that he'll get two or three phone calls this afternoon."

"I hope none of the calls are from his bishop."

"Do you think their bishop cares if the pastor's daughter is modeling for an art class? It's not like she's working at a strip club."

Rolling her eyes, Karla shook her head. "I'm sure there's a clause in the SG rule book against nudity of any variety."

I sighed. "I suppose the SG Church is stricter than the Lutherans, and I suppose Pastor Olafson wouldn't be pleased if his daughter posed for the art class."

Karla cocked her head. "How old is your daughter?"

"Amy's three months old. Why?"

"How would you feel about Amy posing nude when she's a college student?"

After weighing shooting whoever hired her, I decided I'd rather strangle the miscreant. Composing myself, I said, "I'd try to be open minded."

"No, you wouldn't. I could see the fire in your eyes while you were thinking about your response. You'd kill the person who hired her."

"Maybe I'd only hurt them badly."

Karla flipped her hand and walked away. She'd hit the nail on the head. As I parked the van, I decided against killing anyone. But I'd be disappointed in Amy for not using better judgement.

Jenny was in the lobby with a resident who was trying to swallow a pill in a spoonful of applesauce. She saw me walk in and nodded toward the aviary where I watched a parakeet pecking at his reflection in a tiny mirror. Once through with the resident, Jenny walked over with a grin on her face.

"I heard Sherry Vogel hasn't got much…upstairs."

The comment caught me off guard. "Um…I think she's pretty smart."

"Peter, you know what I mean."

"I don't have a clue."

"No wonder the guys in Pastor Olafson's poker group tease you about not having a poker face. You're a terrible liar."

"Oh, you mean the art class model. She was facing away from the door when I walked in."

"Was that before she asked if you'd give her clarinet lessons?"

"Honestly, I stayed focused on her eyes."

"And you have no peripheral vision?"

"Can we move to a different topic?"

"Sure. I heard you were negotiating with Melissa on payment for your modeling services."

"I told her I wouldn't model."

"I heard you wouldn't accept $300, but she was trying to negotiate you down from one million."

"Who said that?"

"I won't give up my sources, but you might want to talk to Nancy before the news gets to her."

"Do you think she cares if there's a nude model at Melissa's art class?"

"Is the art class one of your sanctioned recreation activities?"

"Aw crap." I looked down the hallway and saw that the lights were on in the director's office. "It looks like she's in her office. I'll talk to her now."

Nancy was staring at her computer with her fingers poised over the keyboard when I knocked on her door frame. "Do you have a second?"

Nancy turned and took off her readers. "Sure. What's up?"

I sat in one of her guest chairs. "We had a situation at the art class today." After I explained the nude model and being kidded about modeling, Nancy got up and closed her office door. I steeled myself for a tongue lashing. Instead, the director sat in the guest chair next to me and smiled.

"Karla said the art class would be moving to more challenging subjects."

"I take it that you're okay with them using nude models?"

Nancy shifted and crossed her legs, like she was framing her reply. "I heard it was being handled tastefully. Isn't that true?"

After searching for the right words, I said, "I suppose it's tasteful. I was unprepared to see a nude model when I walked into the studio."

Smiling, Nancy moved to another topic.

"Thank you for going to the art exhibit. I heard you pointed out the mate of the

Evenson painting we'd displayed, and that the two of them were moved together."

"They were painted as a pair. Seen side-by-side, they were quite remarkable."

"That was a good catch that the museum curator had missed. Dr. Blankenship called to thank me for your attendance and help."

"It was a nice evening."

Nancy nodded. "How was the movie you watched after ducking out of the art exhibit?"

Busted, I composed my thoughts. "We hadn't been out without the children since Amy's birth. The movie was so-so, but the evening alone with Jenny was wonderful."

Nancy patted my arm and stood. "My children are grown, but I remember those special moments when my husband and I slipped away without them." She paused, standing by the door. "I'm glad you enjoyed your getaway. Be forewarned that I won't pay Wendy to babysit for your next date night."

I stood, walked to the door, and nodded. "We really appreciated the night out. Thank you."

* * *

I heard my office phone ringing while still a few steps from my door. I snatched the receiver out of the cradle without looking at the caller ID. "Whistling Pines, this is Peter."

"I just got off the phone with Nancy. She said you'd be sitting in for her at the Chamber of Commerce meeting." Recognizing Meg Cochran's voice, I knew the evening of babysitting was about to be repaid.

"Hi, Meg. When's the meeting?"

"We're meeting at Judy's Café in fifteen minutes. I'd asked Nancy to develop some ideas to leverage the upcoming Tall Ships Festival. She said she'd passed a few thoughts onto you."

I covered my eyes with my left hand and exhaled. "She didn't have many ideas."

"Bring whatever you've got." Meg paused. "By the way, there won't ever be another lutefisk toss, like you arranged for the Pirate Days Festival. I spent a lot of time on the phone explaining that the city hadn't violated any EPA rules by washing the lutefisk into the lake."

I saw no point in blaming the Sons of Norway for the lutefisk toss suggestion. "I think the gulls ate all the lutefisk before it got to the lake."

"That's the excuse I used. Then, the woman from the state pollution control agency told me that fishermen had reported a gull die off in the week following the festival. The PCA veterinarian couldn't determine the cause, but he was unaware of the gulls eating lutefisk, so we may have dodged a bullet."

"People eat lutefisk, and I assume a gull's digestive system is more robust than a human stomach."

"Let's just let that idea die quietly and move on. Suggest something else that will keep people in town for a few extra hours during the Tall Ships Festival. The Chamber accountant estimates that each family unit spends $250 an hour while they're in town. If we can get a hundred families to spend an extra three hours in town over two days, the businesses will have an additional half million dollars in sales. That's a lot of money coming into town."

"I'll put on my thinking cap," I said.

"Don't think too long. You need to leave for Judy's right now."

* * *

Meg was calling the Two Harbors Chamber of Commerce meeting to order as I walked into Judy's. Kerry waved at me from the back of the room and slid an empty chair away from the table. I sat between Kerry and Ray Bandeau, the harbormaster. Ray flipped a coffee cup over and poured from a thermal carafe on the table.

"Haven't seen you since the sailboat murder," Ray whispered as he slid the cup in front of me.

"There hasn't been an excuse for me to visit the harbor," I replied.

Meg reviewed the minutes from the previous meeting, recapping the discussion of finances and the revelation that the Tall Ships Festival was moving from Duluth to Two Harbors while their waterfront was undergoing reconstruction after a tremendous November storm. After reading the minutes, Meg took a swig from a water bottle and set the paperwork aside. "I've asked everyone for suggestions on how to expand the tourism options during the Tall Ships Festival. Our goal is to provide interesting activities that will keep each family in town an extra one or two hours."

A female voice from the opposite side of the room said, "While spending their hard-earned cash in our shops."

The anonymous comment drew a chuckle from the crowd. Meg nodded. "I'd express that in less predatory terms. But, yes, we want our guests to have options that will lead to a positive financial impact for our businesses."

Butch Oldham, who owned a bait shop, stood up. "The food trucks were a nice draw. I think we should do that again."

Meg looked at the café owner. "What do you think, Judy? Did the food trucks negatively impact your business?"

"There were more people in town than we could feed. My tables were full all day long and we closed early because we ran out of pie and meatloaf."

A male voice announced, "The Rotary Club is planning to have a pancake breakfast in the park Saturday morning."

Meg nodded. "Those are good. But we need some daytime activities to keep people engaged."

Ray elbowed me and leaned close. "Don't mention the lutefisk toss."

Meg glared at him like a teacher who'd overheard children speaking in class. "Do you have something to share, Ray?"

"I just told Peter we shouldn't repeat the lutefisk toss. In case all of you haven't heard, the gulls swept in and ate all the lutefisk chunks as the firemen hosed down the street. The next day, there were dead gulls falling from the sky. Thor Thoreson had a group of guys from the Cities out on a fishing charter. A gull died over his boat and…well he said it looked like a Kamikaze coming in for the kill." Chuckles filled the room. "It wasn't funny. That bugger hit one of his fishermen in the chest and broke two of his ribs!"

Meg cut off the laughter. "The lutefisk toss was a one-time event. We need some other ideas. Peter, what do you have?"

Flustered by hearing my name called out and not having any suggestions, I improvised. "Let's do a dunk tank and the chamber members can take turns sitting on the platform. We can charge five dollars for three throws."

Clearly unhappy with the suggestion, Meg frowned, but looked around the members. "What's the consensus on a dunk tank?"

Patty Patterson, the owner of the hair salon, stood. "We'd have a line a block long if the mayor was in the dunk tank. I'll call around and see how much a dunk tank rental will cost."

Resigned to the idea of the dunk tank, Meg made a note and looked around. "I need at least two more activities."

Melissa, the art instructor, waved at Meg. "I have some very talented artists at the studio. I could set up a couple easels outside and we could draw caricatures of the visitors."

I felt Kerry's hand on my arm and turned. His lopsided grin told me he had something impolite to say. I leaned toward him. "I wonder if the minister's daughter would pose while art students drew her portrait?"

I couldn't stifle my laugh, causing Meg to turn to me. "Peter, it sounds like you and Kerry have another fun idea."

I tried to hide my laugh as a cough, then took a drink of coffee, like I had swallowed wrong. Meg didn't buy it. "Okay, Kerry, what's your idea?"

"I thought people might like to see one of Melissa's art classes sketching a model in the park."

Meg looked at Melissa, who was sipping from her mug. "What do you think about the Chief's suggestion?"

Melissa's eyes sparkled. "My Whistling Pines class might be willing to do that. But we'll need a model who's willing to sit for two days. Perhaps Peter would consider modeling for us."

"I can't commit to spending two days sitting in the park," I pleaded. "I've got to help with my kids."

Meg scanned the room, and no one dared even scratch their nose, fearing the motion would be taken as a signal they'd volunteered.

I watched Melissa pour something into her mug from a brown bag buried in her purse. After taking a big swig, she cleared her throat. "Sherry Vogel has modeled for a couple of my classes. If the chamber was willing to pay her a few hundred dollars, she might be willing to pose during the festival."

My brain seized with the image of Sherry posed in front of the Whistling Pines artists with only a sheet draped over her thigh. I didn't know I'd made a sound until I realized the entire room was staring at me. Speechless for a second, I took a breath, counted to ten, then let the breath out slowly. "Sherry's a college student who's been modeling for the Whistling Pines art class. She might like the extra cash."

Melissa's Cheshire Cat grin chilled me. She turned to Meg. "Sherry's been modeling in the nude for the Whistling Pines art class. In order to make this a family event, I'll ask if she has a cute bikini or maybe a body suit."

Not realizing I'd been holding my breath, I let out a sigh of relief. "That would be good."

The meeting wrapped up after the Two Harbors City Band offered to play a Saturday night concert of Sousa marching tunes, and the Sons of Norway offered to host a book signing by some local authors.

Kerry took me aside as the membership filed out of the café. "You seized up when Melissa suggested using Sherry Vogel as a model."

"I walked in on an art class when Sherry was modeling in the nude and…"

Kerry chuckled. "That was the vision in your mind when Melissa mentioned having Sherry model."

"Yeah. It wasn't a G-rated event."

"You know, every sailor I've ever known had a sixth sense for finding naked women."

"I was deployed with the Marines."

"Same thing. The Marines report to the Secretary of the Navy."

"That's not the case for you Army guys?"

"Nah, the Army is too busy slogging through swamps and sleeping in the boonies. Unlike the Navy, who releases sailors in every port to do heaven knows what."

Ray Bandeau, who'd retired from the Navy before becoming the harbormaster, nodded. "Yeah, you Army guys had it tough: Crappy food. Sleeping on the ground. Being shot at. No women. I don't know how you put up with it when you knew we Navy guys were eating steak and sleeping in safe comfortable bunks." He paused. "Will I see you guys at the VFW tonight to continue this discussion?"

I shook my head. "I've got two kids at home. My drinking days are over."

Kerry slapped Ray on the shoulder. "I'll have one beer with you after I get off duty."

Chapter 7

Kathy Christensen and Karla Telker were retelling the rumors they'd heard about Deborah Evenson as they ate yogurt topped with granola and fruit. Noticing people entering the dining room in my peripheral vision, I saw the police chief and Whistling Pines director approaching.

Kathy, a master of wry Scandinavian wit, wiped her mouth and whispered, "I think they've finally come to arrest you, Peter."

"Why would they arrest me?" I asked as I stood to meet the visitors.

"It must be something to do with the minister's daughter. They're onto you."

I met Nancy and Kerry halfway across the dining room. "This looks ominous."

"The Chief is getting very clever," Nancy said. "He came directly to me, requesting your time and assistance."

I glared at Kerry but addressed Nancy. "I assume that's because he didn't want me to refuse to help with the Evenson investigation. I routinely use my job as an excuse for not assisting him."

"As good stewards of community service, it's our job to put Whistling Pines in the best possible light. I'd like you to provide Kerry with whatever aid you can offer."

"That's easy," I said. "I have nothing to offer. I'm the Whistling Pines recreation director and there is no overlap between providing recreation to the residents and the investigation of a suspicious image on a painting."

"As I recall, Peter, it was you who informed me of the hidden image in the painting and suggested that it might be more than an artistic representation of death."

After tipping my head back and contemplating a water stain on the ceiling tiles, I drew a deep breath. "What do you need, Kerry?"

"Evenson's studio is for sale. I contacted the realtor and he's going to meet me there in half an hour. I'd like another set of eyes looking around the building and grounds."

"I'm sure it's nothing but an empty shell. What do you hope to find?"

"It's not empty. Evenson's trustee is planning to have an estate sale, but the auctioneer is booked every weekend until September. The house is as it was when Evenson died after her fall."

Seeing several residents taking too much interest in our conversation, Nancy steered us toward the dining room door.

79

"You two can discuss the details of the death and the studio on your drive into the hills."

"I've got to set up the movie and make popcorn this afternoon."

Nancy put her hand on my elbow and urged me toward the door. "I'll have Wendy take care of that if you're not back in time."

Kerry's police cruiser was parked under the portico. I was unhappy to be dragged into yet another police matter especially with Kerry's appeal to Nancy for my help before he'd spoken to me. "That was underhanded," I said, buckling my seatbelt.

"You always use Nancy as an excuse for not helping me. I decided to break down that hurdle before you had a chance to throw it up."

"What do you expect to find in Evenson's studio?"

Kerry steered through the parking lot and onto the road before answering. "Investigations are a lot like a carnival grab bag, you don't know what's inside until you put your hand in it."

"Really? That's the best analogy you've got?"

"At this point, I don't know what I don't know."

"That's profound. It sounds like a Yogi Berra quote."

"Stop being a Debbie Downer. This is an adventure. Evenson's studio might be filled with partially completed artwork and

80

mementos of her life. It might be a very interesting look into the life of a reclusive woman."

"Or it might be a monumental waste of our time."

* * *

The only things identifying the driveway to Evenson's studio were a mailbox and a FOR SALE sign. After turning into the driveway and winding through a half mile of secluded forest, Kerry commented, "I've never seen a concrete driveway through the woods. Most people have a gravel driveway full of potholes."

"I think pouring this driveway cost more than my house," I replied.

The pine forest opened into a glade filled with ferns and bushes. The entire east side of Evenson's studio was covered with huge windows reflecting the morning sun. A black Cadillac Escalade was parked near a four-stall garage. The driver's door opened as Kerry parked, and a man whose face I recognized but had never met, stepped out.

"I've never actually met Oscar Pederson," I said as I stepped out of the cruiser. "But I've seen his face on a dozen billboards advertising his realty office."

Kerry paused with his car door open. The side of his face that wasn't covered with scars when he'd been trapped inside a burning military vehicle, smiled. "That picture must've been taken twenty years ago."

Oscar walked toward us, his face beaming as if we were potential buyers. "Chief Stone, I'm pleased to meet you."

After shaking Kerry's hand, Oscar introduced himself to me. "I don't think we've met."

"I'm Peter Rogers, the Whistling Pines recreation director."

Oscar glanced at Kerry, an unasked question on his face.

"Peter's also a reserve police officer. He has a keen eye and I've used him as my investigator in the past."

Oscar continued to smile, offering me a view of the tiny scars above his ears where the plastic surgeon had *lifted* his face. His eyelids had also been lifted, giving him a surprised look to go with his salesman's smile.

Turning toward the house, Oscar pulled a set of keys from his pocket. "The trustee asked me to have the locks changed because we're unsure how many keys may have been made or who might have them. There are several paintings in the studio that may be quite valuable."

Following Pederson up the sidewalk, Kerry commented. "This is a very remote structure that's not visible from the road. I suggest that you and the trustee consider

82

moving anything valuable to a more secure location."

Pederson inserted a key in a deadbolt lock, then nodded toward the doorbell. "The house has security cameras in several locations, and there's an alarm system."

As soon as the door opened, an alarm system started beeping. Pederson turned to the wall next to the door and entered a four-digit code into a keypad, stopping the beeping.

Kerry watched silently, watching the realtor shut down the alarm and close the door. "Security cameras are great if someone's living here. However, they only help us catch the thieves after the crime."

Pederson continued to smile. "The alarm system is remotely monitored and if there's a breach, the security company calls 911, and your officers will respond."

"Alarm companies usually wait for two minutes for someone to enter the code and turn off the alarm. *If* someone at the monitoring site sees the breach immediately, then, they call the house and ask for someone to answer a security question. If they don't get a satisfactory response, they call 911. Under the best circumstances, that takes ten minutes, and if my officers are in town, it'll be another ten minutes before they arrive at the driveway. An astute burglar will be long gone before all of those steps are completed."

Pederson continued to smile. "I believe that most burglars shy away from houses with security systems."

"Most security companies have a sign at the driveway.   Without that, how will a burglar know there's a security system before he breaches a door or window?"

Pederson's smile faded. "I'm sure the security camera doorbell would be an obvious deterrent."

Kerry shook his head. "Your FOR SALE sign is welcoming to a burglar, especially anyone local who knows that the owner recently died. The local people would also suspect that there are valuable works of art inside."

Pederson gestured toward the living room behind him. "Perhaps we should look around before we get too concerned about a burglary."

One wall of the living room was field stone with a fireplace in the center. Split birch logs were stacked in a wrought iron rack set on the oak plank flooring. Aside from a loveseat in front of the fireplace, the living room furniture looked unused. An oak bookshelf built into the wall opposite the fireplace was filled with the awards Evenson's art had earned over a lifetime. End tables displayed tasteful sculptures where I would've placed lamps, and a coffee table in front of a leather couch had a large book of Craig Blacklock North Shore photos.

The walls between the fireplace and bookcase were filled with paintings.

I studied them, in awe. "Some of these must represent Evenson's early work, during her realism stage. During her years as a student, she painted landscapes and people. I think her paintings became more complex as she'd refined her technique. Later works included the influence of other 20th century artists like Picasso, O'Keeffe, Bourgeois, and Dalí."

Kerry saw me studying the art. He walked beside me. "What?"

"A lifetime of artistry." I swept my arm from right to left. "Her years as a student, followed by refinement of her technique, and finally the establishment of Evenson's unique style." I paused. "What do you see?"

Kerry pointed to a bare spot on the wall where the wood paneling hadn't faded. "I see a missing piece of artwork." He looked at the realtor. "What had been here, Oscar?"

"How should I know? I'm just a realtor, not a museum conservator."

"You didn't catalog what was in the house when you signed the listing agreement?"

"The contents aren't part of the sale. I only make a walkthrough and generally note what's in the house."

Intrigued by the realtor's vague response, I asked, "Did you take interior pictures for the online ad?"

Pederson's eyes narrowed. "Sure. They're part of the marketing package I assembled."

"That's perfect," I said. "If anything's missing, you can notify the trustee so he can make an insurance claim. Unless that painting is in your living room."

"Are they valuable?" Pederson asked.

"I'm not an art expert, but I'd guess the works on this wall would sell for hundreds of thousands of dollars at an art auction."

Ignoring the issue of the missing painting, Pederson said, "The trustee asked me to have the collection appraised. It hasn't been a priority."

Kerry's withering glare melted the realtor's smile. "You should look at the listing to see which piece is missing. We can use your photos to start a theft investigation. I'll give you a file number for the insurance claim."

Pederson stared at the window overlooking the driveway. "I thought that piece looked valuable, so I put it in my Escalade…for safe keeping."

Kerry clenched his scarred fist, obviously irritated and struggling to control his temper. "Oscar, I think the painting would be safer on the wall where it's apparently been for years than wherever you were going to transport it."

"I'll bring it in after we finish our walkthrough."

"You will, or I'll arrest you for theft." Kerry let his words sink in. "Contact the trustee and suggest he hire a guard until you get the collection crated and placed in secure storage."

"Where would I hire guards?"

"I've got part time officers who'd be happy to have some extra income. Sitting here would be a pretty nice gig."

Pederson threw up his arms theatrically. "Fine, arrange for a few days of security. I'll hire a couple high school students to box the art. The mini storage in town probably has an open unit."

I clenched my teeth, framing a tactful response. "Oscar, these can't be boxed in cardboard and put into the Two Harbors mini storage. They need to be carefully set in wood crates and placed in a temperature and humidity controlled secure warehouse. Or they should be shipped by a bonded carrier to an art auction house."

Obviously unprepared to hear that assessment or to accept that responsibility, Oscar nodded toward a door. "Let's go into the studio."

Kerry took one step inside the door and froze. The room had huge windows lighting a bright studio. The walls were knotty pine covered with urethane that made them look wet. Aside from a huge canvas mounted behind a step ladder, apparently a work in progress, were dozens of completed paintings on easels stacked around the walls. "Holy Hannah," Kerry uttered.

"What?" Pederson asked.

I walked to the giant canvas that was 20 by 30 feet. Evenson had laid a base layer of landscape and clouded sky. On top of that, she was adding minute details. In the lower left corner were tiny, winged books flying into the sky. Close up, they looked like Bibles rising from fire. Hidden in the flames was a reflection of the devil's face. From across the room, the scene looked like smoke rising from a campfire. What appeared to be blades of brown grass were tiny men in suits, lined up and walking into the burning campfire. It took a second for me to recognize them as businessmen, politicians, and bankers lined up, marching into hell.

I stood back, taking in the larger canvas, unable to speak. Kerry saw me staring at the campfire and knelt to examine the painting more closely. "It appears Evenson didn't think much of our current political and economic system."

The realtor was staring at a different easel across the room. "I think I recognize the nude woman in this painting."

Kerry looked over Oscar's shoulder. "Please don't mention this painting to anyone in town."

I joined them but didn't recognize the face that was mostly obscured by brown hair. Moving closer, I saw frown lines on the model's forehead and crow's feet at the corners of her eyes. Her brown hair was a tangle of tiny brown snakes. A quick glance at the naked body revealed tiny bugs as the shadows cast by curves of the model's body. "Evenson didn't like her model much," I said, stepping back.

"I've arrested her a couple times," Kerry replied. "She's been in and out of rehab repeatedly and made a lot of bad life choices. I think Evenson captured the model's self loathing."

The realtor turned away from the nude, then looked through a stack of canvases stacked against the wall. "These appear to be complete, but the images are crazy. I see bits and pieces of things, but they're not artwork I'd hang over my mantel."

I placed the front painting on an empty easel, then stood back. Kerry and Oscar stood alongside me as I took in the entire painting, then refocused on the minute detail. "When I unfocus my eyes, I see an old man's face. When I look at the details, I see a North Shore seascape with crags and waves washing against the cliff that is the old man's chin."

Kerry got into it. "Yes, the man's gray hair becomes storm clouds."

Oscar looked baffled. "I think you two have been smoking something."

Walking away, he led us into a kitchen that would've made a beautiful magazine cover. The appliances were huge and stainless steel, the countertops black granite, and the cupboards hickory.

"The appliances don't look like they've been used," I said.

Looking around the space, Oscar said, "Someone in town said Evenson was a cleaning nut who binged. She'd spend twelve to eighteen hours painting, then crash. When she woke up, she'd cook something, then scrub the kitchen until her hands bled."

I nodded. "I suppose she painted when the light was right, and she had inspiration."

"It sounds like she had obsessive-compulsive disorder," Kerry said. "She might've had a hard time working if everything wasn't perfect. What do you think, Peter?"

"In general, artists work in spurts. I know composers who go for months with random notes playing in their heads. Then the magic starts, and they pick up their guitar or sit down at a piano and write a masterpiece in an hour or two."

Oscar frowned. "You're shitting me?"

"Robert Louis Stevenson completed *Dr. Jekyll and Mr. Hyde* in one twenty-four-hour writing session. Paul Stookey said he was divinely inspired when he wrote *The Wedding Song*. He was convinced God's hand guided the composition—he released the copyright so anyone could play it without paying royalties."

The realtor was unconvinced. "Look in the bedroom and convince me someone with OCD lived here."

We walked down a wood-paneled hallway lined with small sketches to an open door. Inside was a master's suite with clothing strewn everywhere. Wading through the clothes, we walked into a bathroom that looked like an explosion had dispersed towels everywhere. Beauty supplies and moisturizers were arrayed randomly around the sink. In the bedroom, I looked at the dresser that had bottles of Chanel No. 5 and hand lotion next to candles and an open jewelry box. The jewelry consisted of semi-precious stones set in rings, necklaces, and dangly earrings. Inside the walk-in closet were rows of stylish shirts, pants, and jackets hung in neat rows, arranged by color. Shelves above the coat racks held hundreds of silk scarves. Racks of shoes filled the back wall, all arranged by style and color. To the side were shelves of sweaters, most cashmere, but many were wool or silk.

"This closet screams OCD," I said. "Everything neatly sorted and arranged. The bedroom and bathroom are the flip side of her compulsion—being overwhelmed by the choices and suddenly rushing to move on to whatever was calling to her."

After staring at the realtor for a second, Kerry commented, "Unless someone dug through her drawers looking for valuables, there isn't any diamond jewelry among the cheaper pieces. Was it like this the first time you walked through the house, Oscar?"

The realtor's face darkened. "Are you accusing me of something, Chief?"

"I'm just asking a question. It looks like her drawers and jewelry box were searched by a burglar."

Swinging his arm in a broad gesture, Oscar said, "It was a mess when I got here. She was a slob."

I pushed the closet door open so Oscar could see inside. "The closet says otherwise."

Raising his hands, Oscar shook his head. "I haven't touched a thing."

"What else is down the hallway?" Kerry asked.

The realtor led us to another bedroom suite that looked unused. The bed was made, and clean towels hung from the racks. Oscar opened the closet exposing rows of men's suits, shirts, ties, and shoes. "At some point, Evenson had a well-dressed boyfriend." He went to the tie rack and held up a tie. "This width and pattern were stylish in the '70s. Look at the wide lapels on the suits. These are expensive clothes, but they're from a different era."

Closing my eyes, I flashed back to a Whistling Pines conversation. "Evenson had a rich male patron. It was rumored that he stayed with her when he was in town."

While Oscar and I were talking, Kerry opened the dresser drawers. "The upper drawers are filled with men's underwear and socks, the lower drawers with shirts that look like they just came from the store." He opened a wooden box on top of the dresser. "Hmm, cufflinks and tie bars. Based on the gaps, I'd say a few are missing, perhaps the ones that had precious stones."

"Are you accusing me of stealing those, too?"

Closing the box, Kerry locked eyes with Pederson. "You're the only person who's had access to the house."

Oscar crossed his arms. "I'm a respected and trusted realtor and I object to your insinuation."

I walked to a dressing table with a mirror. "There's a bottle of Yves St. Laurent Opium perfume here. Evenson had Chanel perfume."

"There's a perfume called Opium?" Kerry asked.

Oscar frowned. "Not anymore. I think it was popular in the '60s."

Opening a drawer, I lifted a plastic bag half-filled with crumbled green leaves and two rolled joints. "This looks like marijuana and there's a package of cigarette papers here, too."

Kerry looked at Oscar. "You didn't want the dope?"

Oscar colored. "Look, Chief, I didn't loot this place. If you think someone stole stuff, you should get a forensics team in here to check for fingerprints. You won't find any of mine."

Smiling, Kerry said, "I imagine you're too smart to leave fingerprints. I think we'd have better luck looking for the stolen jewelry, but I don't imagine there's any record of what's missing."

After replacing the marijuana, I opened the other drawer. "There's a hairbrush here with long, blonde strands, lipstick, and other cosmetics. I think Charlie Crowder was sharing this room with a woman."

"Everyone in town knows he and Deborah Evenson were an item," Oscar said, dismissively.

I held up the perfume bottle. "This isn't the perfume in the other bedroom. The women I spoke with said Evenson was a natural beauty who never wore cosmetics. These items belong to someone else."

After making a scoffing sound, Oscar shook his head. "There aren't any women's clothes in here. I think old Charlie had his girlfriend make herself up to suit his taste. They'd smoke a doobie and pretend she was his naughty maid."

Kerry glanced at me. "The pictures of Deborah Evenson all show her with short hair. The hairs in that brush are long blonde hairs."

Oscar rolled his eyes. "There's probably a blonde wig in the closet or under the bed."

Kerry led us into the hallway. "I didn't grow up here, so I don't know the history. But I know this town is famous for its rumors and innuendo. If a man spent a night here, I'm sure everyone in town assumed that he and Deborah Evenson were lovers, but the items in the dressing table make me think he was entertaining someone else."

"If the Whistling Pines rumor mill is to be believed, Deborah Evenson had a string of male lovers who visited here. There wasn't much said about women visitors."

"Yeah," the realtor sighed, "if a single woman has a male visitor, it's assumed they've rushed to the bedroom to have wild sex. There are widows in town who won't order pizza delivery because the neighbors will assume she's had a tryst with the delivery boy."

"That rumor mill contains a thread of truth," Kerry said. "Peter and I witnessed some of the basis for those rumors at the marina during last year's pirate festival."

Oscar's smile said he was aware of that. "There's another bedroom."

He led us across the hall to the third bedroom. The dusty mattress, dresser, desk, and tables indicated the room's long-term disuse. Kerry opened an empty drawer and closed it. In a second drawer he reached far into the back, then lifted out a woman's bra too large for the home's owner. "I don't recall anyone mentioning Evenson's mother staying here," Oscar said, "but there was a female visitor who spent a significant amount of time here in the past."

I looked at Kerry. "The missing art professor."

Raising his unscarred eyebrow, Kerry replied, "Could be." After checking the other drawers, which were all empty, he led us back into the hallway.

I studied one of the pencil sketches we'd walked past earlier. A flash of inspiration hit me. "We should bring the Tweed Museum curator up here to render an opinion on the value of the art in the living room and studio."

The realtor looked disgusted but resigned. "Sure. Bring the whole UMD art department, too."

"What's the problem?" I asked.

"I'm trying to get this place ready to sell for the trustee."

"Have you had a lot of interest?" Kerry asked.

"Not so far. The price point, location, and interior layout put most buyers off."

Kerry nodded. "What's the asking price?"

"There are no comparable sales, so I really had to reach to price it. The wooded acreage is valuable by itself, and the structure, with the location and outbuildings, make it easily worth two million dollars."

"Wow," I said. "That's a hefty price for Two Harbors."

The realtor led us to the front door, keys in hand. He turned to lock the door after we stepped out but froze when he heard jangling behind him. Slowly turning, he looked at Kerry, who was swinging a pair of handcuffs from one finger.

"Is the painting returning from your Escalade, or are you riding to the police station in handcuffs?"

Red crept up from Oscar's neck until his entire face was the color of a beet. "It slipped my mind." He unlocked the door and walked to the SUV.

Kerry and I watched him open the rear hatch and remove the painting that was nearly two feet square. "Would you have arrested him?"

"Nah, I knew his memory would return when he saw the handcuffs. I do want to talk to the trustee. I don't think Oscar is as trustworthy as he tries to portray."

I held the door for the realtor, who passed without thanking me. As he locked the door, Kerry asked for the name and phone number of the trustee.

"He's a Chicago lawyer. I don't have the number with me." Pederson stepped down from the door but stopped when he realized Kerry wasn't following. "What?"

"Check your cell phone's call log. I bet you either called him, or he called you on your cell."

"It's in my office."

"Oscar, you work out of the Escalade. Your only phone listing is your cell. Look up the trustee's name and number."

Pederson glanced at his Rolex impatiently. "I have a showing in fifteen minutes."

Kerry didn't budge. "The longer you stall, the later you'll be for that showing."

Blowing out a breath, Pederson pulled out his cell. Flipping through screens with his finger, he found the number and read it to Kerry, along with the lawyer's name. "I hope you warn him that there's going to be a bill for security."

Kerry nodded as he entered the lawyer's number into his phone's address book. "I'll warn him about that. I'll also mention that you seem uninterested in protecting the interests of the estate beyond selling the real estate."

"I *am* a realtor. The contents of the house are the trustee's problem."

Kerry's half-face smile was scary, the burn scars not flexing with the rest of his skin. "I'm sure the trustee will be happy to have that information. He may find it unsettling and will, perhaps, find an agent who cares about the house sale *and* the rest of the estate."

Pederson's eyes went wide as he calculated the potential loss of sales commission on a two-million-dollar house and whatever additional fees the trustee had promised for dealing with the estate. "I was just yanking your chain. I'll take care of the contents."

"The paintings aren't chattel," I said, using the legal term for belongings left behind by sellers after they move out.

"I understand that," Pederson said, checking his Rolex again. "I'll try to find someone to appraise the estate."

"Let's be clear, an auctioneer who specializes in farms and antiques is not an acceptable evaluator."

With a flip of his hand, the realtor left. Kerry hesitated, rather than walking to his car. "What's wrong?" I asked.

"How many people in Two Harbors wear a Rolex?"

"Oscar Pederson wears the only Rolex I've ever seen in town."

Deep in thought, Kerry stared at the house. "Most businessmen are attuned to the sensibilities of their clientele, so they don't drive a Cadillac or wear a Rolex, even if they can afford it."

"Oscar is apparently trying to project the successful realtor image. 'Look, I am so good at what I do, I can afford an expensive SUV and a Rolex.'"

"I think being ostentatious would put people off rather than attracting business."

"It seems to work for Pederson."

Walking up the driveway, Kerry said, "Let's see if the garage is locked."

Trailing behind I asked, "You don't really think the realtor would leave the garage unlocked, do you?"

The side door wasn't locked. Kerry flipped on the lights, illuminating the two garage stalls and shelving. "That Nissan is only a couple years old."

"There's a car under a canvas cover in the other stall," I said, edging past the Nissan. I lifted the car cover far enough to reveal the taillight of a 1960s Corvette. "Look at the dust. This hasn't been driven in years."

Lifting a front corner of the cover, Kerry threw it back exposing the driver's door and half the hood. He opened the door and bent down. "Wow, there's only 38,000 miles on the odometer."

"It must've flipped over and it's actually 138,000 miles," I said.

"The interior is pristine. I've seen a lot of these old 'Vettes and they usually have cracked vinyl seats and dashboard. This is pristine."

After replacing the cover, I walked to the shelves farthest from the door. "These boxes are all marked. Here are Christmas lights, Christmas balls, garland, and a Christmas tree stand."

Kerry bent down. "The plastic tubs on the floor are fertilizer, weed killer, and gardening tools."

One shelf higher were tax records and business receipts. My eyes fixated on a banker's box. "Here's a box marked 'art records.' I wonder if she kept records of what she'd painted?"

"Bring it over to the workbench," Kerry suggested, turning on fluorescent lights over a dusty, but clear workspace next to a rack of lawn tools.

I removed the lid, exposing rows of small business planners, each marked with a year on its spine. I removed the book marked 1998 and flipped through the pages. "These are her calendars. Here's Tuesday, April seventh. She went to the Two Harbors high school at 10 o'clock to speak to the art class. In the afternoon, she worked on a painting she called, *Equestrian*."

Kerry pulled out an untitled book with a cracked binding, and a splotched black and white cover. It reminded me of a high school lab notebook. Opening it to the first page, were written in neat cursive, a list of titles and dates. He flipped through the pages. "I think we've found a catalog of Deborah Evenson's art. Here's a note—on December 12, 1964, she sold a painting called *Midnight Terror* to Maude Evans for $750." Kerry flipped back a page. "*Midnight Terror* was started on June 12 and completed on October 3rd."

"Seven hundred and fifty bucks isn't much pay for four months of work."

Closing the book, Kerry looked at me. "It might've been a big payday for a college kid in 1964." He set the notebook back in the box. "Put the calendar in here and close the lid. We're taking the box with us."

"Is that legal? I mean, it's part of the Evenson estate."

"Given the lack of concern exhibited by the realtor and the fact that the garage was left unlocked, I'm concerned about the security of the contents. As officers of the court, we're required to protect these records."

Kerry pulled an unmarked box from an upper shelf. The flaps were loose, and dust billowed when he lifted them. He reached in and lifted out a bulky sweater. "I guess Evenson kept her winter sweaters in the garage."

I took down another unlabeled box exposing jeans, shirts, and underwear that had been thrown in randomly. I lifted out a pair of bell bottom jeans. "This looks like something Jenny would wear to a retro party." Setting them aside, I lifted out women's shirts, pants, and dresses. "I've

102

never heard of the BIBA brand, or Krist. Here's a sheer bodysuit. I don't recall any woman wearing a halter top like this since I was a kid."

Intrigued, Kerry pulled down a third box that was filled with bras, panties, and camisoles, all thrown in without folding. "Here's a Janet Reger camisole. It looks like someone just tossed these into the box. They must've been left by a previous female resident."

"Why wouldn't they be donated to a charity or put out in the garbage?" I asked as I lifted down a box of vinyl records." Flipping through the titles I shook my head in disbelief. "I've never seen some of these except in pictures. The Guess Who, Gordon Lightfoot, Carole King, and a Bill Cosby comedy recording. Wow. These are collector items."

After closing the box of clothing and returning it to the shelf, Kerry said, "Maybe someone thought the owner was returning."

"People thought Annika Banks was taking a sabbatical in Paris. Maybe she packed up her clothes," I said, returning the records to the shelf.

Kerry wrinkled his nose. "Would Jenny dump her clothes into boxes for storage, or would she carefully fold them? I think someone dumped these because they knew the owner wasn't returning."

"They knew Banks wasn't coming home from Paris," I said.

Kerry's stare was disturbing. "Or she never left."

"You are so cynical," I said, picking up the box of papers.

"It's not cynicism, Peter. I deal with a reality that most civilians don't want to know about."

I carried the box of business planners out of the garage, then waited for Kerry to turn off the lights and lock the door. "I think we have a catalog of Evenson's work. The trustee might be very interested in comparing these records to the art in the house."

Nodding, Kerry led me to his car and opened the trunk. "Evenson's OCD might be a big help in organizing and valuing her estate." With the box in the trunk, we got in the car and Kerry turned around near the garage. "I'd like you to look through Evenson's records."

"Why me?"

"I view you as a disinterested third party who can assess the extent of Evenson's art collection."

"Geez, Kerry. You need someone to go through the records and create a spreadsheet of the paintings, which were sold, who they were sold to, and which remain unsold and in her collection."

"Great suggestion. Go for it."

I stared out of the windshield. "I said what *should* be done. I didn't volunteer to do it."

"You know how to create a spreadsheet, right?"

"That's not the point! It's not my job to catalog Evenson's life work. I have a job and a family. Creating that spreadsheet could take...weeks."

Glancing at me, Kerry smiled. "Nancy said I could have whatever of your time I needed. None of my city cops know how to create a spreadsheet or the significance of the painting titles."

"Hire someone to do it!"

"You're already a reserve cop."

"No! I resign. I have a full plate as it stands. I have no interest in taking on another part time job for weeks."

"I didn't offer to pay you, Peter."

"That makes it even worse! You expect me to do this for free!"

Chuckling, Kerry drove through town. "I'll talk to the trustee. I suspect he'll authorize a stipend to cover the time required to organize the catalog."

"Are you deaf? I don't have time to do this!"

Kerry was silent until he pulled under the Whistling Pines portico. "I'll talk to Nancy. I'm sure she'll be okay with you taking this on."

I went to the medical office and found Jenny updating a computerized medical chart. She looked up and smiled.

"Kerry and I aren't speaking."

A smile curled on Jenny's lips. "What?"

"Kerry torpedoed me."

"What do you mean, he 'torpedoed' you?"

"Kerry got Nancy's permission to use me as a resource before he asked me to help. Nancy told him that he could use whatever of my time he needed."

Jenny's grin broke into a full smile. "Kerry's become devious."

"He's always been devious. He's just never used his deviousity on me."

"Is deviousity a word?"

"No, but you understood exactly what I meant, didn't you?"

Chapter 8

I'd shut down my computer and was thinking through the things I needed to do when I heard someone behind me. Brian stepped into my office and sat in the guest chair.

"I was on my way out the door," I said, hinting for him to leave.

"I started a tuba quartet. We're calling ourselves the tuba fours."

I closed my eyes and shook my head. "That one almost made me chuckle."

"You can tell that one to Jeremy."

"I don't think it'll work until he understands lumber."

"Huh, an adult-themed tuba joke."

Apparently inspired by the thought of telling me an adult tuba joke, Brian was about to speak when I cut him off. "Is there a reason for your visit beyond tormenting me with tuba jokes?"

"I heard there's a hidden image in the pair of Evenson paintings."

"I'm constantly amazed at how quickly news spreads in Two Harbors."

"It's not general knowledge yet. I heard it through the art community."

"You're part of the art community?"

"Sure. The band considers itself part of the community's artistic talent pool. Many musicians are also artists, engineers, and mathematicians."

Metal clanking against my door frame diverted my attention from Brian. Hulda banged her walker against the door frame twice before she got inside the door. She looked at Brian. "Show me a trick."

"I'm sorry, but I don't understand," Brian replied.

"It's a simple request. Do a trick for me. Don't you have a deck of cards?"

Brian looked from Hulda to me, hoping I understood what she was requesting. "I think you need to explain yourself."

Hulda glared at Brian. "I heard you tell Peter that you were a magician. I asked you to do a trick."

Recognition swept over Brian. "I said many musicians were mathematicians, not magicians. I can play the tuba, but the only magic trick I can perform is making my wife disappear from the house when I start practicing."

"Was that supposed to be funny?" Hulda asked.

"I thought it was clever," Brian replied.

"Bah. Your jokes are no better than your tuba playing." Hulda turned to me. "Are you modeling for the art class tomorrow?"

Brian's eyes went wide, and he broke into a smile. "I'd pay to see that."

"I have never posed nude, and I don't plan to start now. Please don't spread that rumor."

"Well, who *is* going to pose tomorrow?"

"It's not my responsibility, and I don't know if anyone is posing tomorrow."

"I hope Melissa doesn't have that skinny minister's daughter back. I'm tired of drawing girls. I'd like to see a beefy male model on the stool." Hulda sized up Brian who was lost by the discussion. "You're probably too old and chubby. I'd like a beefcake model like one of those lifeguards from *Baywatch*. They had sculpted bodies. There would be some challenging muscles and curves to shade in."

After catching the direction of the discussion, Brian joined in. "I could pose in my band uniform with the tuba. There would be a lot of curves to draw."

The image caused Hulda to pucker like she'd sucked a lemon. "I want to draw six-pack abs, not a stupid tuba."

Banging the walker against Brian's knees, my feet, the desk, and the door frame, Hulda turned around in my tiny office and walked out the door while muttering to herself about tubas and beefy hunks.

Once she'd left, Brian looked at me. "Your job is much more challenging than I'd thought. Do you have many people who'd confuse a musician with a magician?"

"There are a few," I admitted.

Brian stood and walked to the door. He stopped in the door frame and turned back to me. "I think you'll solve several mysteries when you determine whose face is depicted as the devil in Deborah Evenson's painting."

"It was rather abstract," I replied.

Shrugging, Brian cocked his head. "I saw a lot of things in her paintings and all of them had meaning. I had to stare at some of the images for a while before they became clear." Brian paused. "There were several men in Evenson's life. It would be interesting to find pictures of them and compare them to the devil's face in her painting."

"The only man I've heard about is Charles Crowder."

In uncharacteristic silence, Brian weighed his words. "Debbie was adopted as an infant. She has an adoptive father, and a biological father."

"How do you know that?"

"There aren't any secrets here. You should know that by now." I sighed, waiting for Brian to leave, but he wasn't done. "Who's the woman? Is it Debbie Evenson being tormented by one of the men in her life, or is it someone else?"

"The museum curator suggested that the diptych contained so many images it could be a doctoral dissertation for an upcoming Ph.D. candidate."

"If I know you, Doc, you won't leave that mystery for some future college student." A smile spread over his face. "Did I tell you one of my neighbors was pounding on my door at three this morning? Luckily, I was still awake, practicing the tuba."

Brian was gone as quickly as he'd arrived. His questions about the images were insightful and intriguing.

* * *

Jenny ordered pizza for supper, which suited everyone. Jeremy had a ton of homework and no clue how to solve the math problems he'd been assigned. We sat at the dining room table for hours while he reasoned through the homework. I tried to guide him to the solutions without doing the work for him.

Jenny fed Amy, then put her to bed. Jeremy and I read another chapter of *Treasure Island*, then I turned off his bedroom light and walked downstairs.

Jenny turned off the television when I walked into the living room. "You were distracted all evening. What's wrong?" she asked as I sat next to her on the sofa.

"Brian stirred my brain. I've got dozens of questions swirling."

"About the city band?"

"No, he knew about the Evenson diptych and asked me whose faces were in the shadow images."

"Aren't they abstract?"

"Brian suggested that they may represent actual people from Evenson's life. He asked if I had pictures of the men in her past for comparison to the devil figure. Then he asked if Evenson was the woman being stabbed by the devil, or if the stabbing victim was someone else."

Jenny took my hand in hers and squeezed. "It's not your problem."

"He also told me Deborah Evenson was an adoptee. He suggested the devil might represent her adoptive or biological father."

"Is he suggesting that she might've been abused?"

"The suggestion about her biological father made me think she had psychological, rather than physical problems."

"I wonder about that with Jeremy. He used to ask about his *real* dad before you adopted him. I'm sure he'll have more questions later in life." Jenny paused. "Did his comments make you want to dig more deeply into the images in the paintings?"

"I'm not sure. He caused a lot of thoughts to swirl around."

Pulling my arm over her shoulder, Jenny leaned into me. "Forget about the painting tonight and snuggle with me. I had a tough day and I need you to be here with me."

I pulled her close and leaned my head against her. "I'm sorry I checked out."

"We've got so many outside influences tugging our sleeves that I sometimes forget about us."

"We had a date night this week. That was *our* time."

"Our date opened Pandora's box in my head. I realized how consumed I've been with Amy's needs. We need to plan a date night away from the children."

"A monthly date night would be nice."

"One of my aides offered to babysit. I'll talk to her tomorrow and ask about setting up a schedule."

Our snuggling was interrupted by my cell phone. Jenny gripped my arm tight, preventing me from reaching into my pocket. "You're right. Whoever it is will leave a message."

The ringing stopped, replaced by a vibration signaling that someone had left a message. I bent my head down and kissed Jenny, who pulled me into a tighter hug. She was unbuttoning my shirt when the phone rang again.

"Don't even think about answering that," she whispered.

"People never call twice unless it's something important."

Jenny grabbed the hand reaching for the phone and pulled it to her hip. "Priorities, sailor boy."

Urged on by Jenny's kisses and caresses, I was sliding my hand under her t-shirt when the phone rang a third time. I leaned away from her and drew a breath. "I *have to* answer it."

She slid out of my arms and stood. "I'll be naked in the bed when you come to your senses."

Without checking the caller ID, I answered.

"Peter, why haven't you been answering your phones?" My mother-in-law asked.

"I was putting Jeremy to bed."

"Jenny wasn't answering her phone either."

"It's probably in her purse, upstairs. What's up, Barbara?"

"Howard is in an ambulance. They're taking him to Duluth."

Bounding up the stairs, two steps at a time, I asked. "What happened?"

"He was short of breath, then had chest pain. Against his wishes, I dialed 911. The EMTs said he's having a heart attack."

Barging into the bedroom as Jenny slipped under the sheets, I handed her the phone. "Your father is having a heart attack. Talk to your mother."

Five minutes later, Jenny was in the car, driving to Duluth.

I tried reading Steven Thayer's bestseller, *The Weatherman* but was too distracted by Howard's situation to concentrate. I fell asleep watching QVC's special birthstone jewelry night. I remember hearing about April diamonds, and the announcer's admonition that diamonds were both a gift and an investment, before nodding off. The phone woke me during the October opal segment of the show.

"Yeah," I said, pushing myself up on one elbow.

"The cardiologist just spoke with us. Dad had a near total occlusion of three coronary arteries. They inserted stents and his prognosis is good."

"There's no permanent heart damage?"

"The doctor says Dad should make a full recovery."

I let out a sigh of relief. "How long will he be hospitalized?"

"Probably three days. They want Mom to meet with a dietitian, and he's going to get some cardiac exercises." Jenny paused. "I'll be home in an hour."

"You're not going to stay overnight with your mom?"

"She's sleeping on the couch in his hospital room. Since everything is okay, I'm not really needed here."

Chapter 9

I shut off the alarm and snuck quietly off to the shower. Amy apparently woke up to the sound of running water and decided it was time for breakfast. She and Jenny were sitting in the nursery rocking chair when I checked in on them.

"I tried to be quiet so you could get another hour of sleep."

The dark rings under Jenny's eyes contrasted with her attempt to be upbeat. "Amy had other ideas about Mommy sleeping in."

Feet shuffling down the hallway preceded Jeremy's entrance into the nursery. He yawned and rubbed his eyes. "What's for breakfast?"

I ran my fingers through his mussed hair and urged him toward the stairs. "Same as usual."

"Could we get cereal that already has sugar on it? I mean, what's the point of getting Cheerios, then adding sugar, when you could buy Frosted Flakes that don't need extra sugar?"

"We're humoring your mother," I said as I measured ground coffee into the basket of the coffee machine.

"Why does Mom get to choose? You're in charge now."

Laughing, I retrieved milk from the refrigerator as Jeremy poured cereal into a bowl. "Your mother makes all food decisions."

"Why?"

"Because she's a nurse and understands nutrition and having a balanced diet."

Jeremy pouted while he poured milk on his cereal. "I liked it better when we went to your house before you married Mom. You had fun food."

"You also had to smell the milk before you drank it."

After spooning too much sugar on his cereal, Jeremy shoveled a spoonful into his mouth while I put bread into the toaster. "Why did your milk always spoil? Ours never goes bad."

"I didn't drink milk fast enough to use it up before it expired. That's not a problem with you around because you drink half a gallon a day. We should own a cow."

The cow comment stopped Jeremy's chewing. "We can't have a cow in town."

"I was joking."

"Why joke about a cow?"

"Because you drink as much milk as a cow produces in a day."

"So what?"

The coffee maker ended its brew cycle at the same time the toast popped up, giving me an excuse to end the cow questions. After smearing the toast with peanut butter and grape jelly, I poured two cups of coffee.

As I sat down, I remembered Brian's jokes. "A tuba player walked into a bar. It cost him $300 to repair the dent."

Jeremy stopped eating and thought. "That's stupid. Why would it cost him..." Recognition swept Jeremy's face. "Oh, he dented the tuba when he walked into the bar. I get it."

Jenny entered the dining room with Amy on her hip. She sat at the table, snuck a piece of toast off my plate, and slid a coffee mug in front of her.

"What do you call a musical instrument on the bathroom counter?" I asked.

Jeremy cocked his head, deep in thought. "I don't know."

"It's a tuba toothpaste."

Jenny rolled her eyes, but Jeremy laughed out loud. "I'm going to tell that one to Jacob Stone."

Jenny looked dead tired and chewed slowly as she ate bites of toast. "Are you going to be functional today?" I asked.

"I plan on an early bedtime tonight."

"Not too early," Jeremy replied. "Dad and I are up to chapter thirteen in *Treasure Island*." Jeremy turned to me. "Are we halfway through it?"

"I suppose we're through about half of the book."

"It's really good, Mom. You should read it."

"Maybe when you and Dad are done." Jenny gave me a look that said that was never going to happen. Then she asked, "What are your plans for the day?"

"Kerry asked me to organize Deborah Evenson's records into a spreadsheet. Today might be the perfect time to lock myself in my office and plod through data entry."

* * *

After drawing a cup of coffee from the urn, I walked through the dining room, smiling and greeting people. Sensing no rumor fueled fires, I topped off my coffee and went back to my office. Going through the Evenson list of paintings was tedious, mindless keyboarding as I entered painting names, dates, subjects, and buyers into the spreadsheet I'd created. I'd completed all the 1960s entries and was working my way through the early 1970s when someone rattled my doorknob, then knocked.

Blanking the computer screen, I stood up, stretched, and opened the door. Karla Telker peeked over my shoulder, trying to determine why I'd locked myself in my office. "You usually have an open-door policy."

"I'm trying to catalog Deborah Evenson's art history. It's easier if people aren't poking their head in with rumors and distractions." As soon as the words were out of my mouth, I regretted the comment that sounded like I'd just told Karla she was pestering me.

"The ladies are lining up for the van trip to the art studio."

"Um, they've already been there twice this week."

"We have to go when Melissa can get models. She notified us yesterday afternoon that she had a model this morning."

"Are you finishing the drawings of Sherry Vogel?"

"She has someone different today."

I was reaching for the keys when my office phone rang. "Hi Peter, I've found a couple newspaper articles about an art professor's disappearance in 1968."

I glanced at the caller ID that showed *THLIBRARY.* "Thanks for getting back to me, Margaret. I'm making a trip into town in a few minutes. I'll stop at the library after a bit." I paused, recalling the question about whose faces were represented by the devil and victim in the diptych shadows. "Can you find anything about Deborah Evenson's family in your research? I'd like to get photos of her parents and siblings. Someone said Evenson was adopted. Pictures of her biological parents would be good, too."

"I can look up her birth certificate and get her adoptive parents' names. They might be pictured in yearbooks or newspaper articles. Her adoption files are probably sealed, so I'm not sure how to access the identities of her biological parents."

I chuckled. "Margaret, your predecessor worked miracles."

"That's really cruel," Margaret said, laughing. "You've thrown out the questions and I suppose I'll have to rise to the challenge."

"Thanks." Another thought popped into my head. "See if you can find a photograph of Charles Crowder, too."

"He was a very public figure. There should be lots of photos of him in the newspaper."

Karla was staring at me when I turned back toward the door. "Why do you want pictures of all those people?"

"A person at the museum suggested that the shadowy faces in the diptych might be real people from Deborah Evenson's past. I thought I'd get photographs of as many of them as I can. Then, I'll take them to Duluth and compare them to the images in the painting."

While considering my comments, Karla stood blocking the door. "I wish you luck, but shadows don't yield recognizable images. They define shapes, like the shadow of an egg looks different than the shadow of an apple. But you can't recognize someone's face from their shadow."

"I thought we were rushing to get the van for a trip to the art studio."

Watching me lock my office, Karla chuckled. "Some of the art students are more in a rush than others."

We fell in step walking down the hallway. "I take it that you're not as excited about this trip as some of the other ladies?"

"Melissa's stories are getting…repetitive. I'm not sure if it's because she's drinking all the time, or if her life really was a series of romantic encounters with the same type of air-headed men while smoking pot and swilling cheap wine."

"My guess is that the pot smoking and wine swilling made the encounters all run together in her brain."

"I guess I can't relate," Karla said as we walked into the atrium. She put her hand on my arm and smiled. "Melissa has three children. I'm not sure her husband fathered any of them."

"It makes for colorful stories, I suppose."

"I knew she had a reputation, but geez, Peter. I'm surprised she wasn't pregnant for half her adult life."

I guided Karla toward the door where the rest of the art students were lined up. "It was the '60s and everyone was on the pill." Karla joined the line while contemplating that comment.

* * *

Melissa was standing on the sidewalk with a coffee mug in one hand, and her other hand on the arm of a swarthy young fellow who appeared to be enduring, rather than enjoying, whatever she was saying. The man stepped into the studio when Melissa moved to greet the art class.

Hulda pressed past the other women, stepping on toes and garnering insults. She was out of the van, with a spring in her step, before I took her arm. "Is that our model?" she asked, getting into Melissa's personal space.

"I take it you like Ricky's looks," Melissa said. Even from several feet away I could smell the bourbon on her breath.

"He's a hunk," Hulda said, walking into the studio without waiting for me to unfold her walker.

Several of the other art students were on her heels. Kathy and Karla were the last off the van. Kathy reached out and grasped the handles of Hulda's walker. "I'll bring this inside. I'm sure Hulda will need it for her return trip to the van."

Melissa waited for Kathy and Karla near the studio entrance. As they passed, Melissa whispered, "He's well endowed."

Karla glanced at me and clenched her eyes shut, clearly unimpressed with the comments about Ricky's endowment. After the last students passed, Melissa looked at me. "You can watch if you want."

"Margaret, the librarian, is waiting for me."

Melissa's eyes sparkled. "Is Margaret the new brunette librarian? The one with the curly hair and perpetual smile?"

"Her name is Margaret Jensen."

"She's cute. Ask her if she'd like to model for the art class."

"Um, no. If you want her to model, *you* can ask her."

I drove the van away before Melissa expanded on our conversation.

The library was only a few blocks from the art studio. The plentiful open parking spots suggested that the library wasn't terribly busy on weekday afternoons. Margaret was working at a computer, her back toward the counter, obviously engrossed in whatever she was reading. I cleared my throat. The librarian spun around so fast that she nearly fell out of the chair. "Peter!"

"You were intent. I feel bad for interrupting you."

Rising from her chair, Margaret smiled. "No worries. I was creating announcements for the children's summer reading program." She hesitated. "Is *Treasure Island* capturing Jeremy's imagination?"

Having not visited the library since Margaret's arrival, I was surprised she'd connected me with Jeremy. "We're reading a chapter every night. He'd happily go through it more quickly, but I want him to understand the context and different time it represents. It's generated some…interesting discussion."

"If you're up for the discussion, he might enjoy *Adventures of Huckleberry Finn.* The language and discussion aren't politically correct, but a few parents have thanked me for suggesting it because the story led to teachable moments."

"I'm not sure I'm ready for those discussions. Jeremy is really into the idea of pirates and buried treasure."

"A lot of boys Jeremy's age have enjoyed the Alex Rider series. *Stormbreaker* is the first."

"Thanks."

"I did some research for you," Margaret said, handing me two printed sheets of paper. "The Minnesota Department of Health manages all birth records. They're not accessible on-line, and only available to adoptees through written request, and are only released with the permission of the biological parents. The exception is that direct descendants of deceased adoptees can request the information."

"So, we can't look up the name of Deborah Evenson's biological parents."

"No, and she couldn't either, unless they gave their permission to the state." Margaret pulled out two more sheets of paper and handed them to me. "Here are pictures of Charles Crowder. I printed the top one off the microfiche reader. The photo is from a 1958 fundraiser—the woman standing next to him is his wife. The second photograph is a copy from the *Duluth Tribune* on-line archives. It's from 1969 and the woman with him is Deborah Evenson. The caption says it was taken when he endowed her as the artist in residence at UMD."

"What's an artist in residence?"

"The endowment apparently provided Evenson with a monthly stipend in return for coaching art students and continuing her own artistic projects."

"Deborah Evenson had a sugar daddy."

Margaret cocked her head. "I think the term 'sugar daddy' implies a quid pro quo arrangement. The artist in residence endowment appears to be without strings except for her obligation to mentor students and continue with her art."

"Ah, that's right. You're not from here. The town is convinced that Charlie Crowder kept Evenson as his Two Harbors…concubine."

"Really?"

I smiled. "Once you've lived here a while, you'll understand that reality becomes whatever the prevailing rumors say it is. For all I know, Charlie Crowder was a benefactor of the art community, and his endowment was completely altruistic. That's not what most of the locals believe."

"Oh my. I thought I'd left those issues behind when Justin and I moved here from Isanti."

"It's not that big," I chuckled. "By the way, Justin has a reputation as being a really tough teacher. Jeremy told me he hopes he doesn't have Mr. Jensen for any classes when he gets to high school because he's really tough."

Margaret's eyes twinkled. "He'll be thrilled to hear that. He's afraid he's being too easy on the kids." She paused. "I'm sorry I couldn't help with the adoption information. Please call if there's anything else I can do."

"Thanks."

I turned to leave, but Margaret called my name. "We're always looking for children's programming. Jeremy told me you play the guitar and accordion. Would you consider a weekday morning program?"

"Jeremy tends to inflate my capabilities. I do okay on the guitar. The accordion is a work in progress."

"Justin and I heard you play with the Gin Fizzes at Hugo's. You're way beyond okay on the guitar."

"That wasn't the night the woman tried to French kiss me between sets, was it?"

Margaret snorted. "I don't remember that. I might've been in the bathroom." After a pause she asked, "Does that happen much?"

"That is literally the only time I've been kissed by a strange woman since I proposed to Jenny."

Margaret's smile disappeared and she leaned close. "I suppose a kiss in front of a crowded bar started all kinds of rumors."

"I probably got a pass on the kiss. But when the woman licked my tonsils, it started tongues wagging."

"I really can't tell when you're serious or when you're kidding."

"Assume I'm kidding, and we'll get along well."

"There is one request that came from the previous librarian."

"What's that?"

"I'm not sure just what she meant, but she said not to let your neighbor into the library with any loaded guns."

"I had an elderly neighbor who used her husband's collection of antique firearms to shoot vermin in her yard. Dolores moved into Whistling Pines and left her house to Jenny and me."

"Jeremy mentioned your haunted house. Do you need a book on exorcism?"

"The ghosts are gone."

"Peter, seriously. If you have research I could do, please let me know. I have unstructured time here and weekday mornings are dead. I've got lots of research data at my fingertips. You only have to ask."

"Thank you, Margaret. I'm sure I'll be back."

The wind had changed directions while I was in the library. Now sweeping in from the south, it carried a chill after traveling over miles of frigid Lake Superior water. I started the van and turned on the heater, thinking about how most of North America expects a southerly wind to carry warm air. Here, on the north shore of the world's largest air conditioner, Lake Superior, a southerly breeze means that residents put on the spare flannel shirt kept in the trunk.

On the drive to the art studio, I went through downtown Two Harbors. Passing a tourist shop, I watched a family of five exit the store in their brand new, matching, Two Harbors logo sweatshirts. They were unprepared for the sudden twenty-degree temperature drop brought about by the wind shift.

While waiting for the art class to end, I sat in the van and read the on-line *Duluth News Tribune* headlines. Three men had been sentenced to lengthy prison terms after dumping a body in Lake Superior. One of them testified that they'd heard bodies didn't float to the surface in the frigid lake water. He'd missed the other half of that knowledge, that well-refrigerated bodies don't decompose at all. Divers searching for shipwrecks found the body and notified the authorities. They quickly identified the victim and tied him to his three buddies who'd had a falling out while drinking and playing cards.

You should've hung out with a nicer crowd. I said to myself, setting aside the phone and picking up the printouts Margaret had given me. The article accompanied by a picture of Charles Crowder with Deborah Evenson expanded on Crowder's charity work, and briefly mentioned his support of Evenson as the artist in residence at the university. Studying the grainy newspaper photo, I was struck by Crowder's bearing. He wore a tuxedo and stared at the camera like a movie star on the red carpet. Although he'd been in his eighties when the photo was taken, he was trim and carried himself with almost military bearing. Deborah Evenson was beautiful, wearing a long gown and striking jewelry. None of it fit with the unhappy look on her face.

"I wonder if the photographer caught you at a bad moment, or were you unhappy about being led around as Crowder's eye candy?"

The studio door opened, and the art students filed out. Opening the van door, I stepped out to help the ladies up the two steps into the vehicle. Melissa and the blond male model followed the students onto the sidewalk. Melissa took a wad of currency out of her pocket and stuffed it into Ricky's hand. A lopsided grin appeared as he quickly counted out the money before jamming it into his jeans pocket. Hulda stumbled, distracting me from Melissa and Ricky.

I caught Hulda before she fell, but not without garnering a glare. "The city should fix these sidewalks!" she muttered as I helped her up the steps.

Kathy Christensen was immediately behind Hulda. As she passed by me, she whispered, "That crack in the sidewalk wouldn't have been a problem if Melissa had cut Hulda off after one glass of wine."

Hulda, whose hearing was selective when she wanted it to be, turned and glared at Kathy. "That was sacramental wine like they serve for communion at church. There's not any alcohol in it."

Kathy's sly grin made me smile. "I'm sure Pastor Olafson uses a box of wine for communion. Don't you agree?"

Karla was the last person in line. She took my arm and led me a half step away from the van's door. "I think you need to supervise the classes. Hulda tried to pull the sheet off the model's lap. He was quick enough to catch it before a complete revelation, but it could've exposed more anatomy than most of us were prepared to draw."

I tipped my head back. "I'm sorry, but I don't think protecting the art class models from Hulda is in my job description."

"Every job description has a final disclaimer. 'And other duties as assigned.'"

Melissa stepped to the van as Ricky swaggered away. The alcohol on her breath made my eyes water. "I think the ladies had a good time. Hulda requested another class session with Ricky so she could complete her drawing."

"I heard there was a sheet incident."

Melissa looked down the block at Ricky, who was unlocking a yellow Camaro. "Yeah, we nearly had…an overexposure. It's not a big deal. Ricky posed without the sheet for several of my evening adult classes. I use the coverup with this class because some of the Whistling Pines students are a little prudish and I didn't want to offend anyone."

"I think that's a good plan. You might also want to moderate the wine servings. Some of the ladies are unstable even when sober. I'd hate to have one of them fall and injure themselves."

"They're adults and I let them decide how much is enough. Besides, the wine helps them open their inner artist. Their drawings become more fluid and creative, instead of blocky and rigid."

"Hulda doesn't realize there's alcohol in the wine."

Melissa smiled. "Are you always so naïve, Peter?"

* * *

Jeri Westfall met us as the art class was unloading from the van. She pulled Karla and Kathy aside for a whispered conversation. I was ready to park the van when Jeri wiggled her finger at me.

"Karla and Kathy had been kidding me about being on the television cooking show, but never sharing the actual recipe we'd prepared. I made a black magic cake and brewed a pot of coffee. Come up to our apartment after you park the van, and you can sample a slice."

The sweet aroma of Jeri's cake wafted through the hallway as I approached her apartment. The door was ajar, so I knocked gently and stepped in. Kathy, Jeri, and Karla were seated in the small dining area. The table was set with four slices of cake and cups of coffee. Jeri's husband, Lee, was reading in a living room recliner.

"Lee's not joining us?" I asked as I took a seat.

Glancing past Kathy, Jeri shook her head. "He's into some goofy book about a pirate festival. He won't set it down." Lee chuckled and turned the page, oblivious to Jeri's comment.

Kathy spread a napkin on her lap and inhaled the aroma of the warm cake. "This smells wonderful. It's no wonder that Jonathan Edwards showcased this recipe on his television show."

Karla put a piece of cake into her mouth and closed her eyes. After swallowing, she wiped the corners of her mouth and said, "Jeri, this is heavenly."

"Like I explained on the show, this recipe was given to my mother by a Czech woman whose family owned a bakery. This was their signature dessert."

We all agreed that the cake was wonderful. Jeri reminded us that the recipe was in the Whistling Pines cookbook. As we finished our last bites of cake Kathy sat back and looked at me. "Our art class was…interesting."

"In what way?" I asked.

"I've never actually studied a man's physique before. I mean, my husband dashed past on his way into the bathroom, but to have a man sit there for hours letting us stare at his muscles and..."

Karla gestured with her hand. "I was uncomfortable. I mean, it's not like the view was unpleasant or X-rated, but it was strange to have a naked man just sitting there."

Not being one of the art students, Jeri leaned forward. "Was he totally...?"

"No," Karla replied. "The instructor carefully draped a sheet over his hip so there weren't any male parts showing, but there was still plenty of exposed skin."

"Speaking of discomfort," I said. "I got copies of newspaper articles about Charles Crowder and Deborah Evenson. Mr. Crowder was very striking."

The silence was deafening until Jeri gathered the plates and forks. "Would anyone like me to refill their coffee?"

Kathy was staring at me, waiting for more. When I didn't speak, she leaned back. "Charlie Crowder was a rich old bastard who used his money to buy people."

"Are you talking about Deborah Evenson?" I asked.

"She was one of his victims, but a quarter of the town worked for his railroad or his mines. He exploited his workers, barely paying them a living wage, while making himself rich. He owned them and their families. There weren't many other jobs except fishing and mining. Crowder knew those were tough, physically taxing jobs. He used this town and manipulated everything to his advantage."

"That's a strong accusation," I said.

Lee, who'd become interested in the conversation, set his book aside and stood. "Crowder made known who he supported for the city council and mayor, and expected his employees to vote them in. He threatened to bust the union and hire replacement workers if their wage demands were too high. All the while, he got richer and richer."

"I thought he generously supported the arts and the community," I said.

Lee shook his head. "Many a man sees his end on the horizon and tries to make up for a lifetime of sins. Charlie tried to put frosting on his exploitive life in the hope of making things right with the community and his God. I'm not sure either was fooled."

Karla looked uncomfortable. "I understand your anger, but I saw his generosity and the good it brought to our schools and artistic community. No one else has ever done more."

Removing the newspaper reprints from my pocket, I spread them on the table. "Deborah Evenson doesn't look happy in this picture."

The ladies passed the pictures around, then handed them back. Jeri wrinkled her nose like she'd just had a whiff of ammonia fumes. "Charlie looks equally happy with his

136

wife and with Evenson. I find it…disturbing that he's willing to show up at a charity gala with an attractive young woman a couple months after his wife passed away."

Kathy nodded. "It doesn't look like Deborah Evenson is happy about it either."

"The photographer may have caught her at an awkward moment," I said, picking up the printouts and refolding them.

Kathy shook her head. "Photographers take dozens of photos at those events. Either this represents Evenson's expression in all the photos or the editor chose this particular photo to express his own displeasure with Crowder's choice of escort."

Lee snorted. "Escort might be a polite word for Debbie Evenson's relationship with old man Crowder."

Chapter 10

The afternoon dining room crowd consisted of a foursome playing bridge, three former farmers arguing the wisdom of a new-age couple who'd transformed a farm from cattle to alpacas, and Wendy, who was engrossed in a crossword.

I brought a cup of coffee to the farmers' table and sat in an open chair. "What's wrong with raising alpacas?" I asked.

"It's the wolves," Vernal Hanson replied. "It's the same reason people don't raise sheep here. A herd of wolves show up and say, 'It's a mutton smorgasbord!' The next year the farmer wises up and buys cattle."

"Bah," George Classen said. "Farmers use alpacas to chase the wolves off."

Vernal leaned forward, stabbing the tabletop with his fingertip. "That's llamas, George. Alpacas are hardly bigger than a sheep, they have to be dewormed every month, and they cost ten thousand dollars each!" He leaned back and crossed his arms, exposing the worn elbows of his flannel shirt.

I looked at Bud Swanson, who had turned to George, awaiting the return volley of the argument. "What do you think, Bud?" I asked.

"I don't have an opinion," Bud replied. "I just like to watch the fireworks."

Vernal, obviously more irritated by the alpaca argument, glared at Bud. "You mean you've been sitting here for two cups of coffee and neither of us have swayed your opinion?"

"Hell, until Peter showed up, I thought alpacas were those green vegetables with the leaves you peel back."

Throwing up his arms, Vernal looked exasperated. "Those are artichokes, Bud. They don't even grow in Minnesota."

Bud nodded. "That's what I thought, which is why I thought it was so amusing. You two are arguing about raising artichokes that don't even grow here."

Vernal's blood pressure was rising, with his face turning red. I pulled out the library printouts and spread them on the table to change the topic before Vernal had a stroke. "What can you tell me about Charles Crowder and Deborah Evenson?"

Bud looked at the picture of Charles and Evelyn Crowder and smiled. "Old Charlie Crowder was the best thing that ever happened to Two Harbors. Before he ran the railroad into town, there were no jobs except fishing and trying to scratch out a living on forty acres of rocky soil. He brought good paying jobs here."

Shaking his head, George obviously disagreed. "Everything Crowder did, he did for himself. Yeah, he brought jobs, but he fought the unions every step of the way. I was on the negotiating committee, and we had to fight for every nickel an hour we got in raises. Crowder was making millions off the railroad, but all the workers got were crumbs from his table."

After gathering the printouts, I let the men move their argument to a different topic. Wendy looked up when I sat in the chair to her left. "I need a four-letter word for center," she said while twirling her pencil between her fingers.

"Try FOCI," I suggested.

She wrote in the letters, then went on to fill the crossing words. "Hulda asked me to model for her art class."

"I hope you declined," I replied.

"The negotiations are ongoing." Wendy completed more words, then looked up. Her eyes twinkled as she said, "I heard Melissa is negotiating with you, too."

"There are no negotiations. Melissa asked me if I'd pose for a million dollars. When I said, 'I'd consider it,' she laughed and said that even I had a price. I'm not modeling. And, neither should you."

"She offered $300 an hour."

"Posing in the nude would compromise your professional reputation with the residents."

"You mean *further* compromises my professional reputation. I'm sure you think my ethics are already tarnished because of the naturist cruise during the pirate festival."

"Your ethics are untarnished. You wore a bathing suit on the cruise."

The change in Wendy's expression made me uneasy. "I had a bathing suit on when we left the dock…"

I stood, not wanting any additional information.

Satisfied with my discomfort, Wendy moved on. "The Gin Fizzes have a gig at Hugo's Saturday night. You're welcome to sit in."

"My plate is full at work, and we have a baby at home."

"You might like a break from the kids."

"Thanks. I'll pass."

The bridge game had ended, and the ladies were putting the cards away as I passed. Karla Telker stood and guided me to a spot out of earshot from the other occupants of the room. "Kathy Christensen is a very talented artist. While most of our drawings look like they've been done by school children, Kathy has an eye for the lines and proportions that the rest of us lack. With a few lines, she captures the model's features. Her drawings are minimalistic, but incredibly good."

"Another talented person in the residence. I'm really pleased that she's had an opportunity to hone her skills."

"She's got her drawings taped to the walls in her apartment. They deserve to be on display where everyone can appreciate them."

"Perhaps we can set up an art show in the music room. All twelve of you can post your drawings so the other residents can see them."

"Make it a contest, Peter. Have the residents vote on the best drawings and offer prizes."

"My prize budget is limited to the dimes given to the Bingo winners."

"I'll give you five dollars if you can find donors to match it."

"I'm sure Nancy will match your gift. I'll mention your idea to her when I see her."

About to step away, Karla touched my arm. "Hulda will browbeat her friends into voting for her drawings. Make sure to discount those votes when you do the final tally."

"You want me to stuff the ballot box?"

"Not at all. I just want to make sure that the best drawings win."

I found Nancy reading in her office. She looked up and removed her reading glasses when I knocked on her door frame. "What can I do for you, Peter?"

"Karla Telker suggested that I arrange a competition to showcase the drawings from the art class. She offered five dollars for the prize if I could get someone to match her donation."

Raising her eyebrows and grinning, Nancy said, "And you hoped I might provide the matching donation." Without hesitation, Nancy opened her wallet and offered me a five-dollar bill.

"It's rumored that Kathy Christensen is a very talented artist."

Nancy looked surprised. "Really? I suppose Kathy's experience as a hairdresser gave her a sense of proportion and an eye for facial features. I can see how that could translate into artistic talent." After a pause, Nancy motioned for me to close her office door. "Tell me what's going on with the Evenson art exhibit."

I sat in Nancy's guest chair while composing my thoughts. "The diptych has created a stir. Deborah Evenson specified that those paintings could not be displayed together until after her death, and that's apparently because of the hidden themes visible when they're displayed together."

"The devil is in the details," Nancy said.

"Quite literally," I replied. "An art student working at the museum noticed images in the shadows cast by the morning sun. The shadows appear to depict a devil stabbing a woman with his pointed tail."

"How is that only visible in the morning?"

"Evenson created a sublayer of texture that creates shadows not visible when the paintings are lit from the front. She was very clever with her use of texture and color, and the diptych shows that to the extreme."

Nancy cocked her head, deep in thought. "Peter, Paul, and Mary sang, 'I Dig Rock and Roll Music'. There's a line in the last verse, 'the radio won't play it unless I lay it between the lines.'"

"That's a great analogy. I'm sure that's why Evenson didn't want the diptych displayed until after her death. She'd hidden a shadow image that displays something she didn't want revealed while she was alive."

"Who are the devil and the victim?"

I spread the printouts of the grainy newspaper photos on Nancy's desk. "These are pictures of Charles Crowder, who was Deborah Evenson's patron. He endowed her position as the artist in residence in the UMD art department."

Putting on her reading glasses, Nancy studied the photos and read the articles. "This is a terrible picture of Evenson and Crowder," Nancy said, handing the printouts back to me.

"Or does that picture really capture the nature of their relationship?"

"Are you still working with Chief Stone on this?"

Standing, I folded the printouts and put them in my pocket. "I've been developing a spreadsheet of Evenson's art catalog. She left a notebook with a list of all her paintings, their titles, the dates they were painted, and who bought the pieces."

"How long is the list?" Nancy asked, standing and moving to the door.

"I'm two pages into the list and I've already got over forty lines. I'm barely through the 1960s."

Placing her hand on my shoulder and gently pressing me toward the door, she said, "I hope you find something worthwhile in her notebook."

* * *

In my office with the door closed and locked, I continued transcribing Evenson's notebook into the spreadsheet. I flipped to the third page, prepared to make the next entry when my eyes were drawn to a scrawled message a third of the way down the page. All the entries before that point were neat, printed notes, confined between the notebook's grid lines. The message I read was in cursive and sprawled across four lines. "*The bastard took the painting.*"

There was a notation of the date she'd started, July 17th, 1975. And the title, *Nikki*.

There wasn't a completion date, nor was there a buyer listed. A notation after the title said, "Annika nude."

After contemplating the written comment for several minutes, I dialed Kerry's cell phone number. "What's up, Peter?"

"I found a curious comment in Evenson's notebook. Until this point, all the notations have been neatly printed and unemotional. This is scrawled in large cursive letters. It says, 'the bastard took the painting.'"

"Does it say which painting was taken?"

"The title is, *Nikki*. The notation says, 'Annika nude.'"

"I don't suppose *the bastard* is identified?"

"It only says *bastard*, which I assume to be a man. Given the emotion of the comment, I assume it would've said, '*bitch'* if a woman had taken it."

"Hmm," Kerry said. "I assume she knew who took it, and that it wasn't stolen without her knowledge. Does Annika have a last name? Maybe we can contact her to find out who took the painting."

"Well, it was taken in 1975, nearly fifty years ago. Even if the model was a college student, then, she'd be in her late sixties or seventies now."

Scanning the entries on the page, I searched for a clue to Annika's identity. I stopped at the notation after the scrawled note. "The next painting after *Nikki* is *Cottage/Cabin diptych*."

"So, someone took a painting of a nude, and the next painting Evenson does has the image of a devil stabbing a woman?"

"Right," I replied.

"There aren't any coincidences in law enforcement. I wonder if that's true in art as well?"

"If we identify the devil, we may know which bastard stole *Nikki*."

Kerry was silent for a moment. "Do you think Annika's father found out she was posing nude for Evenson, and he took the painting to keep her naked image from hanging in an art gallery?"

"I suppose that would be a motive if Annika was a teen model."

"Or if she was someone's wife."

I sighed. "Sometimes I hate living in a small town."

Kerry laughed. "Do you think some city teenager's father would be less unhappy than a small-town father if he found out his daughter was a nude model?"

"The librarian found photos of Charlie Crowder, his wife, and Deborah Evenson in newspaper archives. I have copies we can compare to the shadow images in the painting."

"Do you think the faces in the paintings are actual people and not just artistic creations?"

"I won't know if I don't look," I replied. "The museum curator was going to have special lighting erected to highlight the shadows. I should call him to see if they're through with the installation. Direct lighting should sharpen the shadows and that might make the faces more recognizable." I froze for a second, then pulled Evenson's book open to the page with the scrawled note. "See if any women were reported missing around July of 1975. That would coincide with the bastard taking the nude painting."

"I think it'd be more likely that 'the bastard' beat the crap out of Evenson for using his daughter as a model. That would be a hospital report."

"Humor me."

"You do realize that none of the records before 1990 are computerized, and some are on microfilm."

"Like I said, humor me. Ask your dispatcher to look through the records. There can't be more than a couple calls coming in on a shift."

"I'll figure something out. You keep at the spreadsheet. Call me if something else jumps out at you."

Needing a break from the spreadsheet, I walked to Kathy Christensen's apartment. "Come in!" She called out from inside the apartment.

While most people kept their apartments tidy, I often visited people who had coffee cups on the counter, newspapers spread on chairs, and snack crumbs on their tables. Kathy's apartment was spotless, with tasteful decorations and family photos on the walls and end tables. Between the framed photos, she'd taped five of her drawings to the walls.

"You've been busy at the art class," I said, stepping up to a charcoal drawing of a fruit bowl on a table. As Karla had observed, Kathy's style consisted of a few quick strokes that defined the outline of the subject matter. Her orange was easily discernible from the apple and pear in the bowl. Smudges defined the shadows cast by the fruit and bowl, giving the drawing depth and reality.

"This is fabulous, Kathy."

Many of the residents were embarrassed by compliments, but Kathy smiled. "Thank you."

"Have you taken art classes before?"

"Not art, per se. I took classes to become a beautician. Over the years I developed an eye for shapes, colors, and proportions."

"There's an artistry to creating a hairdo. You must've been good at it to have a career that spanned decades."

Kathy cocked her head. "No one has ever described my work as artistry, but I suppose there's a certain artistic flair to it, at times."

The next drawing was Ricky. Kathy's location has given her a view looking over the model's left shoulder. The only facial feature was his ear, but she'd captured the sculpting of his back muscles, buttocks, and triceps. Even the folds of the sheet over his leg showed depth in the shadowing she'd done.

"I'm arranging an art competition. I'm asking all the art students to bring their drawings to the lounge where we'll display them. I'll ask the residents to vote on their favorites."

"I'm not sure my art is ready for prime time, Peter."

"You may be the most talented artist in the group. Choose two of your favorites and we'll add them to the display."

Kathy pointed at an easel sheet nearest her window. "That's probably my best."

I stepped in front of a drawing of Sherry Vogel. Kathy's vantage point had been nearly straight in front of the model, whose head was turned to the side and tipped forward, so her hair obscured her face. With a few dozen lines and some charcoal shadowing, Kathy had captured Sherry's youth and beauty.

I'd been so consumed by the simple beauty of the drawing that I didn't realize Kathy was standing behind me. Her voice startled me. "You know, she's a perfect model. I mean, her body doesn't look like a girly magazine, but she has curves and dimensions. The way her hair draped across her face was perfect."

"It reminds me of a seated *Venus de Milo.*"

"I think that's a little much."

"Really, Kathy. This is lovely. What did Melissa say?"

"She wanted to have it framed and displayed in her gallery."

"If I didn't have a young son who'd appreciate the model for all the wrong reasons, I'd buy it myself."

I turned when Kathy drew a deep breath and let it out. "I'm not sure I'll ever do anything like this again. I can't explain it. I felt like my fingers were being guided by a higher force when I put down the original lines."

I gestured for Kathy to sit down, and I sat on the end of her couch. "I get that. There are times when I'm playing guitar when suddenly, it's not me strumming the guitar or singing. The music flows through me, not out of me."

"Like when you and Jenny sang the duet in the band shell."

Reflecting on that moment, I felt deeply moved and speechless. "Yeah."

"It sounds like that's happened to you more than once."

"Almost every time I play a guitar session, there comes a time when a higher power takes over."

"God is playing through you."

I shook my head. "I can't get my mind around the thought of God caring about Peter Rogers' guitar playing. But yes, there's something more there than just me." I paused and looked at the Sherry Vogel drawing. "That's not the last inspired drawing you'll do, Kathy. Just let your hands be guided. Don't force it, but let it happen."

"Thank you."

"For what?"

"For arranging the art studio opportunity. For offering encouragement." Kathy stood and walked to me. I got up and she pulled me into her arms. "Thanks for being…you. You're a gift to everyone here. Thank you."

I patted Kathy's back. "I do what I can."

Kathy released me and shook her head. "In the words of my daughter, 'bullshit!' You give your heart for us. For some people, this is a job. It's apparent that we're more to you than a bunch of demented old farts."

"You are."

"So, you're having an art competition. What's the prize?"

I tried to look shocked. "Bragging rights aren't enough?"

"Come on, what's the prize?"

"The winner gets a crisp ten-dollar bill."

Kathy's eyes sparkled like she was impressed by the prize money, but I knew she would've been happy to participate regardless of the prize. "It'd be nice if there was a blue ribbon I could hang on the drawing after I win."

"You're getting pretty cocky, young lady."

"Listen, Peter. I've seen what the others have been drawing. A paint-by-numbers sketch would be an improvement over most of them."

I wiggled my eyebrows. "I guess we'll see."

I turned to leave, but Kathy stopped me. "I was serious about the blue ribbon."

"I'll see what I can do."

Glancing at the kitchen clock, Kathy asked, "What's the afternoon movie?"

I dashed for the door. "I'll tell you in about five minutes."

Chapter 11

After starting a batch of popcorn as people filtered into the small auditorium, I looked at the Netflix offerings and found *The Proposal,* starring Sandra Bullock. The popcorn stopped popping as I got the movie started. I turned down the lights, passed bags of popcorn to the attendees, and slipped out the back door.

I locked my office door and took Evenson's book from my drawer, then pulled up the spreadsheet I'd started. Opening the records to the page with the note about the nude that had been taken, I thought about the pages of remaining records that needed to be transcribed into the spreadsheet. Struck by sudden inspiration, I entered the sequential dates of all the paintings, without entering any of the other information. In less than ten minutes I was up to 2022, where Deborah Evenson had entered the name of the last work, *Sunburst* which was still incomplete on her easel.

I leaned back and scrolled through the four pages of entries, trying to grasp the enormity of her body of artwork. After a moment of reflection, I started filling the column of painting titles. It was a slower task than keying in dates, but in less than an hour, I'd entered the name of every painting. Some were fanciful, like *Fairies on the Shore*. Others were inspired by other artists like *Starry Starry Night*.

After reading that title, I felt the need for a break and picked up my guitar. I picked the notes from Don McLean's song, "Vincent", and sang the opening line, "Starry starry night, paint your palette blue and gray…" Having played the song hundreds of times the lyrics were etched in my memory. Looking at Evenson's notebook made me sing them with different images playing in my head.

Halfway through the four-minute song, there was a knock on my door. I set the guitar aside, realizing that the movie was nearly over, and I needed to shut down Netflix and stow the popcorn machine.

Jenny walked in and closed the door behind her. "Finish the song."

"I need to…"

"I never get to hear you play anymore. Please finish the song."

I restarted the song and played with my eyes closed. As I started the third verse, I looked at Jenny who was gently swaying with the music with her eyes closed. The final chord faded, and her eyes opened. "What inspired you to play that song?"

155

I nodded toward the open notebook as I put the guitar in the corner. "Deborah Evenson painted a picture titled '*Starry Starry Night*.'"

"Are you making headway with her notes?"

"I have all the dates and painting titles entered in the spreadsheet."

"Have you found any surprises?"

Feeling suddenly guilty for not telling her about the scrawled message, I flipped to the third page and handed Jenny the notebook.

"Oh my." Jenny flipped through the pages. "Did she leave a hint about the identity of the 'bastard?'"

"I couldn't find any other reference to a bastard, nor does she identify the subject of the nude painting other than saying she was Annika. Kerry suggested that the model may have been a young woman whose father discovered his daughter was a nude model, causing him to destroy the painting to protect her reputation."

After handing me the notebook, Jenny stared at it. "If the theory about an angry father is true, someone in this small town would know who the model was."

"Kerry is checking records for a missing woman."

"A missing woman?"

"Maybe the model was so disgraced that she moved away." I nodded to the notebook. "The diptych in the museum has hidden

156

images of a woman being stabbed by the devil. Maybe the answer is in the shadows."

Jenny stared at the ceiling over my head. "Maybe the people depicted in those images lived in the shadows of Evenson's life."

"Wow," I replied. "I've been trying to identify the people closest to her. If you're right, I should be thinking peripherally, at the people who touched her, but weren't close."

"Be careful. They might've been physically close, but emotionally distant." Jenny paused. "We all have people like that in our lives."

I pictured Jenny's relationship with Jeremy's biological father. They'd obviously been intimate, but when Jenny revealed her pregnancy, he quickly disappeared from her life. Not wanting to pick off that emotional scab I said, "People like that can cause more pain than the people who remain distant."

Jenny nodded and stood. "There are a couple hundred people who know about Deborah Evenson. I imagine there are a few of them who knew her well enough to know the characters from the darker parts of the artist's life." Before opening the door, Jenny stopped. "Mom said my father is bouncing off the hospital walls, and ready to come home. The doctor won't release him until he completes tomorrow's cardio therapy session."

"I'm sorry. With all the other things going on I'd forgotten to ask about your dad."

"You knew he was past any danger."

"But still…"

"He's fine. Go ahead with your investigation."

* * *

The dinner crowd was gathering in the atrium in anticipation of the doors opening at five o'clock. It was a time of socialization more than a rush to be among the first people served a meal. Howard Johnson was standing near the mailboxes speaking with Bud Larson, so I decided to test Jenny's theory on them. "Good evening, gentlemen."

Bud lifted his arm, consulting his watch. "Technically, it's still afternoon."

Howard's look was precious. "It's afternoon, unless you're a senior citizen who'll be in bed before eight o'clock."

"Peter's not quite there yet," Bud replied.

"With a full-time job, a middle-schooler, and an infant, eight o'clock is often bedtime," I replied.

"You look like something's weighing on your mind, Peter," Howard said. As usual, he was perceptive and inquisitive.

"I'm going through a list of Deborah Evenson's paintings. In 1975 she was painting a nude. She made a note that someone took the painting before it was completed. Do either of you remember that being a topic of discussion back then?"

Both Bud and Howard shook their heads. "The '70s are a haze," Bud replied.

Howard glanced across the atrium, "I'll be right back."

Bud and I watched as Howard threaded his way through the people standing and sitting in the atrium. He avoided a group who tried to engage him in conversation and walked up to a person standing alone in front of the aviary. A moment later he had Ginny Johnson's elbow and was leading her across the room.

Ginny is a sweet woman whose memory had slipped over the years I'd been at Whistling Pines. She'd recently moved to the locked memory care unit after wandering away from her apartment one night.

"Peter, I'm sure you remember Ginny, my sister-in-law."

"Have we met before?" Ginny asked, offering her hand to me.

"I'm Peter Rogers, the recreation director."

Ginny smiled. "Are you the person who arranges the movies?"

"I am," I said.

Then I looked at Howard, trying to discern his reason for bringing Ginny over. He raised his hand and gestured for me to be patient. "What do you remember about 1975, Ginny?"

"That was the year the Vietnam war ended. I remember seeing helicopters pulling Marines off the top of the U.S. Embassy."

"What else happened that year?" Howard asked.

"The movie *Jaws* had everyone afraid to swim in the ocean, and some crazy woman tried to assassinate Gerald Ford."

Realizing that Ginny's short-term memory was terrible had left me with the impression her entire memory was gone. Howard had demonstrated how well she could bring back older thoughts. "Ginny, do you remember Deborah Evenson?"

"She was the artist with the studio up in the hills."

"That's right," I said.

"She was a pretty woman who did a lot of teaching at the schools." Ginny stopped, like her mind had frozen. "Mind you, she wasn't a teacher. She just came into town and coached the art classes. My Becky said, 'Ms. Evenson is so talented and pretty. I want to be just like her.'"

"Is Becky an artist?" I asked.

"Becky? No, she's not an artist. She does something with computers down in the Cities. But she thought Deborah Evenson walked on water."

"I'm looking through Deborah Evenson's notebooks and something happened in

1975. Do you recall an incident at her studio?"

Ginny frowned. "Is it proper for you to look through her notebooks?"

"It's okay. She gave me permission to catalog her artwork."

That answer seemed to satisfy Ginny, who nodded. "She had a lot of paintings. There was a show of her paintings in town in 1972. She had dozens of paintings. They were rather abstract, but the colors were beautiful and…"

After a minute's pause I tried to restart Ginny's thoughts. "You were talking about her studio show in 1972."

"It was a beautiful show. They had paintings from two artists. Deborah Evenson had a studio in the hills above town and she had some lovely abstract paintings. The other artist did more realistic works; things like landscapes and scenes along the Lake Superior shoreline."

"Do you recall the other artist's name, Ginny?"

"She was a university professor. I think she was Deborah Evenson's teacher when she went to the university in Duluth."

"Do you remember the UMD professor's name?"

"It was an unusual Swedish name, the same as that golfer."

"Annika?" I suggested.

"I believe that was it, Annika Banks. She was older than Deborah, but just as talented. She was pretty, in a fifty-year-old way, and always carefully made up. Deborah was striking and the men hung on her. Professor Banks was like her wingman, who steered her out of uncomfortable conversations, and was always after her to make sure she didn't drink too much." Ginny stopped abruptly. "Deborah Evenson never married. People in town knew that Annika Banks lived with her, so they assumed they were lovers."

"Is that what you thought, Ginny?"

"No, I don't think so. Annika treated Deborah like a protégé. They had chemistry, but the professor was a divorcee and twenty or more years older. I don't think they had anything sexual going on."

"What happened in 1975? Someone took a painting Deborah Evenson was working on."

"It was after the fall of Saigon. The news had settled down after the war ended. I think Evenson and the professor had a falling out because Annika Banks stopped shopping in town. She was the one who bought groceries. We never saw Deborah Evenson except when she went to the schools. Then, in the summer of 1975, Deborah Evenson started buying her own groceries. I commented on that to Marcie, at the grocery store over Independence Day. Marcie said the professor had taken a sabbatical and moved to Paris." Ginny looked at me. "People usually come back from sabbaticals, but Annika Banks never did. I guess she liked Paris better than Two Harbors."

Residents started filing into the dining room and Ginny became fidgety. "I'd best go for dinner. Ralph's probably looking for me."

I looked at Howard Johnson as Ginny walked toward the dining room. "Who's Ralph?"

"He's my brother who died in 1999."

I must've grimaced at the realization that Ginny was going to look for her husband who'd been dead nearly twenty-five years.

"Don't worry about Ginny's long-term memory. Her facts about Deborah Evenson and the events in the 1970s are spot on; Ginny was the hub of Two Harbors information from the 1950s to the 1980s."

"Did she have a job?"

"She ran the Two Harbors tourist information bureau for thirty years. Any outsider who stopped at the kiosk got the latest information from festivals, restaurants, and motels, to where the fish were biting. The locals got the hottest gossip. Ginny had it all."

"She must've had an encyclopedic memory," I said.

"She did, right up until my brother died. Ralph's death slowly sapped her drive. She slowed down, then started to forget things, like taking pills and eating meals. But as you heard, if you ask her anything about the period of her heyday of information, she'll give you the facts."

Chapter 12

I called Kerry while browning hamburger and onions for chili while Jeremy did homework on the dining room table. "I found a resident who remembered the events at Evenson's studio in 1975."

"Someone from town or one of your demented residents?"

"Not all of them have dementia."

"Assure me that your source of 1975 information is lucid and reliable."

After a moment, I'd framed my answer, without answering Kerry's question. "Ginny was definite about the events of 1975 from the end of the Vietnam war to *Jaws* being the thriller of the year."

"So, she can't remember what she had for breakfast, but she can remember 1975." Kerry sighed. "What did she tell you?"

"Deborah Evenson had an art exhibit with her mentor, Professor Annika Banks, that summer. She remembered Evenson as a striking young woman, and Banks as an attractive fifty-year-old woman who was very protective of her student. Contrary to the 'lesbian lovers' rumors of the day, Banks wasn't Evenson's lover. Ginny was convinced they were teacher and student who lived together."

"That's amazingly open-minded for someone of that day. Did she say how she came to that conclusion?"

"Ginny operated the tourist information kiosk. She was the hub of all information for both tourists and local gossip."

"Did she have a rumor about someone disappearing that summer?"

"Annika Banks took a sabbatical from the university to spend a year painting in Paris. She never returned."

"Good," Kerry replied as I drained the browned hamburger/onion mix and added a can of tomatoes to the kettle. "The case of the missing woman is closed. We can move on."

"I don't think so. Tenured professors return from sabbaticals. They work hard for tenure. They don't walk away from the university to 'find themselves' in Paris."

"Why can't you just let that door close? Maybe she met the love of her life while walking along the Left Bank and stayed there."

"See if you can find her in Paris," I said as I stirred kidney beans, minced garlic, and chili powder into the kettle.

Kerry coughed. "Yes, sir. I'll jump right on that, sir."

Bristling at his military mocking of my order, I counted to five. "I suggest that we look for Annika Banks in Paris. I have an uneasy feeling about her departure."

"*We* can do that as long as we are you and the mouse in your pocket. I don't have time to look for college professors who ran away fifty years ago."

"She's dead, Kerry."

"What makes you say that?"

"Intuition."

"If you feel strongly about it, dig around to see if you can find anything to substantiate your feelings." Kerry paused. "Are you thinking she's the woman in the shadows of the diptych paintings?"

"Jenny had an interesting insight. She asked if the devil and victim were painted as shadows because they were people from the shadows of Evenson's life."

"That seems reasonable. They were people who weren't directly connected to her."

"Or they were in her life but weren't engaged with her. Like the acquaintances who call you friend, but who wouldn't buy you a cup of coffee."

"Huh," Kerry said. "There are a lot of people who want to slap me on the back and buy coffee because I'm the police chief. As soon as I resign, or get fired, they won't recognize me in the grocery store."

"That's a great analogy."

"Who would've had that relationship with Deborah Evenson?"

"All the people who wanted to hang out with her because she was a famous artist, but who would've been gone from her life the day she set aside her paints and canvas."

"How do we find those people?" Kerry asked.

"I hate to say this, but it may have been everyone in her life. I remember a quote from Janis Joplin commenting about the loneliness of being a performer. 'Every night I make love to ten thousand people from the stage but go to bed alone.'"

"Wow. I'd never heard that quote before. It's tremendously sad."

I heard Jenny's car door slam in the driveway. "Jenny's home and I've got supper ready. I'll talk to you tomorrow."

"Peter…"

"Yeah?"

"Call your friendly librarian. She might have resources you don't know about to help search for the missing professor."

"Good thought! I'll talk to Margaret tomorrow."

Chapter 13

After checking the dining room rumor mill, I went back to my office and called the Two Harbors library. Margaret answered on the first ring. "Hi, Margaret. I hope you can help me with another mystery."

Margaret laughed. "If you can wait a couple hours until I check in the overnight book drop then read to a group of preschool children, I can try to help. What do you need?"

"A woman named Annika Banks was a UMD art professor. She was living at Deborah Evenson's studio until she disappeared during the summer of 1975. The likely explanation for her disappearance is that she took a sabbatical from the university to paint in Paris. I'm uneasy with that explanation because she was a tenured professor, and she never returned."

"Off the top of my head, I can't think of any way to trace her. I'll think about it while I'm doing my other chores and get back to you."

* * *

Making up voting sheets for the art show was easy. To prevent stuffing the ballot box, I made the first line the resident's name. After that, they were asked to rank their first, second, and third choices for best drawing. I set out a box with a slot on top to collect the completed ballots. I found an online clipart site and created blue, red, yellow, and white ribbons. The first three places would get the blue, red, and yellow ribbons. Everyone who got at least one vote would get a white 'honorable mention' ribbon.

I posted the rules. I planned to award everyone a ribbon whether they got a vote or not.

The logistics of locating display easels, getting the art class to bring their drawings to the movie room, and mounting the drawings, took way more effort than I'd expected. Some of the artists, like Kathy and Karla, showed up as requested, an hour before the judging was scheduled to begin. We mounted their pictures with art gum, assigned them a random number written on a Post-It note, and set the easels along the wall. The other artists straggled in, some excited about having the residents see what they'd drawn, and the others, like Hulda, came in at the last second, then argued about where their art was displayed.

"Don't set mine in the back corner," Hulda scolded. "No one will make it that far before they cast their votes." After consultation, we rearranged the display so that each artist's works were interspersed with the drawings of others.

At 10 o'clock, we opened the door and handed residents the voting sheets and pencils as they entered the room. Hazel Pearson grabbed my arm and pulled me aside. "This is so much fun, Peter. You should do more activities like this. We could have a knitting and embroidery show, just like the county fair."

Assuring her that I'd consider that suggestion, I let momentum take over the art show, and I picked up my guitar. Signaling Wendy, we went to stools I'd set up near the window. I picked the opening notes of Don McClean's *Vincent*, and Wendy sang the opening verse. We sang the second verse in harmony, then alternated verses until we sang the ending in harmony. A round of applause rippled through the room, blocking out the dozens of discussions.

We sang *Mona Lisa, Painter Man,* ending my repertoire of art related music. Wendy suggested *Let It Be Me,* then requests from the residents included *That's Amore,* and Chad and Jeremy's *Summer Song.*

The crowd had finished rating the artwork and were listening to the music, so I announced the last call on voting, then walked to the cardboard ballot box. Bud was standing in front of Kathy's drawing of the male model while complaining to Howard Johnson. "You can't even tell who the models were," Bud lamented.

Howard, always tactful and supportive, smiled and said, "Bud, it doesn't matter who the models are. They're obviously people blessed with natural beauty. Look at the muscles on the man's back, his curly hair, and the detail of his ear."

"But you can't see his face."

"This artist was sitting behind the model, so this is the view she had."

Bud stepped to his right and pointed to the next drawing. "The artist was sitting right in front of this model, and I still can't make out her face.

"Yes, Bud. Her head is tipped forward and her hair obscures her face. Ignore that and look at the lovely curve of her side and the detail in her fingers where they're resting on her thigh."

Hulda, leaning on her walker in front of the next drawing, snorted. "Is this supposed to be a bowl of fruit? It looks like a stack of tennis balls in a bowl."

Karla edged up next to me. "We certainly have a roomful of art critics."

Bud stepped in front of a drawing of the female nude, drawn from the side. It was a little crude, but Evelyn had captured the curvature of the model's arms, legs, and back from a side perspective. A bit of the

172

model's nose and chin peeked through her hair. "This one has no face. I can't tell who it is."

Chuckling, Karla leaned close to my ear. "We've done it. We've displayed twenty drawings of nudes, and no one can identify the model in any of them."

"Why is that perfect?"

"Because the rumor mill can't throw out names to ridicule. It's going to drive them crazy."

Bud threw up his arms in exasperation. "Hell, this could be someone from town, but it could just as easily be someone from Duluth or Grand Marais."

Kathy approached me from the other side. "Poor Bud, he doesn't know whose family to criticize. I'm sure he thinks our models are outcasts who grew up in families of big drinkers with loose morals." She paused. "I love it."

"What's this?" Bud asked, pointing at the tastefully draped towel. "Why didn't they draw in the boy parts in this model? What is he, a 1960s Ken doll with nothing between his legs?"

Karla leaned past me and winked at Kathy. "Good thing we didn't draw the part that was dangling below the sheet."

I looked back and forth between them. "Really?"

Kathy's eyes sparkled. "You'll never know for sure, will you, Peter?"

I snatched the ballot box from the table and took it to my office. I was certain Kathy's drawing of Sherry Vogel was the very best of the drawings displayed, but I was curious to see how the residents voted.

Ten minutes later, I'd completed the tally and carried the ribbons and ten dollars back to the movie room. Standing on a chair, I clapped my hands to get everyone's attention. "First of all, I'd like to thank the Whistling Pines artists for sharing their talents with us."

A round of applause followed and I waited for the sound to die down. "The voting was close, but there are three works of art that deserve special recognition." I let the anticipation build for a moment, then announced, "The first-place blue ribbon goes to Kathy Christensen for her female nude. Second place goes to Kathy for her male nude, and third place goes to Amanda Jennister for her female nude. Every other drawing got at least one vote, so I'm awarding honorable mention white ribbons to all the other drawings."

I stepped down from the chair and walked to Kathy's drawing of the minister's daughter and attached a blue ribbon to it. Kathy beamed when I handed her the ten-dollar prize for first place. Wendy helped me attach ribbons to the remaining drawings. Several residents gathered around Kathy to congratulate her on the drawing. Hulda pushed her walker through the crowd, stopping with the wheels nearly on Kathy's feet. "I don't see it. You hardly showed her little boobies."

* * *

It took an hour for the maintenance man and me to clear the room and stow the easels. A man of few words, Bingle stared at me for a moment. "You did good, kid. The artists got to show off, and the residents enjoyed being able to vote on the best drawing. It was a nice change of pace."

"Thanks, that means a lot coming from you."

"It would mean more coming from Nancy. She could make you hear it through your wallet. From me, it's just words."

"Not at all. You only speak when you've got something worth saying. Your words mean a lot to all of us."

He nodded thanks and left me to turn off the lights. I was walking toward my office when my cell phone rang. "Peter," I answered without looking at the caller ID.

"This is Dr. Blankenship. I've got the lights installed on the diptych. You should drive down and take another look at it. The shadow images are much sharper than they were in the morning light."

Weighing my interest in seeing the sharper shadow images against my distaste for another drive to Duluth, I acquiesced. "I'll be on my way momentarily."

"Excellent!"

* * *

I found an open parking meter, paid for an hour, and rushed into the building. Although the museum wasn't open, the right-hand door was ajar, and I let myself in. The new lighting drew me from the darkened exhibits to the room where the diptych was displayed. Blankenship, a lanky man in coveralls, and a chunky man wearing a sweater with a camera, were staring at the paintings. A camera on a tripod was aimed at the paintings. A young woman, in jeans and a ratty t-shirt, was adjusting a bank of lights. She placed a red lens over a spotlight when I joined the men.

"Why the red?" I asked.

The chunky man turned and glared at me. "You're a little old to be a student."

Blankenship put his hand on the man's arm. "Dr. Quill, this is Peter Rogers, the person who identified the two paintings as a diptych. Peter, Dr. Quill is the photography expert I mentioned."

Quill, pushing his glasses up, seemed unimpressed. "I'm the chairman of the graphic arts department. Not 'the photography expert.'"

Trying to appeal to the professor's ego, I said, "Dr. Blankenship suggested your eye might note some detail we've overlooked."

Quill looked away from me and considered the paintings. "Sylvie, try the green lens."

The student swapped out the red lens for a green lens and stood back, awaiting the professor's next order. Quill cocked his head and considered the shadows cast across the paintings. Then he sighed. "That's about the best contrast we've had."

He stepped to the camera, adjusted some settings, and snapped a photo. The image immediately displayed on a tiny screen mounted on the rear of the camera's case. Without looking away from the camera, Quill motioned for us to approach.

Although the screen was small, the displayed image was more distinct on the screen than the shadows on the paintings. I stepped back, looked at the paintings, then looked at the camera again. "Why is the image clearer in the photo?"

Quill let out a sigh and looked at Blankenship, as if pained to be explaining himself yet again. "The photo is black and white, which takes away the color that tricks your eye. The image is displayed in two dimensions, instead of three. Step back and look at the paintings with one eye closed."

I closed my left eye, and the image was indeed different. With the depth gone, the shadows looked sharper. While I stared at the photo, Quill put a different filter on the camera lens and snapped another photo.

"Yes, the polarizing lens cuts out the reflected horizontal light. Look at this."

Moving behind the camera, I stared at the now sharper image on the screen. "Can you blow that up?"

Sighing, Quill stared at me. "Of course, I can enlarge it. I only use the LCD screen to preview the image and make sure it's focused and centered." He looked at the student adjusting the lights. "Sylvie, take my XD card to Dr. Blankenship's computer and print a copy of this picture."

As the student trotted away with the tiny card from the camera, Quill shrugged. "It'll be better when printed on photo quality paper on a high-resolution printer, but we'll get an okay image to look at immediately."

We all stared at the paintings while awaiting Sylvie's return. I took the copies of the newspaper articles out of my pocket and unfolded them. "I thought the man and the woman in these articles might be the people depicted in the paintings."

Quill snatched the printouts from my hand and held them up to the light. "These are copies of poor-quality newspaper images."

"But the subjects are recognizable."

"Barely," Quill said, handing the printouts back to me. "Can you get the originals?"

"The Two Harbors librarian printed these from microfiche."

"That's not what I asked," Quill said. "Can you get the original photos? Or better yet, can you get the negatives?"

"I don't know."

"Well, find out."

Quill was apparently unaccustomed to dealing with anyone but students or people he felt were beneath his position as department chair. "I'm doing this as a favor for the Two Harbors Police Chief. If we discover something promising, I'm sure he'll assign an officer to follow up on it."

"Who are you?"

"I'm the recreation director at Whistling Pines Senior Residence."

"And, what's your interest in any of this?"

"To be perfectly honest, I'm mildly curious about the images. Beyond that, I have no vested interest in this...academic exercise."

Sylvie walked back before Quill could render further comment. She handed each of us a printed copy of the image and handed the tiny card back to Dr. Quill. I showed her the library printouts and saw her eyes light up. "That's the guy in the painting! The one with the devil's horns!"

Obviously unhappy about being upstaged by a mere student, Quill puckered. "There is some resemblance. Who is the man in the newspaper photos?"

Blankenship accepted the printouts and read the caption. "Oh dear, that's Charles Crowder. He was the artist's patron."

Quill cocked his head. "Her patron?"

Holding out the printouts, the curator pointed to the second photo, with Deborah Evenson on Crowder's arm. "Crowder built a studio for her in Two Harbors and paid her a monthly stipend while she honed her craft."

From the mouths of babes, often comes the truth. Sylvie shook her head. "He may have been her patron, but she didn't like him much. Look at the expression on her face."

"I wish I had a picture of Annika Banks," I said. "It's obvious the woman laying under the devil is neither of the women in these pictures."

Blankenship rubbed the tiny diamond stud in his left earlobe. "There's probably a picture of her in the university archives. When was she a professor here, Peter?"

"In the '60s and early '70s."

"I doubt the faculty photos from that era are digital."

Quill sighed. "They're probably in a dusty file cabinet in our darkroom. Sylvie, take Peter over there and see if you can find those files."

While leading me through the maze of interconnected walkways running between the buildings, Sylvie was quiet. We met a few students, but for the most part, the university was quiet. "Mr. Rogers?"

"Please call me Peter."

Sylvie stopped outside a door marked *darkroom* with keyring in hand. "I was wondering…"

Thoughts raced through my mind about potential topics that might've piqued Sylvie's interest. I expected her to ask about some aspect of the diptych that she'd seen. "What?"

"You're the recreation director at Whistling Pines, right?"

Surprised by the question, but intrigued, I said, "Yes."

Inserting a key in the darkroom lock, Sylvie paused. "My friend, Sherry, modeled for your art group. Her dad found out, so her modeling days are done." Opening the door and holding it for me, she stared at her shoes. "I could model for your class."

Unprepared to address her proclamation, I reached for a light switch while I scrambled for a response. "I'm not the one who hires the models."

Sylvie looked up at me. "I get it," she said, leading me back to a closet in the rear of the room. Flipping the switch, I saw a room filled with tan and gray metal file cabinets. Judging by the dust on top of the cabinets, I guessed the university had moved from battleship gray office furniture to tan after military surplus office furniture was unavailable, about 1950. The older cabinets were all five drawers high, the drawers built to contain paper correspondence. The labels indicated the year and months of the contents.

Scanning labels on the drawers of the tan cabinets, Sylvie and I quickly found the 1960s. I pulled open a drawer marked June-November 1960 and leafed through the folders, each tab marked with a date, but not the contents. Sylvie watched silently as I leafed through the photos developed and filed by date. "What's the matter?"

"Sherry's face is cuter, so I can see why you'd want her to model."

Intent on my search, I replied. "The instructor actually tipped Sherry's head forward so her hair obscured her face. The students focused on drawing her body."

"I have a nice figure."

Not finding faculty photos, I moved to the next lower drawer. "I really wasn't the one who hired the models. You need to speak with Melissa."

"Peter, look."

I glanced up from the waist-high drawer. Sylvie had lifted her t-shirt exposing her bare midriff. "I've got rock hard abs. Don't you think I'd make a suitable model for your class?"

I turned away, lost my balance, and tried to break my fall by grabbing the open file drawer. My weight on the open drawer tipped the file cabinet, causing the remaining drawers to slide open. In a cascade of events that occurred so quickly I couldn't react, I felt the file cabinet tilt forward. Pushing myself back, the cabinet crashed to the floor, spewing file folders and pictures. My backward momentum pushed me into Sylvie and the two of us tumbled to the floor.

I landed on top of Sylvie, eliciting a grunt of pained surprise. Quickly rolling to my side to get off her, I found myself looking at her shocked face. I pushed up on my elbow and reached out to her. "Are you okay?"

"I think so," she replied.

The noise of the falling file cabinet brought the pounding of footsteps running through the darkroom. "What happened?" A male voice asked.

"Um, Brad," Sylvie said, pushing herself onto her hands and knees. "We were…"

"I can see what you were…"

The male student with studs in his eyebrows and an array of tattoos on his exposed arms stared at me in judgement. "Aren't you a little old to be necking in the storage room?"

I put up my hands. "I was looking for a photo in the archives when the file cabinet tipped over. Sylvie tried to break my fall." Trying to reinforce my alibi, I knelt down and started gathering the photos and files strewn across the floor.

Unfazed by the file cabinet fall, Sylvie stayed focused on modeling. "So, Peter, what do you think? Will you recommend me to the artist?"

"Sure, I think you'd be great."

"The woman who owns the studio paid Sherry $300 an hour. I could really use the extra cash."

Brad's Doc Martin boots appeared at the edge of the spilled photos. "You're a little old to be hanging around with a sophomore."

Sylvie got in his face. "Gawd, Brad. Get over it."

Trying to ignore them, I shoved photos into the nearest files. As I gathered the spilled photos, I glanced at the folder titles and spotted one labeled '69-70 faculty. Abandoning the clean up, I pushed the pictures back into the file and stood. Brad and Sylvie pushed the file cabinet upright as I flipped through the smiling faces of the primarily White male university faculty members. I flipped each female photo over to check the name printed in black ink on the rear. The fourth woman's headshot bore a resemblance to Deborah Evenson. Annika Banks was a beautiful woman who appeared to be about fifty years old. The camera loved her. Her smile was warm and unforced. Her high cheekbones and perfect teeth made her look like the photo on a magazine cover. But

184

most enchanting were her eyes—they looked right into me.

Sensing someone at my shoulder, I turned my head and nearly bumped noses with Sylvie. "She's a goddess," Sylvie said. "I also think she's the person in the painting. Do you have the printout from Dr. Blankenship's computer?"

I handed the photo to Sylvie and took out the folded printout from my pocket. Brad stood alongside Sylvie as we compared Annika Banks' photo to the printout. "If you change the smiling face in the photo, to the woman's terrified look in the printout, I think they're the same woman."

Comparing the poor-quality reprint from the curator's printer with Banks' photo reminded me that we could get a reprint with higher resolution. "Sylvie, Dr. Quill was going to make a print from his XD card on photo paper. Where would he do that?"

"His office has a photo-grade printer. I'm sure he'd print the photo there."

Sylvie was nearly out of the door before I could stop her. "We need to pick up this mess."

She turned and flashed a dazzling smile at Brad. "You'll take care of this, won't you?"

Dazzled by Sylvie's smile, Brad sighed. "Fine."

Sylvie knocked on Quill's doorframe and waited for his acknowledgement, which was simply, "Come."

Blankenship was leaning over Quill's shoulder, watching as he manipulated the diptych photo on the computer monitor. The shadows got deeper, then lighter. The background faded out of focus, adding definition to the shadowy figures. A final manipulation sharpened the outline of the shadows, eliminating some of their length. Quill leaned back, studying his work. "I think that's the best I can do in a few seconds. Given more time, I might be able to get more out of it."

After pressing a button, Quill stood and stepped to a printer in the corner of his office. While we waited for the printer to spit out copies, I looked around at the dozens of photos hanging on his walls. They ranged from North Shore views, to shadowy woodland trails, to European fountains. Two of his framed pieces were magazine covers, hung alongside his accompanying photo submission. There wasn't a person in any picture aside from two self-photos. His desk was devoid of the usual happy family photos. The man appeared to be a complete narcissist, totally focused on himself and his achievements. I wondered how many times he'd been married and divorced.

Holding a stack of printouts, Quill studied his work. Seemingly satisfied that he'd made us wait long enough, he handed each of us a print. "These aren't suitable for a museum, but I think they're adequate for *your* use."

I was comparing Banks' photo to Quill's prints when he snatched the Annika Banks photo from my hand. "Perhaps a more trained eye will be able to catch the nuances of the subject's facial features."

I glanced at Sylvie, who'd also recognized the resemblance between the photo and the poor-quality printout, but she didn't dare interrupt her mentor.

"Dr. Blankenship," I said. "I think the woman in the painting is Annika Banks."

Quill looked at me like I'd just unapologetically farted. "Perhaps."

Blankenship put up his hand to stop further fireworks. "I think this serves Peter's mission." He waited a moment for Quill to hand Banks' photo back to me. "Would it be possible to view the collection of paintings at Ms. Evenson's studio?"

"I think the police chief would be very interested in your assessment of that collection. We're trying to establish their value."

Blankenship's eyes sparkled. "I'll look at the recent art auctions tonight and get a feel for the prices of her recent sales. Can we view her collection *tomorrow*?"

"I'll contact the Chief and make arrangements to get into the studio. Would ten o'clock work for you?"

Quill, irritated that the conversation was no longer about him, shooed us out of his office. Blankenship bid us farewell and hurried back to the museum. Sylvie stood staring at me expectantly.

"Um, thanks," I said.

Sylvie put out her hand. I went to shake and she frowned. "Give me your phone."

"Why?"

"I'll program my number in so you can give it to the art instructor who hires models."

"Right," I said.

I called Kerry on the way back to Two Harbors. "I'm on my way home. I'm reasonably certain that we've identified the people in the diptych shadows."

"Who do you think they are?"

"The devil figure appears to be Charles Crowder and the female victim is Deborah Evenson's professor, Annika Banks."

"Do you have any idea why Evenson put them into the painting?"

"Not yet. They both obviously had some influence on her. Maybe she thought Crowder was the devil who hated Evenson's mentor. Banks' UMD photo from '69 bears a strong resemblance to Evenson."

"You found a picture of Annika Banks at UMD?"

"There was a faculty picture of her from the late 1960s in their photo archives." I chuckled. "There's a funny story about that."

"A funny story about her picture?"

"No. A student was helping me look through file cabinets full of old photos when the file cabinet tipped over."

"Are you and the student, okay?"

"We're fine. I jumped back when the cabinet tipped and fell on top of her. It was comical. Then her boyfriend walked in and thought we'd been necking in the archive room."

"Why would he suspect that?"

I chuckled again. "The student wants to model for Melissa's art class. She was showing me her abs when the file cabinet tipped."

"Wait. You were in an empty archive room with a female college student who was showing you her cute abs?"

"That's why the cabinet tipped over. I kind of fell against an open drawer when she lifted her t-shirt…"

"Oh, this just keeps getting better."

Realizing I was digging a hole, I backpedaled. "I wasn't encouraging her. As a matter of fact, that was the problem. She thought I wasn't taking her modeling offer seriously so she was showing me how cute her body was."

"Peter…"

"What?"

"Quit digging. You hit the bottom of the hole."

"Really! I was trying to explain that I didn't hire the nude models but she kept..."

"Toss the shovel aside and climb out. You're done."

"I told her I had nothing to do with hiring the models, but she insisted that I give her number to Melissa."

"Uh huh. She gave you her number."

"I didn't have a pen, so she programmed it into my phone contacts."

"What did she file it under, 'hot young nude model?'"

"I didn't actually see..."

"That was sarcasm, Peter."

Suddenly aware of how lame the story sounded I decided to move on. "I'm sure Jenny will laugh when I tell her about it."

"I think that would be among the top ten of all-time bad things to tell your wife."

"But Kerry, we share everything."

"You should forget to tell her this one. A sin of omission."

I sighed. "The museum curator is looking up sales prices of Evenson art tonight. He'd like to look in her studio tomorrow. I think he could put a ballpark valuation of the remaining art. We talked about meeting at ten tomorrow."

"Great. I'll call the realtor and have him meet us at the house with a key."

Chapter 14

I was drinking coffee in the dining room with Karla and Kathy, who broke the bad news that Melissa's female model was *unavailable.* Kathy's eyes twinkled when she added, "I understand her father assigned penance for her sins."

"I thought her father was a Svenska Gotter? I don't think they go to confession or have penance." Karla replied.

Kathy's smile was precious. "The SGs don't go to a *confessional,* but believe me, every Protestant denomination has its own version of penance. Most Protestant penance is worse than reciting a few 'Hail Marys.'"

My cell phone buzzed. "Excuse me," I said, rising from the chair. "This is Peter."

"Meg Cochran and I are parked under the portico. Are you ready to drive up to Evenson's studio?"

Checking my watch, I realized it was nearly ten o'clock. "Yes, I'm walking through the lobby."

With Meg alongside Kerry in the front, I climbed in the back seat. "Good morning, Meg. I didn't realize you were joining us."

"Kerry and I were discussing the security arrangements for the Tall Ships Festival, and he asked if I'd like to see Deborah Evenson's studio and art collection. It was an offer I couldn't refuse."

I buckled my seatbelt as Kerry eased out of the parking lot. "The Tweed Museum curator is meeting us there. I think it'll be good to have someone like you, with an eye for local scenery, along."

"I doubt that I can add much to the discussion, but I'm curious about Evenson and her studio."

Kerry glanced at me in the rear-view mirror. "Did you bring your spreadsheet of Evenson's workbook?"

I unfolded the four-page document and handed it to Meg. "Evenson kept a log of her works, the date they were created, who bought them, and the sale price. Some of her later pieces are listed as 'consigned' without price information."

Meg flipped through the notebook, stopping at the last page. "These early buyers got real bargains. Her first few paintings sold for $100. The last sale was six-figures."

Kerry nodded. "I assume she was a typical starving college student in her early

192

days, and one hundred dollars was a lot of money."

Our discussion of Evenson's notebook and the huge body of her works went on as Kerry drove up the hillside above Two Harbors. We spotted a powder blue Mercedes SL idling at the end of Evenson's driveway. Dr. Blankenship waved from the driver's window and followed Kerry up the winding driveway.

The realtor's SUV was parked in front of the garage with the tailgate open. Kerry clucked his tongue. "I wonder what Oscar Pederson has decided needs to be removed for safe keeping?"

I unfastened my seatbelt and stepped out of Kerry's cruiser. "I thought you were going to have someone here for security."

"Roger was here overnight. I told him he could leave when the realtor arrived."

"Security?" Meg asked.

"There are dozens of paintings in the studio," Kerry replied as we walked up the sidewalk. "And you saw the selling prices of her recent works."

"She must have a security system," Meg said.

Kerry stopped at the top step. "The time lapse between someone triggering an alarm and the arrival of one of my officers might be half an hour. A focused pair of thieves could clean out the entire collection before my officer even got the call."

The front door was open, so we walked into the living room. Meg, in awe of the displayed artwork, froze a few steps inside. "Oh my."

A step behind, Blankenship bumped into her. Unable to see what had caught her attention, he bobbed his head. "What?"

Taking a step aside, Meg continued to take in the art on the walls. Blankenship gasped. "My God, this is incredible. Any museum curator I know would sell his soul to have a collection like this."

Kerry was distracted and stared at the ceiling. "What's the matter?" I asked.

"Someone's walking around in the attic." He motioned for me to follow as he rushed into the studio.

A ladder had been pulled down from the ceiling and dim light showed through the opening in the ceiling. A foot tentatively stepped down, the toe of a well-polished shoe, searching for the ladder's top step. The process was repeated as the realtor slowly descended the ladder.

When he was three steps down, Kerry asked, "Do you need a hand with something, Oscar?"

Startled by Kerry's voice, Oscar's toe missed the next rung of the ladder and he fell, landing with his feet tangled in the bottom ladder rung. A framed canvas was still in his hands.

194

Hearing the commotion, Meg and the curator rushed into the studio just as Oscar, still clutching the canvas, tried to pull his feet free of the ladder and push himself onto one elbow. Blankenship pushed past us and snatched the canvas from the realtor. "My god, man. You might've punched a hole in this!"

Oscar, trying to regain his composure, rolled onto his side and stood. His shirt was sweaty from being in the warm attic and he'd rolled up his shirtsleeves. "You shouldn't have snuck up on me like that."

I walked to the bottom of the ladder and investigated the poorly lit attic above. "What did you find up there?"

"I think Evenson stored this blank canvas up there."

Blankenship looked up from the canvas he was holding. "They call that laying down a layer of gesso. Artists do that to stabilize the canvas and provide a base for future painting." He turned the canvas so we could see it. "They often make a drawing on the gesso as an outline for the future painting. It appears Ms. Evenson was planning to make this a view of her living room."

Pederson turned to fold the ladder and raise it back into the ceiling when Kerry stopped him. "What else is up there?"

"Dust and insulation."

Kerry handed me his flashlight. "Take a look around, Peter."

The realtor held onto the ladder, with it partially folded. "There's no need to do that. It's mostly empty up there."

I reached past Pederson and lowered the ladder. Meg and Blankenship were studying the attic canvas. "Dr. Blankenship, wouldn't an outline of a future Evenson painting have value?"

"Now that Ms. Evenson is deceased and not producing any more paintings, this outline is probably worth nearly as much to a collector as a finished painting. It might be even more valuable because it is so rare."

"What do you see, Peter?" Kerry called from below me.

"There are racks of framed canvases that look like she's just painted a coat of white primer on them. Wait. Most of them appear to have sketches outlined on the primer."

Kerry was glaring at Pederson when I descended the ladder. "I take it you had plans for those, Oscar."

"Are you accusing me of something, Chief?"

"I'm just asking a question."

Oscar drew a breath and glared at Kerry. "I'm acting as the trustee's agent and it's my duty to locate and secure all items of value."

"Are there more sketches in the back of your SUV?"

The question caught the realtor off guard and his façade slipped for a fraction of a second. "They need to be appraised. I can't get any appraiser to crawl around in the attic."

Kerry was about to comment when Meg put her hand on his arm. "Who was going to appraise them, Oscar?"

"I was going to…take pictures and send them to a guy in New York."

Meg's eyes drifted from Oscar's face to his wrist. "That's a lovely Rolex President, Oscar. They're expensive."

"Listen, antique lady, I work hard and earn a decent living. Owning some baubles is one of the perks of my job, like the Escalade."

"Could I look at your watch?"

Oscar reflexively wrapped his right hand around his wrist. Realizing how defensive that appeared, he let go and held out his left arm to Meg. "It has diamonds for the hours."

"It's lovely, Oscar. Could I hold it?"

Oscar glanced at Kerry first, then he reluctantly unsnapped the watch and handed it to Meg. She carefully turned it, looking at all the surfaces. "It's not one of those cheap Far East knock-off watches. This is a genuine Rolex. I can read the registration number on the bezel."

Oscar extended his hand. "Thanks for confirming what I already knew."

"Kerry, write down this number," Meg said, turning to get the best lighting on the inside of the watch."

"What are you up to?" Oscar asked, reaching for the watch.

Meg read numbers to Kerry as Oscar tried to grab the watch. After finishing the serial number, Meg handed the watch to Oscar. "All the pawn shops and antique dealers get a weekly list of stolen property from the nearby counties. There was a Rolex President on last week's list from St. Louis County. It was stolen from a Duluth estate."

"I purchased that from a legitimate dealer," Oscar protested.

"Perhaps you did," Meg replied. "One call to St. Louis County or to Rolex will answer that question. Rolex keeps a list of all their registered timepieces. A legitimate dealer will consult with the company when the watch is resold, and the new owner's name will be registered."

"That is unlawful search and seizure," Oscar said, snapping the watch onto his wrist.

"I don't think so," Meg replied. "I have three witnesses who saw you voluntarily hand the watch to me. If that's the stolen watch, Chief Stone can arrest you for possession of stolen property. I might suggest that he use that information to get a search warrant for your house and office to see what other baubles you might've acquired."

Oscar ripped the watch from his wrist and threw it to Kerry. "The guy who sold it to me swore it was a family heirloom."

Blankenship, who'd been oblivious to the whole watch discussion while looking at his phone, glanced up when the room went silent. We were all staring at him, and he blushed. "Um, sorry. Did I miss something?"

"I assume you were looking for other Evenson sketches available on the internet," I said.

"No one would put something like this on eBay. I have access to auction sites and dealers who handle high-end art. There are no other Evenson sketches currently available for sale. The only one I could find was a very crude sketch she drew as a college student. A collector paid $35,000 for it in 2019."

Kerry looked at me. "How many canvasses did you see in the attic?"

I shrugged. "I didn't count them. Maybe two dozen."

Meg quickly did the math. "That's at least a half million dollars in the attic." Then she gestured to the art around us in the studio. "Dr. Blankenship, I assume these completed and partial paintings are worth more than the sketches."

Blankenship, still clutching the sketch to his side, nodded. "We're standing in a museum. No, I don't think one museum could afford to purchase all of these paintings."

Kerry turned to the realtor and put out his hand. "Give me the house keys."

"I'm the trustee's representative."

Kerry shook his head. "I spoke with the trustee this morning. Your services are no longer required."

"But…"

"The keys, Oscar. Give me the keys."

I watched Meg, who owned an antique shop, now deep in thought. When Kerry had the key in his hand, Meg spoke up. "I don't deal in high-end jewelry and watches, but I think a used Rolex President is worth about $35,000. What level of crime is having a stolen watch of that value, Kerry?"

A smile curled the unscarred side of Kerry's face. "Meg, that would be a felony. It could bring a sentence of up to 20 years in prison and a $100,000 fine. What's even more painful might be restoring the property to the rightful owner and the civil penalty of an amount equal to the value of the stolen property, plus a punitive fine of the same amount." Kerry turned to Oscar. "That watch might cost you $100,000 and your freedom for a decade."

"Hey, I had no idea that the watch was stolen."

"I'm sure that would sway the judge toward the fine and a suspended sentence.

But only if you have a good lawyer, and they're not cheap."

I cleared my throat. "Would you like me to look in the back of Oscar's SUV? He might've carried out a couple sketches from the attic before we arrived."

"I *DO NOT* give my permission to search my vehicle."

"If the back is open, whatever I can see is in plain view and a search warrant isn't needed."

Oscar jammed his hand into his pocket and brought out a key fob. He stabbed a button and his SUV beeped. "The back is not open."

Kerry's lopsided grin unnerved Oscar. "What?"

"Anything I can see through the windows is fair game too."

"Shit."

Kerry took out his handcuffs and cinched them around Oscar's wrists while reciting the Miranda warning. He punched a number into his cell phone while Oscar sat on a stool in the corner, much like an unruly child being punished by his teacher.

I showed Ewell Blankenship my spreadsheet, then he scanned the room. "We should tick off the paintings that are here, so the Chief will have an idea if there's anything missing."

While none of the paintings were labeled, Meg, the curator, and I were able to identify most by Evenson's description. We moved from painting to painting until I realized Meg had stopped to study a piece we'd marked off the list. "Ewell, look at the layering in this painting."

The curator walked back and stood next to Meg. "That's Deborah Evenson's signature style. She puts multiple themes in the same painting. Depending on your physical and mental perspectives, you see different things. The diptych in the museum has visual images, as well as shadow images created by texture."

"I'm seldom speechless," said Meg, who always spoke her mind, sometimes emphatically, "but this painting touches something in me. I see images of places in town from my childhood." She pointed to a diagonal line. "That's Highway 61, running past the old downtown businesses. And here are the two Lutheran churches."

Cupping his chin in his palm, the curator studied the images. "I'd say Ms. Evenson didn't hold the churches in high regard. She depicted the buildings as slanted, biased. I wonder if there's a deeper reason for that?"

Meg drew a breath and sighed. "She was engaged to a Catholic man in the '60's."

"I thought she never married," I replied.

"She didn't. The Lutheran minister refused to marry them unless he converted."

"You're joking."

"It was a different time, Peter. The Norwegian Lutheran church still had one service in Norwegian. Catholics believed Martin Luther was a heretic and only they went to heaven. If you were baptized a Lutheran, you were a Lutheran for life and so it was with the Catholics, too."

"They could've been married by a judge, or something."

"Nope. They broke up," Meg replied. "He moved away. She stayed single."

"That's so…"

"I know. Things were different sixty years ago before Vatican II and ecumenism. Even so, we have a Norwegian Lutheran Church across the street from the Swedish Lutheran Church." Meg grinned. "You do know the definition of a Two Harbors mixed marriage, don't you?"

"A tuba player marrying a clarinetist?" I guessed.

Meg shook her head. "A Norwegian marrying a Swede. And don't get me started on what the locals used to call someone who married a Finn."

Blankenship had been listening in and nodded his head in agreement with Meg's comments. "I don't use that word in polite company."

Kerry walked back into the studio, ending the discussion of Scandinavian ethnicity. "The county attorney is drafting a search warrant for the Escalade and Oscar's premises. The sheriff is dispatching a deputy to take Oscar to the county jail."

"This joke has gone far enough," the realtor said from the corner. "Unlock the cuffs and I'll bring the other sketches inside."

Kerry looked at Pederson and shook his head. "I'm not sure how you got a realtor's license, but your previous arrests should've excluded you from being inside anyone's home without an escort."

I raised my eyebrows. "Old Oscar has been stealing stuff since he robbed the candy store as a kid. The judge has been lenient. I expect that's about to end."

"I'll be out of jail two minutes after they drop me off."

Kerry smiled. "You might want to transfer some money over to your checking account. The court doesn't take kindly to people who bounce bail checks."

"I have friends…"

"Oscar, friends like yours tend to disappear once they hear you've been stealing jewelry and paintings from estates that you're selling."

Blankenship was bored with the legal discussion. "Are there more paintings in the rest of the house?"

I nodded toward the living room. "She's got some smaller pieces in the kitchen and bedrooms."

Pointing to my spreadsheet, Blankenship asked, "What do you know about the nude? It's listed, but there's no indication that it was sold or gifted to anyone."

"There's a note scrawled in her records that says, 'the bastard took it.'"

The curator stopped. "Which bastard?"

"There's no explanation in her notes."

"Someone removed a painting against Evenson's wishes and all she did was write an angry comment in her notebook?" Meg asked.

"That's all I know. There's no mention of it being recovered and I haven't seen it here."

Meg sidled up to the curator. "Pull out your phone and search for an Evenson nude."

The curator handed the spreadsheet to me, then his fingers flew over the cell phone screen. "This will only work if it's on public display. Chances are whoever 'the bastard' was, kept it in his private collection."

I froze as a thought buzzed through my mind. "What if the bastard destroyed it?"

The curator looked at me as if I'd blasphemed the Lord. "Destroyed a painting?"

"Maybe he was offended by the subject or the artist's depiction of the model."

Snorting, Blankenship finished entering his search and waited for the results. "That'd be ludicrous. No one intentionally destroys pieces of fine art." With something catching his eye, the curator looked at his phone. "It wasn't destroyed. It's in the Crowder room of the Naperville Art Center."

"Where's Naperville?" I asked as the curator handed Meg his phone to view the painting.

"It's a Chicago suburb," Meg said before handing the phone to me. "I heard that's where Crowder moved after his wife died."

The phone's screen was small, so the image of the painting was miniscule. Like Evenson's other art, there appeared to be layered images. The small screen forced my eye to focus on the main image without the clutter of her other subthemes. The model was leaning back on a couch with a cat on her lap. "Let's go back to the living room."

I held the phone out to Meg and Blankenship and pointed. "The model was sitting on that couch."

After a moment of contemplation, the curator nodded. "The other things I see are the careful flowing lines and soft colors. Evenson liked this model. There are no angry, crooked buildings like the Lutheran churches depicted in her other painting. This nude painting exudes warmth without being lurid or offensive." He paused. "It's incomplete."

"What do you mean?" I asked.

"The model is complete, but some of the background is missing. Look under the couch."

I took the phone and tried to enlarge the image but couldn't see anything but darkness. "Maybe she intended that area to be in the shadows."

"There is nothing missing in any Evenson painting. Every square centimeter is filled with images and meaning."

Meg had been silent through the entire conversation. I looked at her, knowing how out of character her silence was. "What is it, Meg?"

"Sometimes we say things by not saying them."

"Huh?"

"It's possible that the painting is incomplete. But did the artist intentionally leave a blank space as a statement?"

The curator wrinkled his nose. "Well, it's not gesso white, so she did paint something there."

I took a breath, afraid to throw out the thought that was in my mind. "What if '*the bastard*' painted over what Evenson had depicted there? That's why he took the painting."

Meg pointed her finger at me and smiled. "I think that's the answer."

Chapter 15

After the county deputy loaded Pederson into his cruiser, Kerry locked Evenson's studio and stared at Meg. "I have to call the trustee and tell him he needs a new, trustworthy person to handle the estate disposal."

"Why are you looking at me?" Meg asked.

"You've disposed of estates before, right?"

"I've arranged estate sales. I'd need an elevator to move up to this level of estate management."

"Is there someone more trustworthy in Two Harbors, Meg?"

"Flattery will get you everywhere, Chief."

Kerry handed her the house key. "Do your best until the trustees find a suitable replacement."

Meg paused, fingering the key. "I have a shop to operate."

Kerry nodded. "Trust me, you'll be able to pay someone to fill in at the shop." He mentioned the management fee Pederson was being paid.

Meg grinned. "Well, shit, Chief. I think you just hired a new estate manager."

We were halfway back to town, before Kerry broke the silence. "Did you tell Melissa about your new model?"

I looked out the side window as we approached town. "I passed on Sylvie's name and phone number."

"Did you delete them from your phone?"

I jammed my hand into my pocket and retrieved the phone. Kerry laughed and explained the modeling offer to Meg as I pulled up my contact list and deleted Sylvie's information.

Laughter made me look up. Kerry and Meg were chuckling at the line of ladies under the portico. "It appears you're late for something," Kerry said.

"It's the painting class. Melissa has models lined up nearly every afternoon."

Meg looked over her shoulder as the car rolled to a stop. "I heard the art class is like a book club, more about the wine and less about the artistry."

"I think the class has become more interesting since Melissa found a cute male model to pose for the students."

"Ooh," Meg said, "maybe I'll have to take up drawing. Wine and a cute naked guy. What's not to like about that?"

Hulda was in my face as soon as I stepped out of Kerry's cruiser. "I told you not to drive so darned fast. How many times has the Chief arrested you now?"

Knowing the argument would be futile, I trotted to the van and pulled it around to load the art class. Kathy and Karla were the last two students in line. Both were smiling at me in a way that made me feel like I should run. Karla leaned close and whispered, "I heard you've recruited a new model to replace the minister's daughter."

"How?"

Kathy patted my arm as Karla climbed the steps. "It's a small town, Peter. You've got to remember that when you do something stupid."

"Stupid like?"

"Recruiting a cute female college student as the replacement nude model for our art class."

"I didn't…"

"Reality becomes what people believe," Kathy whispered. "Your protests mean nothing."

I tipped my head back as Kathy climbed the steps. Steeled for the heckling I was going to receive on the drive, I climbed in and started the engine.

Ardis Anderson was seated behind me. We were barely out of the driveway when she leaned forward. "How are the new model's…qualifications?"

"She's a nice graphic arts student who needs to pick up a few extra dollars. That's everything I know."

"How does Jenny feel about you interviewing nude models for us?"

"There was no interview. I put her in contact with Melissa and…" I stopped. "Did Melissa tell you about this?"

"Where else would we hear about it," Ardis asked. "It's not like we have a lot of outside contact."

Melissa and Ricky were standing in front of the art studio, awaiting our arrival. Ricky stepped forward and helped the ladies down the steps, while I unfolded Hulda's walker. Not that she needed it. With spontaneous energy derived from the cute young model's arm, Hulda virtually danced across the sidewalk and into the studio.

Melissa watched with amusement while sipping her bourbon-laced "coffee." She took my elbow after Kathy and Karla passed by us. Leaning so close I was nearly intoxicated by the bourbon on her breath, she whispered, "Thanks for passing on Sylvie's information. We talked this morning, and she sent me a couple pictures of herself in yoga clothing. She's motivated and looks svelte."

"You don't need to tell people I found her."

"You should take credit, Peter. Not everyone is willing to approach young

211

women and ask if they're willing to pose nude."

I was about to protest until I saw Melissa's smile. "Gotcha." She turned away but stopped at the door. "We'll be through in about 90 minutes. You really should stop in to see how much progress the ladies are making. Some of them are quite talented." She left unsaid that some were not as talented.

"I don't need to see Ricky's modeling assets."

Melissa rolled her eyes. "There is always a strategically placed sheet covering his assets."

"I heard that rumor."

"It's the truth. I find the amateur classes get too caught up in details when I'm trying to teach them to take broad sweeps of shoulders, arms, and legs. In part, that's why I have the models tip their heads forward so the students don't spend too much time trying to draw eyes and noses."

"Kathy seems to be getting your message."

After sipping her coffee, Melissa smiled. "Some students are more gifted than others."

"You'd better get inside before Hulda rearranges the carefully placed sheet."

Melissa roared. "Ricky is into karate. No one is going to 'accidentally' slip the sheet off his lap."

"He won't hurt them?"

"No, he's incredibly aware of his surroundings and his hands are quick."

I climbed into the van and thought, *but Ricky hasn't dealt with Hulda.*

* * *

Trying to avoid discussion of the new model, I breezed past the dining room and hid in my office. I stared at the box from Evenson's garage, realizing I'd been focused on her notebook, and hadn't leafed through the other material. With the box on my lap, I flipped through correspondence from fans, birthday cards, invitations to events, and brochures she'd picked up at a variety of art and charity events.

Near the bottom, I felt texture on a piece of paper. I assumed it was a notarized contract, and out of curiosity, I unfolded and read it. Stunned, I re-read Deborah Evenson's original birth certificate. Her biological father's name was listed as unknown. Her mother was Annika Pearson. "*What are the odds that Evenson's college mentor and biological mother were different people, both named Annika?*"

I dialed the library and was relieved when Margaret rather than one of the volunteers answered the phone. "Margaret, I need help."

Laughing, Margaret said, "I'm going to get a complex, Peter. You only like me

213

because I can provide you with information. You could stop in for a cup of coffee occasionally."

"I've got a birth certificate. The mother's name is Annika Pearson. Can you tell me if she married someone named Banks?"

Computer keys clicked in the background. "Annika Banks was Deborah Evenson's mentor, right? So, I assume you're trying to determine if she was also her biological mother."

"Margaret, you should've been a detective."

"Solving mysteries is half my job, in case you haven't noticed." Margaret paused. "Annika Pearson married Paul Banks on July 28th, 1950, in Silver Bay."

"Did they have any children?"

Keys clicked, then paused. "I don't see any birth records with them listed as parents. There's a divorce decree dissolving the marriage in 1955. It doesn't appear Annika ever remarried."

"Hang on," I said. "I'm into an interesting layer of paper in the box. I've got a newspaper clipping announcing the death of a Silver Bay soldier in Italy, dated August 1943. Can you tell me if Annika Pearson and Rolf Magnus knew each other?"

"What? How would I…?" Margaret sighed as the computer keys clicked. "You're going to owe me more than a cup of coffee if this search works. I've got the Silver Bay

High School yearbook from 1941. Annika Pearson and Rolf Magnus were classmates. She was a sophomore when he was a senior."

I flipped to Evenson's birth certificate and read the date. "Holy shit."

"What?"

"I think Annika Pearson was pregnant with Deborah Evenson when the Magnus kid was deployed to Italy. She didn't put his name on the birth certificate because he was dead when the baby was born."

Margaret's fingers flew over the keys. "Annika was only sixteen when the baby girl was born. Only a teenager herself, and without a father to help raise the child, she apparently put her baby up for adoption. Evensons, living in Duluth, adopted the baby girl they named Deborah, a week later."

I continued digging through the last papers at the bottom of the box. I set aside school pictures, report cards, and a commendation for best drawing. I stopped when I removed a card. "I found an announcement the Evenson's sent out. 'We've got a new baby.'"

"At some point, Deborah Evenson must have requested the name of her birth parents from the state. Since no father was listed, they only needed Annika Banks' permission to release Evenson's original birth certificate."

Sighing, I looked at the pile of envelopes I'd removed from the box. "Evenson kept a ton of correspondence. I imagine that request and the state's response are in one of the envelopes piled on my desk."

"I'll bet the request was made while Evenson was a college student. She contacted Banks and they became close."

"I think we've opened Pandora's box."

"What do you mean?" Margaret asked.

"Annika Banks' life was intertwined with Deborah Evenson's adult life for ten years, then she left for Paris. There must've been some triggering event that caused a fallout between them."

"There's friction in all families," Margaret said. "Finding a mother you never knew would be life changing."

"But they became close. Banks lived with Evenson in the Two Harbors studio for nearly a decade." I paused. "And Banks is the female figure in the diptych."

"What are you talking about?" the librarian asked.

"The two pictures recently displayed in the Tweed Museum. They're two halves of one mural that Evenson specified couldn't be displayed together until after her death. There's a hidden image of a woman being stabbed by the devil. Lying on her back, the female image has her hand up to fend off the devil's attack. The woman resembles both

Annika Banks and Deborah Evenson. The devil looks a lot like Charles Crowder."

"When did you put those pieces together?"

"We found Annika Banks' picture in the UMD faculty photos yesterday. I took the newspaper photos of Charles Crowder to the museum."

Chuckling, Margaret said, "You're a regular Sherlock Holmes."

"I feel more like Curly of the Three Stooges."

"What are you going to do with this information?"

"I'm not sure. I'd like to know why Annika Banks never returned from Paris."

"Oh crap. You asked me to search for her and I got sidetracked." Computer keys clicked in the background. "I just did a French 'people' search and didn't find her, but that just means she doesn't live there now."

"That doesn't surprise me. She'd be nearly a hundred years old if she was still alive."

"I have library patrons lining up to check out books. I'm making a note to myself to continue the search, and I'll get back to you later."

"Thanks, Margaret."

I was preparing to look through the stack of envelopes when there was a knock on my office door and Brian swept in, uninvited, and sat in my guest chair. "What's twice as large as a tuba?"

After my intense discussion and discoveries with Margaret, I wasn't prepared for tuba jokes. I sighed and shrugged.

"A four-ba," Brian said, laughing. You should write that down for your son. There aren't many G-rated tuba jokes."

"What's up?" I asked, glancing at the pile of envelopes on my desk, hoping Brian would take the hint I was busy, and leave.

Oblivious to my interest in something other than his tuba, Brian forged ahead. "I heard that you're lining up models for your senior citizen art classes. I thought I'd volunteer."

Although my mind was elsewhere, Brian had a way of yanking me into his reality. I looked at him, nearly seventy, and built somewhat like a fire hydrant. I was unable to come up with a reply.

Confusing my silence for contemplation rather than shock, Brian went on. "It's important for art students to draw a variety of body types. I heard they're drawing a handsome stud today. Perhaps they'd like to move on to a body with more…curves. Heck, I could pose with a Sousaphone over my shoulder, and they'd have tons of curves to draw."

There are times when my mind draws pictures that will never disappear. My vision of tuba-playing Brian sitting naked on the model's stool with a Sousaphone over his shoulder will be etched in my memory forever.

Brian's grin grew into a full smile as he watched me wrestle with that image. He licked his lips. "Well, are you going to call Melissa, or should I?"

"I'm not sure my art class is up to drawing...that many curves." I'd been distracted by the discussion with Margaret and now Brian. I glanced at the clock and realized the art class was nearly over and stood. "I need to pick up my art class."

"Before you go, I've got one more thing." Brian followed me as I walked to the back door. "Deborah Evenson left her estate to the university."

I stopped on the sidewalk and turned to Brian. "How do you know that?"

"It's a small town."

"Truthfully, how did you acquire that information and is it real?"

"My sister-in-law's best friend works in the courthouse. The trustee of the Evenson estate filed Evenson's will with the county. It's going through probate."

"The university gets all her art?"

Brian shrugged. "I suppose so. The entire estate goes to the University of Minnesota-Duluth. They get her studio, the art, and whatever else is of value." He gently pushed my shoulder. "You're daydreaming again. There's a crowd of little old ladies waiting for you at the art studio."

* * *

As usual, the street was nearly empty, so I parked the van right in front of Melissa's art gallery/studio. I was a few minutes late, so I rushed inside, planning to apologize and help the ladies into the van. The gallery was empty, so I followed the sound of laughter to the studio.

From the looks of the class, Melissa had served the ladies more wine than usual, and the volume of chatter was louder than usual. Ricky, facing away from me, was posed on a stool, shaking his head as the ladies kidded him about something. Melissa was sipping from her coffee cup across the room, while studying Kathy's drawing. She saw me in her peripheral vision and looked up. "Peter! You need to see today's drawings."

Hearing Melissa's greeting, the class and model, all turned toward me. Hulda seized Ricky's distracted moment to step past her easel and pull the sheet from the model's lap.

He quickly responded, snatching the sheet from Hulda's hand, but not before the class saw his "covered assets." The class's response varied. The people in front of him had a different view than the people behind, at least until Ricky stood to take the sheet from Hulda. Most of the women tittered. A couple gasped. I saw Karla look away. My gaze ended on Hulda, who appeared triumphant.

Unfazed by the incident, Melissa smiled and shrugged. Ricky wrapped the sheet around his waist and walked to the changing room, seemingly unperturbed, kidding with the ladies as he passed them.

It took nearly fifteen minutes for the ladies to settle down, clean up, and roll up their drawings. Ricky passed through the crowd as he left. He smiled, patted shoulders, and acted like it was a regular day at the studio. He cut a wide swath around Hulda as he passed. Melissa handed him some folded money as he left the studio, and he nodded his thanks.

"You said that would never happen," I whispered to Melissa as the art class left the studio.

"Shit happens," she replied, with a sly smile.

"Did you tell Ricky to let that happen?"

Melissa didn't answer until everyone was out of the studio. "I think your ladies need a little spice in their lives. Whistling Pines is rather quiet."

"Melissa…"

"Hey! You're the recreation director, and the class had some extra recreation today."

Sensing an opportunity to get a touch of revenge, I leaned close to Melissa. "I have

221

another person who's offered their services as a nude model."

Melissa raised her eyebrows. "Who?"

"Tuba-playing Brian said he'd pose with his Sousaphone."

Melissa broke into a coughing fit and bourbon sprayed the floor.

I patted her back. "He thought he and the instrument would provide a great opportunity for the class to sketch a lot of curves."

Wiping her nose with a tissue, Melissa glared at me. "That was evil."

"You can't get that picture out of your mind, can you?" I asked.

"Where did you dream that up?"

"Brian stopped by my office. He'd heard I was recruiting nude models and he offered his services. I suspect his modeling fee might be somewhat less than Ricky's. On the other hand, his wife might end Brian's modeling career before it begins."

Kathy was waiting at the van, watching the banter between Melissa and me. She put out her hand and let me help her up the steps. "What did you say to Melissa?"

"I told her about someone who'd offered to model for the class."

Kathy stopped at the top step. "Whoever it was must've been a doozy. Melissa blew bourbon out of her nose. That had to burn like hell." Kathy stood next to me while I closed the van door and buckled my seatbelt. "Well, who was it?"

222

After starting the engine, I shook my head. "You don't need to have that vision burned into your brain."

"It was either really good, or really bad," Kathy said as she took her seat.

"Yes, it was."

Chapter 16

Jenny's parents were conspicuously absent from church and Sunday school. After the service, Jenny called to check on them. "They decided not to attend today because Dad's supposed to restrict his activity. Mom wants us to come over for lunch."

Sunday dinner was a tradition we'd fallen into. After church, we'd drive to Jenny's parents' house, her mom would give me a Scandinavian hug (touching shoulders but no other body parts), her father would open a bottle of wine, and we'd have pot roast with potatoes and gravy.

As usual, Barbara met us at the door with hugs, which Jeremy ducked, and we removed our shoes inside the door, lest we deposit a spot of dirt or dust on a floor clean enough to dine on. The aroma of roast chicken filled the air. I sniffed and looked at Barbara with surprise. "Chicken?"

Shushing me, she grabbed my elbow and led me to the edge of the white living room carpet, carefully stopping short of stepping on the carefully groomed expanse of white that was never trod upon. "The dietitian told me to cut beef and salt out of Howard's diet. He's not happy about the change."

"A dietary change after a heart attack isn't uncommon," I replied. "I suppose all of us would benefit from a reduction in fatty meats and salt."

Apparently standing around the corner, Howard appeared looking unhappy. "I told the dietitian that it was too late in my life to overcome six decades of beef and pretzels."

Barbara chose to ignore the discussion and sped away, through the dining room.

"How do you feel?" I asked.

"I feel great, and that's part of the problem. The doctor said removing the blockages in my coronary arteries improved my heart function and gave me renewed energy. Barbara, on the other hand, thinks that I'm made of crystal and could break if handled roughly."

"What's your rehab?"

"I walk a mile a day and go to the hospital twice a week for my AA meeting."

"Your AA meeting?"

Chuckling, Howard nodded toward the living room where we walked across the forbidden white rug and sat in the unused white chairs. "I'm in a cardiac rehab group that's rather like Alcoholics Anonymous. There's no formal twelve-step program, but the first thing we do is accept that we have

225

heart problems and accept the need for change. I'm currently at the part where I'm asking forgiveness for the people I've wronged."

"What people have you wronged by having a heart attack?"

Glancing at the door to make sure we weren't overheard, Howard said, "Apparently I nearly left Barbara a widow and that was damned inconsiderate of me."

"That's your biggest transgression?"

Howard raised his eyebrows. "It is in Barbara's mind."

Jeremy skidded to a stop in the hallway, his stocking feet sliding on the polished oak floor. "Grandma says lunch is ready." Jeremy looked suspiciously at the footprints we'd left in the plush white carpeting. "Did Grandma say you could walk on the carpet?"

Smiling as he stood, Howard said, "Grandma doesn't make all the rules in this house."

Clearly, Jeremy didn't believe that. But he didn't argue.

Jenny was rearranging her blouse, having fed Amy while Howard and I talked. Barbara entered the dining room with a platter of roasted chicken, ringed with potatoes and carrots. Jeremy threw himself into a chair, then tried to peek over the top of the chicken pieces. "Can I have a leg?"

I expected Barbara to chastise Jeremy for speaking before praying. Instead, she smiled as she spread her napkin. "After prayers. Okay?"

Howard usually said a short prayer. Instead, Barbara reached out. "Let's join hands." She offered a prayer of thanks for the meal, but also for her family and their health.

Jeremy leaned over the table and grabbed a drumstick as soon as his hands were free. "We never eat chicken," he said.

Howard chuckled. "At least someone is happy about our menu change."

As usual, the conversation stayed clear of politics. Barbara asked about the sermon, and Howard spoke about his new exercise regimen. Jeremy gnawed the meat off his third drumstick, and Amy slept in a car seat next to Jenny. I was unprepared for the bombshell.

Howard wiped his mouth and smiled. "I hear there are some very talented artists at Whistling Pines. My therapist said Kathy Christensen's nudes are particularly realistic."

With a fork full of potatoes halfway to her mouth, Jenny stopped. She shook her head almost imperceptibly, and glanced at Jeremy, who hadn't caught Howard's comment.

"The ladies are having fun with their art class," I said, dodging the landmine of a nudity discussion.

Barbara's reaction was predictable. She changed the topic. "I heard the Twins won yesterday."

Howard's eyes sparkled, knowing how painful it was for Barbara to try and skirt the issue he'd raised. "And the Vikings interviewed the New England Patriots' offensive coordinator."

Being a big Minnesota Vikings fan, Jeremy perked up. "They need a new head coach. Jacob says that the current guy doesn't know a pass from…" Realizing everyone was staring at him, Jeremy rethought the word he was about to use. "…his elbow."

I helped Barbara and Jeremy clear the dishes while Jenny set Amy in her father's arms. With the dishes in the dishwasher and Jeremy bored, we hugged Jenny's parents and drove home.

"Dad told me he almost died during the angioplasty."

I nodded. "Howard told me he'd caught a glimpse of St. Peter." When Jenny didn't respond, I added, "There's nothing we can do about it."

"There is," Jenny countered. "He wants to see more of Jeremy and Amy. He's planning to volunteer to help with Jeremy's Cub Scout pack."

"I think both of those things are good."

* * *

Jeremy raced to the house as soon as the car stopped rolling. It took Jenny a minute to release Amy from the car seat. The process woke Amy, who'd been asleep since being fed before lunch. With the baby crying in her arms, Jenny walked past as I held the kitchen door open. "What are your afternoon plans?" she asked.

"I brought the box of Deborah Evenson's papers home. Unless you've got other plans, I thought I'd dig through her correspondence."

"Deb Stone asked if I could bring Jeremy and Amy over. I'm certain she doesn't care if Jeremy or I are there; she wants to play with the baby."

"Go ahead. I'll just read dusty old letters."

With Amy in a fresh outfit and Jeremy carrying his baseball glove, Jenny left. I set the box from Evenson's garage on the dining room table and sorted the contents into piles. The biggest pile was cards of every variety from birthdays to Christmas. I was ready to pile the business envelopes when I was struck by the pile of cards. *We get about a hundred Christmas cards a year. Deborah Evenson didn't accumulate a hundred cards over her lifetime.* Reassessing that, I thought, *maybe she saved the cards that meant something to her. These aren't the one's from the guy who delivers the newspaper and the plumber who installed a new disposal. These are the cards from special people.*

Armed with that thought, I scanned the card stack. The recurring signatures were Edith and Charles Crowders', and Annika Banks'. I set aside three cards signed, "Nettie." There was no last name, nor was there an envelope with a return address.

"Who is Nettie?"

The sound of the back door opening and closing distracted me. I set the cards aside and met Kerry Stone in my kitchen. "The women threw me out. What are you up to?"

I led Kerry into the dining room and showed him the piles of papers. "Here are all the papers in the box we removed from Deborah Evenson's garage. I just sorted through the pile of cards." I handed him one of the cards signed by Nettie.

"Who is Nettie?" he asked.

"I don't know. But Deborah Evenson saved three cards signed by her."

"Who sent the other cards?"

"They're almost all from Annika Banks or Crowders—people who meant something special to her."

Kerry looked at the other two cards. "I suppose Nettie was a close friend." He stopped, then handed the third card to me. "Does this look like a child's signature?"

I studied the somewhat stilted cursive letters, then looked at the other cards. "It appears Nettie's writing improved over time."

Setting the cards side by side, we studied the signatures. "If I had to guess," Kerry said, "I'd say Nettie sent the first card shortly after she learned to write out her signature, and the later cards were sent after she'd mastered handwriting."

My mind swam with possible explanations, and I started throwing them out. "Maybe she had a sister or stepsister. Maybe she had a close friend with a daughter called Nettie."

Without looking up from the cards, Kerry said, "Maybe Evenson gave up a daughter for adoption." He paused. "That would complicate the probate of her estate."

"But there's a will."

"A child who's excluded from the estate could probably protest the will, claiming that it was invalid because there was no provision for her. I remember some rich guy left his ex-wife one dollar, so it was clear she hadn't been left out of the will as an oversight."

"Can you get a copy of Evenson's will?" I asked.

"Not on Sunday."

"Contact the courthouse tomorrow and get her will. I'll call the library. Margaret can search for birth records listing Deborah Evenson as the mother." As soon as I'd fired off those thoughts, I stopped. "Um, sorry, Chief. I suggest that we do those things."

Kerry snorted and raised his hand. "No problem, sir. I'll jump right on it, sir."

"I'm going to make a pot of coffee, then I'll sort through the rest of this. Would you care to join me?"

"Let's see. I can't go home because your wife is still there with the baby. I could drive into town and pay for a cup of coffee. Or, I can have a free cup of coffee and talk to you. Hmm. I choose the last option."

* * *

Because the scarring on Kerry's left hand made manipulating envelopes difficult, I took that pile and let him flip through the loose sheets of paper from Evenson's box. There wasn't much to say as we leafed through our piles. After opening a few envelopes, I realized the contents didn't need to be reinserted, but should remain with the envelope to establish where and when it was postmarked. I stapled envelopes to letters, scanning the requests for donations, acknowledging donations, reminding Evenson of upcoming events, and her accountant requesting the value of items she's donated or sold for less than he felt they were worth.

I refilled our coffee mugs often, and by mid-afternoon, I picked up the empty carafe. "I'll make another pot."

Looking skeptical, Kerry leaned back. "Do you have a couple beers?"

When I returned from the kitchen with beer, Kerry was intently staring at a handwritten note. He set it down and pushed around other papers, searching for something.

"What are you looking for?" I asked, setting his beer bottle on a coaster.

"I hope there's an envelope for this letter."

"Your pile was all loose correspondence. All the envelopes are in my pile and there's a letter in each of them." I stood behind him and read the scrawled handwriting while sipping on my beer. I stopped when the gravity of the words hit me. "Someone was blackmailing Evenson?"

Kerry sipped his beer. "It appears someone *tried* to blackmail her. I haven't seen evidence that she paid anyone or that she responded to the threat."

I picked up the note and reread the message. "The author's handwriting is poor, the grammar is worse, and the punctuation is lacking."

I heard what you did
I think it were worth something for me
not to tell

I flipped the single sheet of paper over, looking for a signature or other identification.

"I assume Evenson blew this off as a crank letter."

"Why would she keep a crank threat?" Kerry leaned back. "If it was just some prank, I'd expect her to throw it away. If she felt threatened, she'd show it to the police."

I shrugged. "Maybe the blackmailer was hoping to prey on her guilty conscience. The writer doesn't say what was done. Maybe Evenson had multiple skeletons in her closet."

Unconvinced, Kerry set his beer aside and flipped through more pieces of paper. "Maybe there's a follow-up threat in here somewhere."

"Maybe the follow-up was made by phone."

Kerry flipped over part of the pile. "There's nothing else here."

"It was just a crank hoping to make a couple bucks."

"How? There's no name, address, or phone number. How was a blackmailer going to get money if he didn't provide a way of contacting him?"

I shrugged. "Like I said, maybe there was a follow up phone call."

"There are notes about every important event in her life. She wouldn't deal with a blackmail threat without recording something."

"Give it up, Kerry. It was an empty threat."

A yellowed corner of paper with a black and yellow logo caught Kerry's eye. Intrigued, he pulled out a smaller sheet of paper. "Deborah Evenson was notified of Crowder's death by telegram."

"That seems impersonal. Who sent it?"

"Cynthia Crowder."

"Daughter, second wife, or other relative?" I asked.

"I've never seen her name before." He pointed at my pile. "There's a legal-sized envelope. What's in it?"

The manila envelope was yellowed with age, and the small denominations of the stamps told me it had been posted decades before. "The return address is 'Schmidt, Fanning, and Bolton, attorneys at law'. Their address is a suite on Michigan Street in Chicago."

"That's the high-rent district," Kerry said. "What's inside?"

The enclosed documents were legal-sized, and the print was double spaced. "The title is 'Crowder/Evenson Trust.'"

"I'd heard she received a monthly stipend from Crowder. I suppose this is the legal document that provides for those payments."

I flipped through the pages quickly, noting headings, but not reading the content. "It's signed by both Crowders, and Deborah Evenson. It was notarized in 1966."

Kerry leaned on the table. "Being curious, how much was she getting?"

I leafed back through the pages. "There's a sliding scale with a base amount of a thousand dollars a month. It specifies adjustments for inflation and a doubling of the base amount every ten years." I flipped ahead in the document. "Hang on. The trust owns the house and is responsible for taxes and upkeep. It also provides for a vehicle of her choice, with the trust paying for replacement every three years, plus paying the insurance and upkeep."

"What happens to the studio when both parties die?"

"The last page says the ownership of the house transfers to the beneficiaries' descendants." I set the documents aside. "Evenson's will gives the studio to UMD, but the trust seems to say the house ownership goes to her heirs. If she doesn't have any heirs, who gets the studio?"

"As far as I know, Evenson didn't have any children. Maybe the house goes to Crowder's family if Evenson doesn't have an heir. I'll ask the trustee."

"Are you planning to write a reminder to yourself about that?"

"I've got a mind like a steel trap."

"Steel traps are known for capturing things. The retrieval is more difficult."

Changing the topic, Kerry waved his beer bottle at the trust documents. "What was expected of Evenson in return for this patronage?"

I had to flip back several pages. "The artist is required to sell at least two pieces of art a year."

"That seems like a 'no brainer.' She was completing a dozen or more paintings a year."

After a moment of thought, I said, "I see two components to that requirement: Her art has to be salable, and Evenson had to part with two of her pieces a year." I read ahead while Kerry pondered my comments. "Hold on, the last line is a doozy. '…and is expected to live a moral and Christian life."

"What do you suppose that means?" Kerry asked.

"It was the '60s. College students were smoking pot, protesting the war, and 'the pill' revolutionized women's sexuality." I handed the document to Kerry. "A good lawyer could bend this to mean almost anything."

Kerry raised his eyebrow. "Crowders could afford the best lawyers. They wrote the document, so they'd be the ones to argue it in court."

I finished my beer and got two more out of the refrigerator. "I suppose the 'Christian life' part could mean at least following the ten commandments."

Kerry pondered that. "Beyond not killing anyone, I suppose it means no bastard children, and no affairs with married men."

"That's Old Testament stuff. There are a whole bunch of New Testament rules."

Kerry cocked his head. "I'm not sure about Lutherans, but when I was in Catholic school there was a list of one hundred mortal sins and ninety-five of them involved sex."

I leaned my elbows on the table. "Like what?"

Kerry snorted. "I was in grade school. They didn't talk specifics. They let our dirty minds wander."

"Did you go to weekly confession?"

"Of course. We all did."

"So, as a grade school kid, what did you confess?"

"Stealing cookies from the cookie jar, not paying attention to the homily." Kerry paused and smiled. "The biggie was the same for everyone; not closing your eyes during the prayer."

"Why would you open your eyes during the prayer?"

"To see who else had their eyes open."

I pointed to the threatening note next to Kerry's elbow. "Someone thought they overheard a sin worse than having their eyes open during the prayer."

"Peter. This is Two Harbors. There's a rumor on every corner and Evenson was outside the mainstream of town life. I'm sure everyone thought she was guilty of violating one of the commandments."

238

"Look at the paper the blackmail note is written on. Was it folded like it had been in an envelope?"

Kerry held the paper up to the window. "It was folded into quarters, but that just means it might've been enclosed in a card."

"Or slipped into the mailbox."

"What else is in the envelopes?" Kerry asked, feeling that we'd wrung all we could out of the blackmail discussion.

"She was audited in 1972. It appears the IRS rejected her valuation of a painting donated to UMD. She claimed it was worth $20,000 and they asked for documentation."

"Did they make her pay taxes on it?"

"It looks like she handed it over to Crowders' attorneys and they dealt with it." I opened another letter from a Minneapolis law firm. "Evenson tried to change the trust in 1997. The lawyers said it was highly unlikely that the courts would allow her to redraft the trust since one of the signatories was deceased."

"All was not happiness in Paradise." Kerry said.

"Maybe Evenson got tired of being the bird in the gilded cage."

Car doors slammed outside. and I set my beer down to gather the papers and replace them in the box. Jeremy ran in and stopped at the table as I packed away the last envelopes. "Jacob drank his root beer too fast and had hiccups for five minutes. Amy thought it was funny."

Jenny walked into the dining room as I gathered our empty beer bottles. "I felt guilty drinking coffee with Deb because I thought you two were slaving away on police business, but you were sitting here drinking beer."

Kerry looked up. "What's the first commandment?"

Jenny looked puzzled, but recited, "I am the Lord your God. You shall have no other gods before me." She looked at me for a hint at the reason for the question.

"Deborah Evenson's trust had a morality clause that said she had to live a moral and Christian Life. Kerry and I were trying to determine what that meant."

"Phew," Jenny said. "That could mean anything from eating fish on Fridays to wearing a head covering in church."

Kerry leaned back. "What would it mean to an eighty-year-old man in 1966?"

"I think it means keeping up the appearance of propriety."

"Just the appearance?"

"As you and Kerry are learning, living in a small town is all about appearances. If people see you acting up, you've become a goof off in their minds, and the minds of the other people they tell. On the other hand, if you treat people nicely, live frugally, and drive an inexpensive car, people respect you."

Jenny was surprised that Kerry was shaking his head. "Not true."

"Sure, it is," she protested.

"Nope. One 'aw shit' can wipe out a lifetime of 'Atta girls.'"

"Give me an example," Jenny said, setting Amy's car seat in the corner with the baby still sleeping.

"Deb brought a casserole to a church potluck dinner. No one stirred the crockpot, so the bottom scorched, tainting the entire crockpot of scalloped potatoes and ham. She will forever be 'the woman who brought the burned hotdish to the dinner.' She could bring perfect Beef Wellington to every church dinner for the rest of her life, and she'd still be remembered as the woman who scorched the scalloped potatoes."

"I'm sure my reputation is pristine," I said, puffing up.

Jenny and Kerry both snorted.

"What have I done?"

Kerry made sure Jeremy was upstairs before saying, "I hadn't even met you and people were telling me about Peter Rogers showing up for his own wedding with a black eye."

Jenny could hardly wait to throw out her story. "Even people who weren't there remember the time you French-kissed the redhead on Hugo's stage."

"I did NOT kiss her. I was backing away and…"

"And she tickled your tonsils with her tongue."

We all laughed until Kerry got serious. "You regained a lot of points with the town with the *Can't Help Falling in Love with You* duet at Pirate Days."

Jenny reached out and squeezed my hand. "That was special, but if you ever drag me onto stage again, I'll have your head."

Chapter 17

The Monday morning breakfast crowd was chattering like normal as I walked from table to table, greeting the residents. I'd caught a snippet of a conversation about the art contest being rigged, but the source was Hulda Packer, and her childish drawings hardly compared to those done by the other students.

Jeri Westfall waved to me from a table near the windows, so I wound through the tables and sat in an empty chair between Kathy Christensen and Karla Telker. Jeri leaned over and whispered, "That poor Vogel girl. I can't believe what happened to her at the Svenska Gotter service."

Unaware of any SG events, I looked at Karla and Kathy, who both shook their heads. "I don't know anything about the Vogel girl."

"Sure, you do. That girl who modeled for the art class. What was her name? Kelly? Nelly? It wasn't Jeri, because I'd remember that."

Karla couldn't stand it. "Sherry Vogel was outed to the Svenska Gotters."

"And?" I asked.

"Her father made her confess her sins in front of the congregation and ask forgiveness."

"Really?"

Kathy nodded. "She stood in front of everyone and told them she'd modeled in the nude for an art class, and she'd drunk wine with the art students," Kathy paused and smiled, "and she'd lusted after her high school chemistry teacher."

"She lusted after her chemistry teacher?" I asked.

Kathy smiled. "Probably not, but don't you think that improved the story?"

"That poor girl," I said. "Then what happened?"

"The congregation rushed forward and laid hands on her to take her sins upon themselves."

I closed my eyes, envisioning the church scene as Sherry received absolution. When I opened my eyes, all three women were staring at me. "What?"

Jeri leaned forward. "I heard three men asked her for a date after the service."

Karla shrugged. "I think someone enhanced that part of the story, too."

"Her career as an art class model is over," Kathy said. "It's good that you found the UMD student to take her place."

"I didn't find a substitute…" Kathy's smile told me she was kidding.

"I heard my niece has been helping with the Evenson investigation," Kathy said.

"Your niece?"

"Margaret, the librarian, is my niece. She told me she's been helping you uncover information about Deborah Evenson and Annika Banks. I would never have guessed they were mother and daughter."

Jeri frowned. "There is a certain family resemblance. You'd think someone here would've noticed that."

"Annika got pregnant during the war," Kathy said. "A lot of good gossip was lost because people were so busy with the war effort."

Karla clasped her hands and closed her eyes like she was praying.

"What's wrong," I asked.

Karla opened her eyes and drew a breath. "A lot of juicy gossip was lost because of the war. Really?"

Jeri nodded. "People were focused on the boys overseas and maximizing the output of the iron ore mines to make tanks and bullets."

Karla clenched her eyes shut again. "I think bullets are made of brass and lead."

"Only because there were steel shortages."

Karla leaned back and spread her fingers like she'd dipped them in something sticky. "Let's move on, okay?"

Kathy stood and looked at me expectantly. "Are you getting the van, or are we walking to the art class?"

I remained seated. "Melissa doesn't have Monday classes."

"We're stepping up the pace. We need to be ready for the Tall Ship Festival."

Karla stood and nodded. "Try to keep up, Peter."

I was walking past Howard Johnson's table when he put his hand on my arm. "Are you taking the ladies to the art studio?"

"Yes, I was just going to get the van."

"Say 'hi' to Kerry and Sparky." His smug smile told me I'd missed something.

"Who's Sparky?"

"He's the fire chief."

"I'm lost. Why am I going to see the police and fire chiefs?"

Howard's knowing smile intrigued me. "It'll be a surprise."

The conversation with Howard bothered me as I helped the art students into the van. I stopped Karla before she stepped on. "Why does Howard Johnson think I'm going to see the police and fire chiefs in town?"

Apparently not knowing the answer, Karla paused. "Are you going for coffee while we're in class?"

"I'll probably go to the library."

"I have no idea. But, if Howard says you're likely to see Kerry and Sparky, I assume it will happen."

As I drove, I asked Ginny Johnson the same question. It was pointless, because she didn't remember we were driving to the art class. "You know why they call Roland, the fire chief, 'Sparky' don't you?"

"Everyone in town has a nickname. I suppose he's called Sparky because he puts out fires."

Ginny laughed and patted my shoulder. "You're so naïve."

"Why do they call him Sparky?"

Ginny was silent, so I looked at her in my rear-view mirror. Her head was cocked, and confusion showed on her face. "Who do they call Sparky?" she asked.

I was about to answer her when I turned the corner onto Second Avenue and saw flashing lights ahead of us. I slowed as I approached the art studio where a half-dozen women, all carrying placards mounted on hockey sticks, were marching and chanting.

Kerry was leaning on his cruiser with his arms crossed. Although it was often hard to read Kerry's expression because of his facial burn scars, his look was one of total disgust. I eased the van behind his cruiser and got out. "What's up?"

"The Svenska Gotter church ladies are protesting Melissa's use of nude models."

As if on cue, the ladies started chanting, "No nude models." The placards were crudely painted. One said, "Svenska Gotters against nudity!" The artist had started the lettering large, then made it smaller and smaller as she realized she'd run out of space on the placard before she'd stated her full message. Others said, ERASE NUDES, and NUDE FREE ZONE.

"What are you going to do?" I asked Kerry.

He glanced at the protesters. "Nothing."

"How will my art class get into the studio for their class?"

After a moment of contemplation, he nodded to Hulda, who was waiting for Karla to assemble her walker. "Hulda can cut a path through that protest like a hot knife through butter."

A man wearing dark blue coveralls sauntered past the assembling art class and joined me alongside Kerry's car. The name "Roland" was embroidered on a patch on his chest. "Morning, Chief."

Kerry nodded. "Morning, Sparky."

We watched Hulda advance toward the protest line. The SG ladies held their positions until Hulda's walker ran over their toes. Amid yelps of pain, Hulda jammed her walker ahead, bouncing the walker's frame off the protesters' hips and thighs.

Sparky cocked his head. "I think that's assault, Chief."

Kerry turned away from the protesters as Hulda's walker rattled and clattered. "I didn't see an assault."

"Uh oh," Sparky said, bringing our attention back to the protest. One of the SG women was blocking the studio door with her hockey stick, ready to throw a hip into the first person who approached, poised like a defenseman protecting her goalie.

Hulda paused, momentarily intimidated by the middle-aged protestor aggressively defending the door. "Get out of the way, you big-nosed Swede!"

I took a step, but Kerry grabbed my arm. "Don't. Someone will get hurt if you get in the middle of this."

"But..." I looked at Sparky for support, but he was grinning, anticipating whatever was about to play out.

A hockey stick fell to the ground and a wail rose from the crowd. Everyone stepped back from the protester blocking the door. Her arms were out, and her head rolled back as she moaned and swayed. A moment later she started chanting in what sounded like Latin.

"She's speaking in tongues," Kerry whispered to me. I must've looked surprised because he asked, "Haven't you ever heard anyone speak in tongues before?"

"It's not a Lutheran thing," I replied.

I looked at Sparky, who shrugged. "I've been to a Lutheran service in Swedish, but

249

I've never heard anyone speaking this language."

Initially taken aback by the outburst, Hulda recovered. "Don't talk Hungarian to me! I was an English teacher and if you can't address me in the king's English, you shouldn't talk to me at all!"

The woman continued to wail, ignoring or unaware of Hulda's rant. Sparky shook his head. "I had Ms. Packer as a teacher. I don't know what the king's English is, but that's not what she taught us." He paused. "You know, there was a Finnish kid in class, and Ms. Packer didn't put up with him speaking anything but English. Poor kid peed in his pants because Ms. Packer wouldn't let him go to the bathroom until he asked in polite English. I don't think the kid knew the word 'toilet' in English. He kept saying, 'käymälä' and holding his crotch. Ms. Packer misunderstood and kept telling him his momma wasn't there."

Hulda ran out of what little patience she had and thumped the front wheel of her walker on the protester's big toe. The speaking in tongues stopped as the woman staggered and hopped on one foot.

The art students walked into the studio while the protesters gathered around their injured colleague. Kerry shook his head. "I gotta hand it to Marla. Her toe got thumped pretty good and she didn't utter one profanity."

Sparky frowned. "How could you tell? She might've been swearing up a storm in Hungarian for all we know."

The protesters glared at us when we broke into laughter. Kerry pushed us behind the cruiser and tried to stop our chuckles. "Have some respect."

Sparky put up his hands. "I just call 'em as I see 'em. Is it just me, or does a cup of coffee sound good?"

We walked to Judy's café where Kerry bought coffee and sweet rolls. Sparky regaled us with stories about a couple of grass fires set by kids burning campfires while drinking beer.

I wiped my fingers on a paper napkin and looked at Sparky. "You have an auto shop. Why were you at the protest?"

"Kerry thought he might need a hose to cool things off if they got out of hand."

"You didn't bring a fire truck."

"Why bring a big old fire truck when a garden hose will do the trick? Melissa showed me her outside faucet and fixed me up with a garden hose and nozzle."

"I didn't see a model. Did she arrive earlier?" I asked.

"She snuck in the back door while I was hooking up the hose."

I glared at Kerry. "There's a back door? Why didn't you send me around the back to unload the ladies?"

Kerry looked at Sparky. "We talked about that but decided it might be fun to watch the fireworks."

"I think I'll pull the van around the back for the pick up."

Kerry and Sparky looked at each other. "Why miss the fun?" Sparky asked.

"The fun?"

"I suspect the exit will be more entertaining than the entrance," Kerry said. "Those church ladies should be really wound up by the time the art class is over."

"Give me a break," I protested. "I have to protect my fragile ladies."

"Wow," Sparky said. "I've never heard Ms. Packer's name and fragile in the same sentence before."

* * *

A light mist started falling as we walked back from Judy's. In the distance, we spotted activity in front of the art studio. Sparky chuckled, "It looks like the protest has drawn a crowd."

I saw the protesters and possibly two additional people. "That's a crowd?"

"By daytime Two Harbors standards, a woman walking her dog is a crowd," Sparky replied, "and I think there are three more people in front of the studio than when we left."

Sighing, Kerry plodded on. "I kind of hoped the church ladies would get bored and cold when the rain started."

With a dismissive snort, Sparky pointed at the onlookers. "They're getting press coverage. There's no way they're leaving now."

"Press coverage?" I asked, looking for a news van with a dish antenna on top.

"That red headed girl is the new reporter for *The Harbor View*."

As we approached, I saw a redhead, who looked all of thirteen, writing on an iPad as she interviewed one of the protesters. "I've never heard of *The Harbor View*."

"It's the new weekly shopper. They run ads for local businesses. There's a 'Good Old Days' column, and one article of local interest."

"They have a reporter to write one article a week?" I asked.

"Steph is the owner's daughter. She gets out of junior high on work release whenever something newsworthy happens." The reporter stepped back from her interview and raised her iPad, taking pictures to accompany the story. Her presence energized the protesters who were chanting "No nudes!"

"Is it just me, or does it sound like they're protesting against newts?" Sparky asked.

Kerry raised his eyebrow. "I think it's their Swedish accents. Nude must be pronounced like newt in Sweden."

We were still a block from the studio when a white van bearing the logo of a Duluth television station parked across the street from the studio. As the satellite dish slowly rose skyward, a man retrieved a television camera and microphone from the back of the van. An attractive young blonde I recognized from the evening news broadcast, held an umbrella over her head to protect her hairdo. She refreshed her makeup in the passenger-side mirror."

Kerry cut diagonally across the street, approaching the reporter. "Ma'am, I haven't blocked the street, so please make your broadcast from the sidewalk."

The blonde, who'd graduated from broadcast school the previous year, looked about the same age as the red headed reporter. Momentarily shocked by Kerry's scars, she quickly recovered her composure. "You're Chief Stone, correct?"

"I am."

"I'd like to interview you for the evening news broadcast."

Pulling Sparky by the arm, Kerry stepped aside. "The fire chief is the incident commander. You should talk to him."

The cameraman rushed forward, handing a microphone to the blonde as Kerry stepped aside. Sparky had a silly grin and was apparently flattered to be interviewed by the attractive young reporter. She stood close to him while covering both of them with her umbrella.

"We're broadcasting from a spontaneous protest in downtown Two Harbors," the blonde said, staring earnestly into the camera. "With us is the Two Harbors Fire Chief, who's the incident commander. What's your name, sir?"

Speaking in his best fake Swedish accent, Sparky replied. "I'm Roland Johnson, but the folks call me Sparky."

Obviously reluctant to address the fire chief as Sparky, the broadcaster composed herself. "Chief, tell us what's happening."

The cameraman focused on Sparky, who drew a breath and turned toward the art studio. The attention further encouraged the protesters who were dripping wet, who started yelling even louder. "Well, it seems the Svenska Gotters have organized a protest."

"Who are the Svenska Gotters, chief?"

"They're an environmental group concerned about all things Swedish."

I turned to Kerry, who quickly covered his smile with his hand. "What is Sparky talking about?"

Kerry shushed me and watched the protesters as they continued to chant, "NO NUDES!" The rain increased in intensity and the protesters' cardboard placards sagged.

The water-color paint on the placards washed away, making it look like they were waving tan flags from their hockey sticks.

"They're protesting something Swedish?"

Sparky nodded. "Ya, they're up in arms over newt imports. Newts don't survive here because the winters are too cold, so they're being imported from Sweden. They're all up in arms over it."

The broadcaster was obviously confused by Sparky's explanation, but the Chief looked earnest, and even a bit concerned. "Why are they protesting in front of the art studio?"

Sparky drew a deep breath, obviously lacking a credible explanation. After stalling for a few beats, he said, "Well, the art studio owner is Norwegian, and she is a big supporter of importing Swedish newts because they're rare in Norway."

Unable to contain his laughter, Kerry grabbed my arm and pulled me into the doorway of a surveying firm across the street. "What time is the art class over?"

"The students should be coming out the front door any second."

Sparky continued to talk about the vagaries of Scandinavian newts while the blonde broadcaster tried hard to look concerned. The front door of the art studio opened, and everyone turned to see who was coming out. I seized up when Wendy emerged wearing a white tank top and denim short shorts that exposed numerous tattoos. She elbowed her way past the protesters, then stopped and struck a pose for the cameraman as the rain soaked her t-shirt. Seeing Kerry and me across the street, Wendy smiled and winked before walking away. The Svenska Gotters, energized by Wendy's nearly indecent display, started chanting louder.

Kerry chuckled. "Another minute in the rain and I'd have to ticket Wendy for indecent exposure."

I groaned.

"Did you know Wendy was modeling for the class today?" Kerry asked.

"Um…no. Actually, I didn't think Wendy was modeling at all."

Kerry ran his tongue inside his lips like he was having a hard time believing me. "It seems unlikely Wendy would show up to take the art class in that outfit."

I weighed the possibility that Nancy wouldn't watch the news against the shitstorm I might face if I didn't tell her. The broadcast team was from the smallest Duluth television station so Nancy might not see the video. Or the editor might deem the image of Wendy's wet tank top too prurient and decide not to show that segment of the video. They'd already been interviewing Sparky for five minutes. A lot of the video wouldn't make it on the air. Or Nancy might see the shot of Wendy, think it was my fault, and she'd fire me in the morning.

I should have Kerry shoot me now, I thought.

Kerry's head snapped around. "I won't shoot you over Wendy's modeling."

Closing my eyes, I said, "I didn't realize I'd said that out loud."

Kerry shushed me, pointing to the cameraman and live mic. "The door is opening. Any bets on who is next in the parade?"

Having no response, I turned to face the studio. Melissa, looking angry and leading with her coffee mug, stepped out. She dipped her fingers into the liquid and flicked droplets of bourbon onto the protesters who jumped back as if they were being burned.

"What's she spraying on them?" the broadcaster asked Sparky.

"I suppose it's Norwegian newt juice. You can see how the Swedes hate it."

The redhead from the newspaper realized she'd become irrelevant when the news van arrived. Getting soaked in the rain, she spotted Kerry and me in the sheltered doorway, and dashed across the street to join us. "Why are they interviewing the fire chief?" she asked.

"We're trying to figure that out, too," Kerry replied. "For some reason, the broadcaster chose him as the spokesperson."

258

"Who was the woman in the tank top?"

Not wanting Kerry to blurt out "*Wendy*," I said, "We think she was modeling for the art class."

"Do you have any comment on the protest, Chief Stone?"

"I think they're all wet."

I broke out laughing, seeing the soggy protesters retreating from Melissa. My smile melted when Hulda pushed her walker out the door. She was walking toward the van, but it appeared she had extra cushions in her hands. The woman whose toe had been crushed limped over to Hulda and started berating her.

Straightening up, it appeared Hulda was going to punch the woman. Instead, a stream of yellow spurted from Hulda's hand and splattered on the other woman's shirt. When a second protester approached, Hulda squirted blue paint from her other hand.

"What's happening?" the blonde asked Sparky.

"Well, those are the colors of the Swedish flag, blue and yellow. I think Ms. Packer is a supporter of the Swedish newts and she's giving them protesters a squirt of their own medicine."

With yellow and blue paint swirling from the sidewalk and down the gutter, I ran across the street and opened the van. Karla ran out of the studio and took the paint tubes from Hulda, then urged her toward the van. Once in the van, Karla handed me the paint as the other art students scurried past the protesters who were trying to wipe the paint off each other, but only succeeded in spreading it around, quickly creating a hideous shade of green as the colors mixed.

I couldn't hear Sparky from inside the van, but he continued to talk and gesture emphatically to the blonde reporter, who seemed to be eating up whatever farce he was spinning. Closing the van door as the protesters realized their attackers were escaping, I turned on the windshield wipers and drove away.

Leaving the scene, the last thing I saw was Kerry talking with the red-headed teen and her father in the shelter of the surveyor's doorway. Karla, who was seated behind me, leaned forward as we drove out of downtown. "What happened?"

"I think you'll have to watch the evening news to get the full view of the events." I turned a corner and asked, "Where did Hulda get the paint?"

"She grabbed it after Melissa went outside to scare off the protesters."

"You didn't stop her?" I asked.

Karla snorted. "No one gets in Hulda's way when she's on a mission. I could've been the one covered in paint."

"Good point."

"How are you going to clean up the paint in the van?" Karla asked.

"There's paint in the van?"

"We all walked through the paint on the sidewalk before getting onboard the van. There are yellow, blue, and green footprints all the way down the aisle. It looks like we've been celebrating something in Brazil."

"Brazil?"

"The Brazilian flag is a blue globe, in a yellow diamond, on a field of green."

"Good eye. I'll tell Nancy we were having a Brazilian Mardi Gras celebration during the art class. I'm sure she'll believe that."

Laughing, Karla said, "You're becoming as cynical and sarcastic as the residents."

Kathy leaned forward and said, "I think the news crew got a good shot of the Whistling Pines logo on the van as we pulled away."

I groaned.

Chapter 18

I spent the afternoon in my office, reading the rest of the correspondence in Evenson's box of papers. There were an amazing number of requests for donations of art or money. Without having her checkbook register, I didn't know if she'd contributed to the organizations or not. Mid-afternoon, I read a request from the Chicago Children's Museum who requested the donation of a painting for their fundraising auction. The name sounded familiar, so I set the request aside and consulted my list of paintings and buyers. A week after the date on the request, I saw that a painting titled "On the Lakeshore" had been donated to the Chicago Children's Museum.

Curious, I went to my computer and googled the Chicago Children's Museum. Listed among the diamond level contributors was the Crowder Family Trust. I checked the correspondence pile to see if there was a letter from Charles Crowder, supporting the donation to the museum. Not finding one, I reasoned that Evenson probably got a call from Charles Crowder requesting that a painting be donated—the cost of his patronage.

I was farther into the pile when there was a rap on my door. Not waiting for an invitation, Brian stepped into my office, smiling. "Why couldn't the tuba player get a date?"

I shrugged.

Brian started laughing and barely got the punchline out. "Because he was too low key."

"I don't think Jeremy would get that without an explanation."

Putting up his hands, Brian said, "Your son isn't my usual target audience."

Intrigued, I asked, "Who is your usual audience?"

"I try all the jokes out on my wife."

"Does Marybeth enjoy them?"

Snorting, Brian shook his head. "No, but she censors them."

"She bans off-color jokes."

"No, she tells me not to repeat the ones that are too...stupid."

"You have a repertoire of jokes worse than the tuba player who couldn't get a date?"

Brian's eyes sparkled. "There are some I only tell after I've had a couple beers. Would you care to join me at the VFW?"

"Not to be unkind, but I'm not interested in drinking this early in the day, nor am I interested in the jokes you'll only tell after a couple beers." I paused. "Is there some reason you stopped by?"

"Annika Banks didn't go to Paris."

The change in direction caught me off guard. "How would you know that?"

"I talked to my mom this morning and told her about your quest to answer the questions about the paintings and Deborah Evenson's life. Mom said Banks never left Two Harbors."

"No one saw her in town after 1975, when they thought she went to Paris on a sabbatical."

"There was no sabbatical. She just disappeared."

"She moved to Canada or Minneapolis?"

"No, she disappeared. As in, she was never seen again. Have your friend Kerry, see if her driver's license was ever renewed."

I made a note to ask Kerry.

"Did you find her Corvette?" Brian asked.

"Her Corvette?"

"Annika drove a red Corvette in the summer. It'd be interesting to know what happened to it. Mom said she never saw Debbie Evenson drive it."

I flashed back to the car under the tarp in Evenson's garage. "There's a red Corvette in the garage next to Evenson's studio."

"I'll bet you twenty bucks the license tabs haven't been renewed since 1975."

264

I made another note to check the license tabs. "That's interesting."

"The Corvette was Annika's toy. She never let anyone else drive it, and she'd have taken it with her if she'd moved somewhere."

"Your mother thinks Annika is dead."

"Since you know that Annika's Corvette is parked in Evenson's garage, the odds are nearly one-hundred percent that Annika is dead."

I leaned back. "Where does your mom think Annika is buried?"

Brian got up and stepped to the door. "I have to leave something for you to solve." And with that, he was gone.

I closed the box and set it under my desk before walking to the dining room. The bridge group was at one table, and Wendy was in a back corner working on a crossword puzzle. She looked up when I sat in the chair across from her.

"Did you really pose for the art class?"

"Is that a problem?"

"Does Nancy know?" I asked.

"Probably." Wendy lifted her crossword. "I need a six-letter word for the town at the eighth mile of the Boston Marathon."

"You need to tell Nancy before a drawing of you shows up on one of our walls."

"She wouldn't recognize the model as me. The art students aren't that good."

"Your tattoos are distinctive."

"Melissa told the class to focus on curves. I don't think anyone was drawing tattoos."

I looked at the crossword puzzle. "Try NATICK."

As Wendy filled in the letters, she asked. "Why do you know that? You've never run the Boston marathon."

"It's part of the useless trivia in my head." Something Wendy said was floating on the edge of my mind. "Melissa told the class to focus on your curves?"

"Melissa called me 'Rubenesque' compared to the hard-bodied models she'd been using so the class learned how the models' muscles shape their physiques." Wendy's Cheshire Cat grin appeared, and I grimaced. "I have many more curves than that skinny college girl you recruited for Melissa."

"Rubenesque will probably be a crossword clue at some point. You should file that away."

"What's the derivation of the term?"

"Peter Rubens was a Belgian painter who studied in Holland. Most of his contemporaries were painting ballerinas and slender waifs. Rubens, however, chose full-figured models because he thought they were more attractive and gave his paintings a greater feeling of reality."

"Are you calling me fat?"

"I didn't make any judgments about you. I was just explaining the derivation of the term Rubenesque."

Wendy wrinkled her nose. "So, Melissa asked me to model because she thinks I'm fat?"

"You're not fat," I sighed. "You're not a skinny or hard-bodied model like the other women who've modeled for the class. You…apparently…have more curves."

While she didn't look pleased, Wendy seemed to accept my explanation. "Why were you at the protest with the police chief?"

"As you may recall, I had to drive the residents to Melissa's art class. Chief Stone was there to make sure the protest didn't get out of control."

"I can't believe those women were protesting the use of nude models in an art class."

"They're very conservative."

"Yeah, someone said they believe everything in the Bible is true. Apparently, Jesus was never naked after he was born, so taking your clothes off is a sin."

"Um, I think it's a tenth commandment issue. They think a naked body stirs up thoughts about coveting your neighbor's wife."

"I'm not married, Peter."

"You're missing the point. Public nakedness creates temptation."

Wendy raised her eyebrows. "Cool, I'm a temptress. I kind of like that."

Giving up on the conversation before it took an even more uncomfortable turn, I stood and walked away. Howard Johnson was reading the newspaper near the aviary, so I sat down next to him.

"What do you remember about Annika Banks' red Corvette?"

"I recall a woman driving around town in a red Corvette, but I couldn't say who was driving, or when. It was quite a few years ago." Howard looked around the room. "You should talk to one of the guys who is into cars. Bud Larson is at the mailboxes. Ask him."

Bud was sorting his mail, with virtually every piece going into the wastebasket. "What do you remember about a woman driving around town in a red Corvette?"

"Recently?"

"In the early '70s."

Tilting his head back, Bud closed his eyes. "If it's the one you're thinking of, it was a beautiful 1966 red Vette with an attractive middle-aged blonde driver. She didn't drive around like she was showing it off, more like she was just running errands. I never saw the car before Memorial Day or after October first, and I never saw a water spot or speck of dust on it. She must've washed it every day."

"The owner was Annika Banks. She lived at Deborah Evenson's studio."

"I never knew who the woman was or where she lived." Bud got a dreamy look. "But that car, it looked like it was going a hundred-miles-an-hour when it was sitting still."

"You didn't know the owner? I thought everyone in town knew everyone else."

"She wasn't a local and she never attended services at our church."

"Did you ever see that Vette after 1975?"

"I can't say. It was around, then it wasn't. I suppose the owner moved away or sold it." Bud smiled. "It had those mufflers that made a low rumble you could feel in your chest. If I still had my license, I'd love to have that sweet ride. Hell, I'd buy it now just so I could sit in it out in the parking lot."

Not getting the information I wanted from Bud, I looked for a different source. The rattle of Hulda's walker caught my attention, reminding me that not all sources were reliable, or even wanted. I tried to re-engage Bud in conversation before Hulda caught me, but he'd finished sorting his mail and didn't hear my desperate throat clearing attempt to catch his attention. I looked toward Howard Johnson, who was suddenly more engrossed in whatever he'd been reading in the newspaper.

Not wanting to be ignored, or just poorly judging distance, Hulda banged her walker into my leg. "Good. I was hoping to catch you."

"What can I do for you?"

"Talk to Melissa and tell her I want Ricky to come back. I didn't finish my drawing of him."

"You can tell Melissa yourself."

"I tried, but she prattled on about finding models with curves." Not one to shrink away from confrontation or inappropriate comments, Hulda continued as the bridge players walked past. "Wendy has too many curves and I'd rather see Ricky's hard body than Wendy's…"

Not wanting to know what curvy part of Wendy's anatomy Hulda didn't want to see, I cut her off. "I'll mention your preference for a male model to Melissa."

Hulda stared at me for a second, and I wondered what she was thinking. I should've known better, because whatever went through Hulda's mind came out of her mouth. "Melissa said the sheet incident might keep Ricky away. I'm sure he thought I was being playful when I pulled the sheet off, because he smiled. He frowned when I pinched his butt."

"You pinched his butt?" I asked a little too loudly, making Howard look up from his newspaper.

"It was cute and looked pretty firm. I wanted to know if he had any body fat at all."

270

"Pulling off the sheets or touching the models is inappropriate."

"Really? Are there sheet rules? I don't remember hearing about any rules."

"I think that's an unwritten rule. No pulling off sheets or touching the models."

Hulda smiled. "Ricky's butt called to me."

The sheet pulling, butt pinching conversation diverted my thoughts from whatever I'd been doing. Consulting the clock, I realized it was nearly time to leave for the day. I punched Kerry's number into my cell phone as I walked to my office.

"What's up?" He asked.

"I spoke to Brian and a few of the residents…"

"Brian, the joke-telling tuba player?"

"Yes, he's the only Brian I know."

"Did he have a good joke I could tell Jacob?"

"I don't remember his joke, so it wasn't one I planned to tell Jeremy."

"Darn. Jacob thinks it's funny that I know someone who tells me tuba jokes."

"Can we move on?"

"Sure. Why did you call?"

"The Corvette in the studio garage apparently belonged to Annika Banks. She drove it around town until she disappeared."

"I thought she moved to Paris?"

"Two people have told me she didn't move to Paris. One said Annika would never move away without her classic 1966 Corvette."

Kerry blew out a breath. "Maybe she left the Vette for Deborah."

"One of the guys said he hasn't seen the Corvette since Banks disappeared. He bet me that the license plates on the Vette expired in 1975."

"There was a lot of dust on that car cover. The tires were all flat, which means it's been sitting there unused for a long time."

"Can you check that? We should also see if Annika Banks renewed her driver's license after 1975."

"There are a few things I can check. In addition to her driver's license renewal, there's voter registration, charge card usage, and telephone listings. I can run a background check on her. That'll show her credit cards, her home address, and telephone numbers."

"How could she just disappear, Kerry?"

"Sadly, tens of thousands of women disappear every year."

"Where do they go?"

"Some are runaways, some are kidnapped, and some are just never found."

"Annika Banks disappeared from Two Harbors. Do you think she's still alive?"

"Deborah Evenson felt Charles Crowder was tormenting Banks. Think about her image in the diptych. Maybe she ran away to escape whatever torment she was experiencing."

After a moment of thought I said, "Maybe we should be more direct in our interpretation. Maybe Charles Crowder killed her."

Kerry chuckled. "I'm sure he stabbed her with his pointy tail."

"That's too literal. But maybe he killed her."

"Before we crawl any farther down this artistic rabbit hole, let me search for her after '75."

Kathy waved at me as I approached my office. "Peter, let's talk about the SGL."

With my mind on Banks, Crowder, and Evenson, I was puzzled by her suggestion. "Remind me what the SGL is."

"It's the acronym we've been using for the Svenska Gotter Ladies."

"Is there an issue with the SGL?"

"I think the news coverage will incite further activism."

I pictured the rain-drenched protesters waving their hockey sticks adorned with the soggy cardboard signs. "Don't you think they got their thirty seconds of fame? They're probably at their church dipping graham crackers in hot chocolate while reliving their time in front of the camera."

"I think they're going to be irate when they hear Sparky talking about Swedish and Norwegian newts."

I broke into a smile. "That was pretty clever."

"You know, Sparky was elected chief by the firemen. The Swedes have a strong voice in the department, and the Sons of Norway paid for the last fire truck. They might feel that Sparky was making fun of their accents. They'll vote and bust him down to apprentice fireman. He'll be moving from in front of the camera to cleaning the toilets at the firehall."

"Really?"

Kathy drew a breath and let it out slowly. "I forget that you're not from here."

"What's that got to do with Sparky's firehouse status?"

"You don't know how much political power is wielded by the Lutheran Swedish Church choir and the Sons of Norway. They're the powerbrokers behind the scenes. No one gets elected without their influence and political donations."

"The choir? Really?"

"Uff da, you're so naïve. The choir practices every Wednesday night, and they sing at two services on Sunday. They sit around, drinking coffee before choir practice and between services. A lot of deals are brokered over a cup of Swedish coffee. And don't even get me started about the Sons of Norway and the lutefisk dinner politics."

"But we're talking about the Svenska Gotters. They're not Lutherans, nor are they Norwegians."

"All that divisiveness gets put aside when someone starts making fun of their accents. Telling the newscaster that the SGL were chanting 'No more newts' is Scandinavian blasphemy. Sparky violated the third commandment."

I pressed fingertips to my forehead trying to stop the headache that was blossoming as my mind exploded over the possibility that making fun of a Swedish accent was equivalent to taking the Lord's name in vain. "What do you suggest?"

"Call Odd Lindback and warn him about the news broadcast."

"Is Odd Lindback a person or a place?"

Sighing, Kathy shook her head. "Odd is the Sons of Norway President."

"How do I address him when he answers the phone? 'Hi, is this Odd?'"

Kathy bit her lip to keep from laughing. "I'd ask for Mr. Lindback. Odd is his nickname."

"Thank heavens for that. I can't imagine parents naming their son Odd."

"Odd is a little strange, which explains the derivation of his nickname. But he's well respected and if you don't stare at his wandering eye, he looks normal. He's a little strange to be around in a group because with the wandering eye, you're never quite

275

sure who he's talking to." Kathy paused, cocking her head. "Well, there are his front teeth, too. They got knocked out playing hockey and he always felt proud that he was tough enough to get by without being able to eat corn on the cob or an apple."

"I'll call him." As soon as the words were out, I knew I was in trouble. "I'll need his first name to look up his number."

"That could be tough. I've never heard him called anything but Odd."

"I'll just look up Lindbacks in Two Harbors. There can't be that many."

"He doesn't live in Two Harbors. I think he lives near Brimson." Kathy looked troubled. "It might be Rollin or Fairbanks. No, he lives closer to Toimi, although his mailing address might be Brimson."

"So, I'm looking for someone called Odd, who lives near Brimson, Toimi, Rollin, or Fairbanks."

Kathy wrinkled her nose. "You make that sound stupid."

"I'm just trying to understand what I'm trying to do."

"Forget Odd. Call Bunny Peterson, the choir director."

"I'm guessing that Bunny is another nickname that won't be in a phone listing."

Kathy exhaled. "It's a nickname. Her real name is…it starts with an E. I think she's Esther or Evelyn."

"I'll look up E. Peterson. There can't be more than four or five hundred of those living around here."

"Just call Pastor Olafson and ask for the choir director's name and phone number."

I walked back to my office feeling like I'd just been part of Abbot and Costello's "Who's on First," routine. I dialed Kerry, hoping he'd tell me to forget about the issue.

"I just had the strangest conversation with Kathy Christensen. She thinks I need to talk to the Sons of Norway or the Swedish Lutheran Church choir director before Sparky's interview airs."

"You're too late."

I looked at the clock on my computer. "The early news isn't on for over an hour."

"Remember the red-headed reporter?"

"Sure. She stood with us in the doorway."

"She took some cell phone footage of the protesters and posted it on YouTube. The Associated Press posted it on their 'news of the weird' feature. It's gone viral and all the Duluth television stations are showing it as a leader for their evening broadcasts."

"No more newts," I said.

"That's it."

"Oh no! Tell me Wendy isn't in the video."

The answer arrived before Kerry replied. Nancy swept into my office and closed the door. "Hang up the phone and pull up YouTube. Type in Two Harbors."

Nancy and I watched the cell phone camera video. I expected her to be furious. Instead, she was chuckling. "Did Wendy really model for the art class?"

"I didn't actually see her modeling for the class, but that's the word among the students. The instructor wanted to challenge the class with the curves of Wendy's Rubenesque figure."

Nancy sighed. "They say there's no such thing as bad publicity."

"We're okay, Nancy. No one knows this has anything to do with Whistling Pines."

Nancy's look told me I was missing something. She pointed at the screen, and we watched Wendy strike a pose for the camera with the protesters chanting behind her. A moment later she walked up the sidewalk. The camera followed her, and she disappeared behind the van emblazoned with the Whistling Pines name and logo.

"Oh boy," I said.

"It gets better," Nancy said, watching the computer monitor. The camera panned back to the studio just as Hulda squirted paint onto the protesters.

Chapter 19

Our family watched the Two Harbors protest video on the evening news. Jeremy asked repeatedly what newts were, then why they were being protested. The phone calls started before the broadcast ended. The first was from Jenny's mother, who was embarrassed. The next was from Kerry, who'd been called on the carpet by the mayor because Sparky wasn't a spokesman any of the Two Harbors power brokers would've chosen to stand in front of a camera. Next came Meg, who laughed so hard she had a hard time thanking me for the great publicity the town received. Sparky had even mentioned the upcoming Tall Ships Festival.

After nine o'clock, we let the calls roll over to voicemail.

* * *

The Whistling Pines dining room was buzzing with newt protest discussions. Most mornings, people ate and returned to their apartments to watch game shows. This

279

morning, it seemed like everyone stayed around to hear different perspectives, or rumors, about the art studio protest. I was drawing coffee from the urn when I heard Jeri Westfall call my name.

Karla, Kathy, and Jeri were sitting at a table near the windows. Jeri waved, trying to catch my attention. After threading my way through the dining room and fending off a few questions about the protest, I sat in the empty chair at the table with the three ladies.

Jeri, who hadn't been at the art studio, leaned close to be heard over the dozens of discussions around us. "You watched the protest from across the street, right?"

"Yes."

Jeri waited for me to expand. When I didn't, she said, "Well, tell us about it."

"Kathy and Karla were there. I'm sure they filled you in."

Shaking her head, Karla said, "We were inside the studio while most of the action occurred. We came out after Hulda had squirted paint on the protesters and they'd dispersed."

Kathy nodded. "I hadn't heard the 'no newts' protest chant until I saw it on the television news last night."

Jeri smirked. "I watched the channel 22 broadcast. That young blonde with the hair like a helmet, was interviewing the fire chief. I giggled through the whole interview."

280

"Kathy and I watched the cell phone video on channels 4 and 9, so we only heard about Sparky's interview this morning," Karla explained. "What did it look like from across the street?"

Leaning my elbows on the table and clasping my hands, I composed my thoughts before answering. "The police chief and I heard Sparky's interview and witnessed Hulda's paint assault of the protesters. It was…distressing."

"Distressing?" Jeri asked.

"I was afraid someone would be upset about the nude models, but I never imagined there would be a protest. I think the hockey stick protest signs were a little much, and the chanting…"

Jeri started chuckling. "'No newts! Sparky sold that line like he was serious. My goodness, he should start a stand-up comedy act."

"There's been fallout," I said, sipping my coffee.

"Fallout?" Karla asked.

Kathy nodded. "I warned Peter that the Swedes wouldn't be happy about Sparky mocking their pronunciation of nudes. Did you call Odd?"

"I'm confused," Karla said. "The whole thing was odd. Peter was going to call it odd?"

"Kathy wanted me to call Odd Lindback, the president of the Sons of Norway. I advised the police chief of Kathy's concerns and left him to make the call to Odd and Bunny."

Karla cocked her head. "He was going to call my Aunt Bunny Peterson?"

"I guess she's the driving force behind the Swedish Lutheran Church Choir. Kathy suggested that Odd and Bunny be contacted ahead of the broadcast."

"I thought a call to warn them about the nude/newt interview might ease their surprise and quiet the uproar," Kathy explained. "Did Chief Stone call them?"

"The cell phone video was already on the internet before I contacted the Chief. He decided it was too late to attempt intervention."

"The video was on this morning's national news," Jeri said.

"For good or bad, Two Harbors is getting publicity," I said.

My chair was bumped from behind, causing me to spill a few drops of coffee. I could tell from the expressions on the faces of my three companions that the intrusion wouldn't be welcome. Hulda pushed her walker between Karla and me. "Willard Scott made fun of me on national television."

"Willard Scott, the weatherman from NBC's *Today* show, died two years ago, Hulda."

"Hmph! Well, that man on the channel 7 news, whatever his name is, said I was a kook! I'm going to sue!"

A voice from a nearby table whispered, "I don't think she'll win that lawsuit."

Hulda spun around. Unsure of who made the comment, she offered a general comment to the rest of the dining room. "I will not tolerate being called a kook! He made me sound like I was completely insane!"

Laughter broke out, which further enraged Hulda. "I'm not insane." She stalked off, ramming her walker into table legs and chairs as she departed.

Karla watched her depart, then leaned close. "I heard the SGL will be back at the art studio in full force today. I think we should skip art class. Can you drive us to the art museum so we can see the diptych? None of us have seen the two pictures together."

Kathy put her hand on my arm. "Please. It'd be a great outing for the art class. We could be back by noon if we left now."

I hadn't booked any recreational programs for the morning, so nodded. "Gather up anyone who's interested, and I'll bring the van to the front door."

My phone rang as I walked to my office to get the van keys. I answered without looking at the caller ID.

"I looked for Annika Banks in the Minnesota Department of Safety database. The Corvette's registration expired in 1976 and hasn't been reinstated. Annika's driver's license expired in 1977. She'd been ticketed for speeding several times, but her last citation was in 1975. Her credit history lists Visa, Sears, and Banana Republic credit cards, but none have been used since June of 1975. Her passport expired in 1978. She didn't vote in the 1976 or 1980 elections, so her voter registration was cancelled."

"She dropped off the face of the earth," I said as I took the van keys out of my desk. "Did anyone file a missing persons report?"

"Not in Two Harbors, Lake County, or St. Louis County."

I walked out the back door, then stopped. "Why wouldn't Deborah Evenson report her missing?"

"Evenson either bought into the story that Banks had flown to France, or she knew there was no reason to report her missing."

"Evenson knew Banks was dead."

"That would explain the cryptic blackmail note," Kerry said. "*I know what you did.*"

"I can't see Deborah Evenson killing her mother."

Kerry chuckled. "No one ever says, 'I knew he was a killer,' when we interview a criminal's neighbors. They all say, 'He was quiet, but nice.'"

"It doesn't fit, Kerry. Evenson was artistic and kind. She volunteered at the schools and donated her time and art to charities."

"Let's say she didn't kill Banks, but knew the professor was dead. If she wasn't complicit in the death, why wouldn't she report it?"

I walked to the van while I pondered that question. "Maybe Banks committed suicide and that's not how Evenson wanted her remembered."

"Where's her body? Did Evenson find Banks dead, then hide her body? Does that seem any more likely than the artist killing her?"

I unlocked the van and got inside. "Let me think about this for a while."

Kerry scoffed. "It's not like I'm rushing to solve a fifty-year-old murder. Take all the time you want. I've got protesters to deal with."

"The Svenska Gotters are back at the art studio?"

"Yes, and they've brought reinforcements. I'm parked across the street from the studio and a dozen people are marching up and down the sidewalk. I'll roll down the car window so you can hear them chanting."

As I pulled under the portico I heard, "*No Naked Models*" over the phone. "Sounds like they've shelved the newt protest. Is Sparky handling the media interviews?"

Kerry chuckled. "The mayor is here. He's got the street crew setting up barricades and they've put up a sign around the corner that says, 'media parking.'"

"Are any media people there?"

"Cassie is standing next to my car. Say hi, Cassie."

The red-headed teen must've leaned into Kerry's car. "Hi, Mr. Rogers. I'm back again today. Are you bringing your art class?"

"The art class is taking a field trip to the Tweed Museum this morning," I said as I opened the van door and stepped out, ready to help the class up the van's steps.

"Too bad, because the news would be more compelling if there was a confrontation."

"Not today," I said.

Kerry came back on the phone. "I appreciate you finding a different activity for the class today. This mob looks a little rowdier than the women yesterday. I heard a rumor that they've got day-old lake trout guts in a cooler. I heard that they plan to throw it at the models and students."

"Who leaked that information?" I asked as I helped Ginny Johnson up the steps.

"The mayor told me his wife went down to the harbor to collect fish guts this morning."

"He didn't stop her?"

Kerry chuckled. "I'm pretty sure he likes the publicity the Tall Ships Festival is getting on the news. He said three networks

286

interviewed Meg Cochran on their morning shows today. She's talking up the festival and promising it'll be a fun experience. I think out-of-state people will come just to hear the locals speaking with a Swedish accent."

"No more newts."

Karla overheard me and stopped. "The protest?"

I put my hand over the phone. "The protesters have rotten fish guts to throw at the models and art students."

"Yuk!"

"Did you hear that, Kerry? My art students are pleased they're going to miss the fireworks at the protest."

"It's just as well. A couple of the Duluth television stations are doing live broadcasts. The protesters are getting wound up. You wouldn't want to get in the middle of this."

With the last of the art students seated in the van, I closed the door and climbed into the driver's seat. "I've got to hang up. We're going to the UMD art museum."

"Uh oh."

I let the van idle without putting it into gear. "What's wrong?"

"Wendy's walking toward the studio. Apparently, she didn't receive the memo about the art class cancellation."

Karla, overhearing the conversation, tapped me on the shoulder. "GO! Drive into town!"

"It's a zoo and about to get crazier."

"I know! Drive!"

* * *

I didn't *speed* into town, but there wasn't any traffic, so I pushed the speed limit a bit. The east end of the barricaded block was empty, with the media and protesters in the middle or other end of the block. I parked the van next to the barricades so the passengers on the right side could see down the street. Almost immediately, I felt the van's weight shift as the ladies on the left side moved across the aisle so they could see the action.

Kerry, in full uniform, was out of his cruiser, facing away from us. Both news crews and the protesters were looking toward Wendy, who was helping Dolores, my former neighbor and the donor of my house, walk unsteadily down the sidewalk.

"What's Dolores doing here?" I asked.

"She wanted to sit in on the art class. I forgot that Wendy offered to drive her into town."

I watched in horror as Dolores and Wendy approached the protesters. I looked for Kerry, hoping he'd intervene, but his back was turned while an earnest looking young man asked him questions. Meanwhile, the mayor was being interviewed by the woman from the local CBS affiliate.

Wendy paused at the picket line as if she expected the women to let them pass.

Dolores, often a force of nature, forged ahead. When a young woman stepped in front of them, blocking their way, Dolores raised her cane and tapped the woman's arm. When the protester didn't move, Dolores drew her cane back and whacked the woman's knee.

Both interviews ended as the cameras abruptly swung to the picket line where the injured picketer was shrieking, jumping on one foot, and shouting unladylike comments at Dolores, who pushed past her and entered the studio.

Kathy, smiling, turned to me. "Some censor will need to bleep a lot of that rant before it airs."

I looked at Karla, who shrugged. "I suppose even Svenska Gotters have their limits."

"They're going to defrock her for that," Hulda said.

"I think they only defrock priests," Karla replied.

Hulda snorted. "Well, they'll do the Svenska Gotter equivalent of a defrocking."

Kathy nodded toward the protest. "It appears the police are getting involved."

The protesters gathered around the injured woman, who'd dropped her hockey stick protest banner and was now holding her knee. Wendy moved through the crowd quickly and followed Dolores into the studio, fish guts splattering the door as it closed.

"Aren't you going to do anything, Peter?" Karla asked.

I started the engine. "Everyone back in your seats. We're leaving for Duluth."

* * *

After unloading the ladies at UMD, I parked the van, and led them through the maze of hallways to the Tweed Museum. "Are we there yet?" Hulda asked as we rounded the second corner.

"We're about halfway to the museum."

"Why didn't you drop us off in the handicapped zone instead of halfway to Hinckley?"

The question brought chuckles from a number of residents who'd either attended UMD's sprawling campus or had visited the museum before."

"I dropped you off at the nearest door."

"They need to either put a door closer to the parking lot or add an elevator."

As often happened, Hulda had twisted her thoughts and words. "The museum is on the first floor. There's no need for an elevator."

"They need a side-to-side elevator for us old people."

"I'll put a note in the museum suggestion box," I replied.

I held the doors open as the ladies entered the museum. Hearing a gasp from

290

inside, I rushed to see if someone needed first aid. Instead, I found Ginny Johnson standing in front of a marble statue with her hand over her mouth. "It's lovely. See how the sculptor captured the shape of the model's muscles, just like Melissa taught us."

Hulda pushed past Ginny and stopped a foot away from the sculpture, which stood atop a pedestal. "Bah! Someone put a leaf over his crotch."

The comment brought a round of chuckles. Kathy, who was standing close to Hulda, said, "Look at the detail the sculptor put into the veins of the leaf. It's exquisite."

"I don't want to see veins in a leaf. If someone's going to take the time to carve a man out of a rock, they should include all the parts." Hulda glared at me. "I suppose they had censors back then."

"One of the popes used a hammer to remove all the male appendages from the Vatican's sculptures."

"I suppose that's in line with that Catholic celebrity thing. He neutered them all."

Karla couldn't stand it. "It's celibacy, not celebrity."

"That's what I said! Don't go correcting me. I said celebrity, and that's what I meant. The Popes all practice celebrity."

Taking Hulda's elbow, I guided her deeper into the museum. "The Evenson show is this way."

Lights flashed from the room ahead. Murmured voices came from the Evenson exhibit. Inside, we found the graphic arts professor set up in front of the Evenson diptych, his camera mounted on a tripod facing the paintings. Two students arranged lights while the curator stood back, watching.

Blankenship walked over to our group when he noticed us enter the room. "Such a distinguished group of artists," he said, offering his hand to each of the ladies.

Wrinkling her nose, Hulda refused his offered handshake. "I know when someone's blowing smoke up my butt."

The look I got from Blankenship was priceless. "My condolences," he said.

Karla nodded. "Well put."

"What's going on?" I asked.

Dr. Quill looked up from his camera, obviously annoyed by what he felt was an intrusion. "I'm capturing the hidden images. By altering the light, I can bring out details that are hidden when lit by the overhead lights."

"Like you talked about by closing one eye to take out the three-dimensional aspects or, using black and white so our eyes aren't drawn to the colors."

Quill sighed. "That's a simplistic view of what I'm doing. There are many techniques: F-stop, exposure time, UV and IR filters, and focus all affect what the camera brings out."

He turned away and directed his helpers to relocate the lights.

"Who stuck a broom up his butt?" Hulda asked, in an outdoor voice.

The curator's eyes twinkled, hearing what he'd probably thought a hundred times. He steered us to a corner of the room where a display table was set up. "Here are some of the photos Dr. Quill took earlier today."

The photos captured aspects of the paintings I'd never visualized. The black and white photos brought out detail hidden by the colors, and his use of light and lens filters brought out different details in other photos. The ladies moved around the table, most with their hands behind their backs, not touching the glossy photos. Hulda pushed her walker against the table and picked up the nearest photo, a black and white image that brought out the landscape in the two paintings.

"That blowhard doesn't even own a color camera. They probably weren't invented yet when he was born."

Karla and Kathy stood on the far side of the table speaking in whispers. Karla gestured for me to join them. "This photo captured a map of downtown Two Harbors," Karla said, pointing to a slightly out of focus black and white photo. Pointing to a diagonal line, she said, "That's where Highway 61 was in the 1970s."

Extending a slender finger without touching the photo, Kathy said, "That cross is about where Evenson's studio is built."

Karla shook her head and pointed to a square near the cross. "You can see the driveway running from the road to the studio. The cross is nearby, but not in the studio."

Kathy spread her fingers and waved them over the photo. "Everything here represents something. She's captured all the businesses, churches, and the residential areas. Here are the harbor and lighthouse. Every single mark represents something. What does the cross mean?"

My look must've signaled a moment of revelation, because the two women looked at me, expecting an answer. "Excuse me. I have to make a call."

I punched Kerry's number into my phone as I walked out of the Evenson exhibit. "How's the protest?" I asked, hearing chants in the background.

"Damned church ladies are a lot of bother. There are five news people here for every one of the protesters, and the protesters are all trying to get their sound bite and five seconds of fame. They step into the street without looking, they're yelling at each other, and they've irritated the mayor. I'm about ready to tell Sparky to turn a fire hose on them."

After checking to make sure I was alone, I said, "I know where Annika Banks is."

"Where is she? Wait. Let me guess first. She's in Montreal, the Paris of North America."

"She's buried behind Evenson's studio."

"Hang on. I have to get somewhere quiet to hear you." A moment later, he was back. "Okay, I'm inside my cruiser. Where is Annika Banks?"

"She's buried behind Evenson's studio."

"Where did you come up with that revelation? Is there something in the box of documents you've been digging through?"

"We're at the Tweed Museum. There's a professor taking pictures of the paintings, trying to bring out hidden details. One of the pictures brought out what appears to be a map of Two Harbors. There's a cross behind Evenson's studio."

Kerry sighed. "I'm not bringing out cadaver dogs and a forensics team based on a cross in a painting. Is this like a treasure map with an 'X' that marks the spot?"

"Everything in that painting means something. She didn't throw a random cross into that composition because of the aesthetics. I think it's marking Annika Banks' grave."

"I'll tell you what I'd like to do. Bring your art class back to Two Harbors, eat lunch, find a couple shovels, then drive into town. The news people are wrapping up and once they're gone, the protesters are going to lose interest. I'll ask the street crew to take down

295

the barricades and then I'll be ready to drive up to the studio. We'll find the 'X' that's undoubtedly spray painted on a tree, and we'll dig."

"I'm serious, Kerry."

"I know you are. But I'm a cynical cop who doesn't believe in witches, ghosts, voodoo, or crosses marking graves in paintings. I'm willing to humor you. Hell, I'm ready to believe you if it'll get me away from these goofy protesters."

The volume of the protest rose suddenly. "What happened?"

"Aw shit. Melissa's got a mister and she's spraying the protesters with blue dye. I've got to go." He paused. "Holy Hannah, Dolores has a gun!"

A moment later I was listening to a dial tone. I hit redial, but Kerry's phone rolled over to voicemail. I tried Wendy, but she didn't answer either.

Chapter 20

After luring the residents out of the museum by promising to buy them lunch at McDonalds, I drove the van down 21st Avenue to the fast-food restaurant. I helped the women carry their meals to tables. When they were settled, I walked outside and called Kerry. Although I expected his phone to roll over to voicemail, he answered after the third ring. "Checking up on the mayhem, Peter?"

"Did Dolores shoot anyone?"

Chuckling, Kerry said, "She came out of the studio leading with the tip of her cane. She had the handle tucked under her arm, covered by her shawl so it looked like a rifle. One of the protesters shouted, 'gun!' which dispersed everyone except for Kirsten Martin, who tripped on the curb and sprawled into the street. She kept yelling, 'Save me, you cowards,' while the rest of them ran to their cars and drove away."

"What happened to Kirsten?"

"Melissa sprayed her with blue dye until she crawled across the street. Last I saw,

Kirsten looked like a Smurf driving off in a Volvo."

"Are Wendy and Dolores safe?"

"We're eating lunch together at Judy's Café. They're just fine, although all of downtown smells like fish guts." Kerry paused. "What's happening with your art class?"

"They're chowing down on Big Macs and fries. We'll probably be back at Whistling Pines in two hours. I'll drop them off and drive home. I've got a couple shovels in the garage."

"I'll pick you up at home." Kerry said. "The department has a metal detector. I'll bring it along."

"Does it have a dead body setting?"

"Um, no. Most bodies are buried with belt buckles, rings, and other metal that a detector can pick up if it's not buried too deep."

"What makes you think she's not buried very deep?"

"In my experience, most killers don't waste a lot of time digging. They excavate the proverbial shallow grave, dump the body, then shovel the dirt back on top. If the metal detector doesn't work, we can dig, but I'd rather use my brain and a metal detector, than digging random holes."

"What if there's an 'X' painted on a tree?"

After sighing, Kerry said, "Peter, if there's an X on a tree, I'll buy you a steak dinner."

* * *

I slipped past the dining room, avoiding conversations with the residents while walking down the hallway. Jenny was talking to one of the aides about a chart when I stepped into the medical office. Surprised to see me in the middle of the day, Jenny wrapped up her conversation with the aide and waved me in. "What's wrong?"

"I'm driving to the Evenson studio with Kerry. I might be late."

"How late?"

After making sure no one could overhear us, I said, "Karla and Kathy discovered a map hidden in the Evenson diptych. There's a cross painted behind the studio where I think Annika Banks is buried."

"Why doesn't Kerry call in the Bureau of Criminal Apprehension forensics team?"

"I'm not *sure* she's buried there. It's more of a gut feeling."

Jenny closed her eyes and looked upward, as if beseeching the heavens. "So, you and Kerry are going up there with shovels to dig holes where a painting depicts a cross. Right?"

"You make it sound stupid."

Jenny opened her eyes and licked her lips. "If you'd said it out loud instead of listening to the voices in your head, you might've realized how stupid it sounds."

"Kerry's bringing a metal detector."

Looking at me as if she thought she needed to move me to a mental health facility, Jenny said, "Metal detectors can't locate buried remains."

"Kerry thinks there might be some metal with the remains."

"I can't believe you talked Kerry into this. He's…sane."

"He's not entirely convinced. He said he'll buy me a steak dinner if we find anything."

"Let's up the ante on Kerry's bet. When you don't find anything, you're going to take Kerry, Deb, and me out for steak dinners with wine."

"Why are you on his side?"

I got the *stupid question* glare. "Maybe you'll learn to keep your nose out of his investigations."

"Um, actually this is more *my* investigation. Kerry's never bought in. He's been unwilling to commit any of his officers to this."

"Perhaps there's a message there." Jenny flipped her wrist. "Go! I've got the kids. Have fun digging holes in the woods. Call me if you find buried treasure."

I wrapped my arms around her, and we hugged. "You're a good sport. This should be the end of this whole Evenson thing."

"How about the nude models at the art class? Is that at an endpoint, too?"

"That is not my thing. Melissa has arranged all the subject matter for the art class. All I do is drive the ladies back and forth."

"Uh huh. You had nothing to do with the UMD student who's been modeling, and you didn't encourage Wendy to contact Melissa."

"I didn't..." I let out a breath. "Okay, I gave the model's number to Melissa, but she handled the arrangements."

"Just go play cop. Okay?"

"I'll try to make it quick."

"Do whatever you need to do. Satisfy your curiosity. I'll be at home taking care of our children like a faithful wife."

* * *

Kerry's unmarked cruiser was idling in our driveway. I retrieved two spades from the garage and set them in the back seat.

"Jenny is not pleased about this adventure."

"Did you think she would be?" Kerry asked as he backed onto the street.

"What did you tell Deb?"

"I said you were dragging me off on a wild goose chase."

"Well, thanks for the vote of confidence."

301

"No problem. My only guilt in this is admitting that I'll be hanging out with you, whose sanity is currently in question."

I turned to face Kerry. "Who is questioning my sanity?"

"Let's see. I had lunch with Meg Cochran and the Mayor. They both think you're certifiably crazy."

"Because we're looking for Annika Banks' body?"

Kerry shook his head. "The mayor is angry because you allowed the whole nude modeling thing to get out of hand." When I tried to interrupt, Kerry went on. "Meg is pleased that you got the Svenka Gotters stirred up and created a lot of interest in the upcoming Tall Ship Festival. She's convinced you're nuts for going about it the way you did, but she's pleased with the resulting publicity."

"Who else was at lunch?"

"Kevin Jenkins and Pastor Olafson."

"They don't think I'm crazy," I said.

"Pastor Olafson is too polite to call anyone crazy. I think he said you were 'somewhat overzealous.'"

"What about Kevin?"

"He never rendered an opinion. He just laughed about the art studio protest and the idea of looking for a missing woman based on a cross in a painting."

When Kerry turned the corner toward the studio, I saw a dark pickup idling near the mailbox. Kerry seemed to ignore it and was unconcerned when it followed us up the winding driveway. We parked behind a Two Harbors cruiser, and the pickup pulled behind us, blocking our exit.

"Do you know who's in the pickup?"

"You'll see in a minute."

I stepped out of the car and watched Pastor Olafson, who I'd never seen in jeans before, get out of the passenger's door. Kevin Jenkins, wearing his Department of Natural Resources uniform, exited on the other side.

"Why are you here?" I asked.

Olafson smiled as he took a shovel out of the pickup. "I've never been on a treasure hunt before."

Kevin hung a set of earphones around his neck and lifted out a metal detector.

"The DNR owns a metal detector?" I asked.

"I use it a few times a year to recover evidence. It's handy for locating spent bullets when I'm investigating poachers."

Kerry removed a metal detector from his cruiser's trunk and closed the lid. "Okay Blackbeard, lead us to the treasure."

Seeing the commotion outside the house, Linda Fouts, the part-time officer providing security at the studio, stepped outside. "What in hell are you guys doing?"

Kerry glanced at me, then smiled. "Peter found an 'X' on a treasure map and we're going to dig up the hidden treasure."

Linda locked the door and fell in behind us. "I've never seen a treasure hunt before. What are you looking for, gold?"

Irritated about all the mockery, I didn't answer, but led the group behind the studio. The unmown lawn ended abruptly in wild raspberries, then open woods under pine trees. I stopped at the tree line and looked at the bed of pine needles covering the podzol soil. I'd expected to see a raised area that looked like a grave. Instead, all I saw was rolling ground covered with pinecones and golden pine needles.

I looked back at the others who were watching expectantly. "I don't see the 'X'. I think this is the general area depicted in the map."

Kevin pulled the earphones up and switched on his metal detector. "Let's start in the middle. I'll go left. Kerry, you go to the right."

We hadn't walked ten yards before Kerry's metal detector beeped. He stopped, swinging the hoop back and forth until the buried metal was centered under it. "Dig here."

My pulse pounded as I scraped aside the pine needles. The ground looked undisturbed, and my shovel only penetrated a few inches before hitting a root. I scooped up the soil I could move and turned it over. Kerry signaled for me to stop, then he scanned the scoop of soil, which caused the metal detector to whoop.

Falling to my knees, I pulled apart the clump of soil, exposing…a pull tab from a 1960s soda pop can. I held it up, showing Kerry.

"Someone sat out here and had a Tab or RC cola back in the day," he said. "Let's keep going."

The pastor and Kevin stopped to our left and went through the same routine, recovering an aluminum beer can that had been opened with a can opener, from the days before pull tabs.

Linda chuckled. "This must've been the party place when the residents were young."

Kerry, Linda, and I found a brass jeans button, another pull tab, and a tiny cast metal car. Kevin and Olafson weren't stopping as often, apparently having an area that was less frequently used by Evenson and her partying friends.

Kerry paused when the metal detector made a different, louder beeping sound. "This is something bigger or more solid."

My shovel sunk into the soil much more easily, hitting only tiny roots in the sandy soil. There was nothing in my first shovel of soil, but Kerry verified I was digging in the correct spot. My shovel hit something solid, with a *click* when I pushed it a second time. I scraped the soil aside with nothing in the dirt I removed. I was about to dig again when I noticed that the shovel's blade had scraped something. Shiny metal reflected the sunlight filtering through the covering pines.

"Stop, Peter," Kerry said, pulling off the headphones. "Scrape around it with your fingers."

Linda pushed close and swept dirt aside with her fingers. "What is it?"

"I don't know yet." I used the edge of my hand like a trowel and scraped aside the soil around the metal that eventually emerged as a small brass belt buckle. I'd nicked it with the shovel, exposing the shiny brass under the patina of corrosion caused by the years it had been buried in the acidic soil. Kerry set the metal detector aside and called to Kevin and Olafson. Together, we gently moved soil until we exposed a zipper and denim.

I heard Olafson speaking softly behind me after exposing part of a skull. I looked up and realized he was praying with his eyes closed. I was going to dig deeper with my fingers when Kerry stopped Linda and me. "Quit. We need the BCA to excavate the body."

"But…"

Kerry stood and picked up his gear. "This is a crime scene. We've already contaminated it. We need to leave the rest for the forensics people."

"But we don't know who it is yet?" I protested.

Kerry put his hand on my arm and turned me away from the excavation. "Your job is done, and I owe you a steak dinner."

"You're sure it's Annika Banks?"

"Is anyone else missing?"

* * *

The remainder of the afternoon was a swirl of activity at the police department. After calling Jenny to explain what we'd found, I typed up a statement explaining how I'd identified the location of the remains and summarizing the details of uncovering the belt buckle. I signed the statement and brought it to Kerry's office. "Here you go, Chief."

Kerry looked away from his computer. "Close the door."

I sat in his guest chair and asked, "What's going on?"

"The BCA mobile crime lab will be here in the morning. I had Linda tape off the entire area behind the house and I'll have an officer stay there until they arrive. Bring back the box from Evenson's garage. I'll need a statement saying it's been in your control and hasn't been altered or tampered with since you removed it."

"Wow. You're taking this seriously."

"Do you think Charlie Crowder killed her?" Kerry asked.

I reflected on the images in the diptych and Evenson's scrawled comments in her log. "I think Crowder killed her, then took the painting of Banks."

"I don't understand why Evenson never reported it."

I thought through the pieces I knew and extrapolated. "We'll never have evidence that'll stand up in court, but I think Crowder killed her and somehow made Evenson complicit in the murder or disposal of the body so she would never tell. That's what the blackmail note was about. Someone overheard Crowder talking about it and was blackmailing Evenson."

"That's a lot of conjecture."

"There won't be a court case. Everyone involved is dead."

Kerry picked up a pen and clicked the mechanism. "There won't be a criminal case, but it sounds like there's going to be a fight over Evenson's trust and estate. Once the Crowder family members hear that we've found a body buried behind the studio, all hell will break loose. The Crowder heirs are already arguing that Evenson violated the morality clause in the trust, so the entire trust and estate are theirs."

"The University won't get Evenson's paintings?"

"I spoke with the Evenson Trustee. He consulted with the UMD legal counsel, and we agreed that the art and studio were Deborah Evenson's personal property, not part of the Evenson trust. They'll go to the university under the terms of her will. The Evenson trust is a charitable foundation which is meant to provide perpetual support to northern Minnesota arts and art education. The trustee said Charlie Crowder added a clause to the Evenson trust that says anyone contesting the Crowder or Evenson trusts can't benefit from either of them. The trustee said once the family's lawyers read the trust, the discussion of lawsuits will be over."

"What about Nettie, the girl who sent her birthday cards? Could she be Deborah Evenson's illegitimate child and the heir to her estate?"

Kerry sighed. "Why don't you make that your next mystery?"

"I'm going home."

Kerry stood and took out his keys. "Have you forgotten that I picked you up and drove you to the studio?"

"Will you give me a ride home?"

"You forgot the magic word."

"Mr. Police Chief, will you please drive me home?"

Pushing me toward the door, he shook his head. "I can pick up the box of Evenson correspondence while I'm at your house."

309

Something tickled the reaches of my memory when Kerry mentioned the correspondence. "I'd like to look through the letters one more time."

"Something is eating at you," Kerry said as we walked to his car.

"Yeah, I read something that didn't make sense, but I can't remember the author or context."

* * *

Jenny was in bed and the kids were asleep when I got home. Still keyed up over discovery of the body, I opened the box of letters and started leafing through them. Having previously read them, I flipped through them quickly, bypassing personal correspondence and cards. My eyes were starting to droop when I found the letter from the Chicago Institute of Art.

September 3, 1975

Dear Ms. Evenson,

Thank you for the donation of your painting, "Reclining Nude." We've displayed it in our collection of modern American art where it's generating significant interest. It's a truly wonderful piece.

Sincerely,
Gerald Matthews
Curator

I set the letter aside and took out Evenson's painting log. Flipping through the pages, I found her scrawled note about the painting, "Nikki", being taken by "that bastard." The painting had been started in June 1975, then had been taken at some later date.

Repeating Blankeship's internet search of the Chicago Institute of Art catalogue brought me to the Evenson painting "Reclining Nude". I immediately recognized Annika Banks as the model. I tipped my head back. "Evenson called her mother Nikki, not Annika."

Closing my eyes, I visualized Annika's room at the studio with an adjoining door to…the room with men's clothing. I punched Kerry's cellphone number into my phone.

"Please tell me you butt dialed me," Kerry's sleepy voice said.

"Crowder wasn't having an affair with Deborah Evenson. His affair was with her mother, Annika Banks."

"That couldn't have waited until morning. No, wait. It is morning. Geez, Peter."

"Crowder became enraged when he discovered that Evenson was painting a nude of Annika Banks. He took the painting and donated it to a museum. I've got a letter of thanks from the curator for a painting called *Reclining Nude*. Having seen Banks' faculty photo, I've realized it's the painting of Annika Banks."

"You called me at two in the morning to tell me the Chicago institute of Art has a nude painting of Annika Banks?"

"It's the key to the whole case, Kerry. I think Crowder was having an affair with Banks and when he saw that Deborah Evenson was painting her nude, he went nuts and killed Banks. He took the painting and donated it to the museum. Evenson got even by painting the diptych depicting Crowder stabbing her mother, but then decided she had to keep the two paintings separate so Crowder would never see the hidden image."

"Go to bed. We'll talk in the morning."

Chapter 21

Kerry called just as I finished my sandwich. "The BCA excavated the body this morning. The driver's license, charge cards, and passport in the grave belonged to Annika Banks. It's going to take the medical examiner a few days to positively identify the remains, but we can assume it's Deborah Evenson's mother."

"Do we know what killed her?"

"Well, it's safe to say she wasn't stabbed by Charlie Crowder's pointed tail."

I sighed. "I was pretty sure of that."

"Do you know what a palette knife is?"

"In general, yes. They're the tools artists use to spread paint to give texture."

"The BCA tech sent me a picture of a wooden-handled knife found in the grave. It looks like a narrow, pointed trowel. There are traces of blood where the metal meets the wood. They're assuming it was the murder weapon."

"The Devil's pointy tail," I said.

"You seemed convinced that a lot of the things depicted in the diptych paintings were real."

"It's only a work of art, not a crime scene photo."

* * *

That afternoon, I sipped coffee and listened to the Whistling Pines rumor mill's version of the discovery of Annika Banks' body and the wrap up of the Evenson case, as retold by Kathy Christensen and Karla Telker. Their version was much closer to reality than the Hulda Packer version that included a downtown shootout involving the Two Harbors Police, Minnesota State Patrol, and the National Guard.

When there was a break in the conversation, I took Karla aside and whispered, "There were birthday cards in Deborah Evenson's things from someone who signed them, 'Nettie.' Do you know who that was?"

Deep in thought, Karla stared at me for a second, then broke into a smile. "That's probably Annette Anderson. She lived down the hill from the Evenson studio and absolutely adored Deborah. I heard she had tea with Deborah and Annika occasionally."

"Was she related to Evenson or Banks?"

"I don't think so. I remember Dolly Anderson being very pregnant with Nettie, and I'm reasonably certain neither Banks nor Evenson were her father."

"Has anyone ever called you a smartass?"

"My very religious brother calls me a smart aleck, but everyone else uses the term smartass." Karla nodded toward the door. "Peter, I think you're being summoned."

Kerry Stone was filling cups of coffee at the urn and the director was beckoning to me with her hand. Kathy, who'd developed an affinity for needling me, smiled. "Was it something you said, thought, or did?"

"Who knows?"

"It's too bad you're not as old as us," Karla said. "Having had a senior moment is a great excuse, but not until you're eligible for Medicare."

Nancy accepted a mug from Kerry. "Let's sit in my office."

I looked at Kerry, but he seemed uninformed about the meeting agenda. "I received an email today that will interest you." She put on a pair of reading glasses and removed a sheet of paper from the lap drawer of her desk. I could see the shadow of a letterhead from the backside of the paper.

Dear Madam Director,

Chief Stone has informed me of the invaluable contributions made by Peter Rogers while aiding in the closure of the Evenson estate. I understand that Mr. Rogers is the recreation director at Whistling

Pines Senior Residence, and has declined our offer of remuneration for his assistance. In lieu of payment for his services, the Evenson trust is making a contribution to the Whistling Pines Recreation fund. We stipulate that this first annual grant be used for art related programming, with a portion supplementing the recreation director's salary.

G. Michael Winston

Deborah Evenson Trustee

Nancy handed the letter to Kerry, then withdrew a bank statement from the drawer and handed it to me. I looked at the highlighted deposit. Unable to believe the numerical amount, I read it aloud, "One hundred thousand dollars."

"Nancy, this is more than my entire recreation budget. How am I going to spend that much on art programs?"

"I had a teleconference with the Whistling Pines board members and they agreed that a quarter of the Crowder Foundation grant will be used for your salary."

Nodding my assent, I said, "That will free up a lot of money for other things."

"You misunderstood me. You're getting a twenty-five-thousand dollar a year raise. Obviously, that will be reduced by Social Security and tax withholding."

316

Kerry elbowed me. "Don't spend it all in one place."

"But..."

Nancy waved off my protest. "I feel, and the board agrees, that your contributions go far beyond the role of recreation director. Your community outreach activities are raising the awareness and value of Whistling Pines to Two Harbors, and we're formally expanding your title to Recreation and Community Outreach Director. You will be the Whistling Pines representative to the Chamber of Commerce and our public safety liaison."

I closed my eyes and tipped my head back. "I barely have time to handle the things currently on my plate."

"Bingle, our part time maintenance man, has agreed to work full time. He'll be driving the van for outings. Wendy, who's underutilized in her current assistant director position, will plan and show the weekly movie."

Looking at Kerry, I asked, "What's involved in the public safety liaison position?"

"You'll be my sounding board."

"Please expand on that."

Nancy cleared her throat. "Chief Stone occasionally needs someone to assist with investigations and to consult on police coverage of city events, like concerts and festivals. He suggested that you meet for

317

half an hour weekly to address the issues he foresees."

"How does ten o'clock Tuesday mornings at Judy's fit into your schedule?" Kerry asked.

"Are you buying coffee?"

"I think the police department can afford coffee *and* a slice of pie."

Nancy smiled, stood, then stepped around her desk and hugged me. "Thanks for all you do."

Unaccustomed to any show of affection or emotion from Nancy, I was struck speechless. I patted her back, then retreated out the door. Kerry shook my hand in the hallway.

"What was your role in all this?" I asked.

"I knew you wouldn't accept a check from the Evenson trust, so I discussed your tiny recreation budget, and your equally modest salary. The trustee suggested an annual art grant. I hope this moves you into a salary bracket where you no longer qualify for food stamps."

"I've never applied for…"

Kerry's grin told me how much he enjoyed kidding me.

"What's going to happen to Annika Banks' body?"

"We found her nephew in St. Cloud. He's working with Pastor Olafson to arrange a funeral when the remains are released." Kerry paused and chuckled. "He's very excited about inheriting a cherry red 1966 Corvette in mint condition."

"I suppose inheriting a classic Corvette would cushion the blow of getting the news that your missing aunt has been found." I paused while a memory tapped on the back of my head, refusing to reveal itself. "What about the blackmail note?"

"I emailed a copy of the note to Mr. G. Michael Winston and asked if there was anything in the trust file indicating that a blackmail payment had ever been made. He's only been the trustee for the past twelve years and had no knowledge of any blackmail claims. The only financial discrepancy he found was a check for $25,000 made out to Evenson shortly after Charlie Crowder's death. He couldn't find any explanation for the payment, and there's no notation of what Evenson did with the money."

"Do you think it was a payoff?"

"My cop instinct says, probably not. Blackmailers tend to return to the well to squeeze more money out of the victim. On the other hand, the grammar tells me the author was unsophisticated, so he or she may have been happy to take the money and run. It's one of those things we'll never know because all the parties to the transaction are dead."

"I just..."

"Leave it, Peter. The statute of limitations has passed, and all the involved parties are probably dead. We solved a murder case because of your bulldog determination. That's enough for one week."

"I guess…"

"If you and Jenny don't have other plans tonight, Deb and I would love to have you over for supper."

"I'm sure Jeremy would like to spend an evening with Jacob, if you don't mind having a sometimes-unhappy baby in the house."

"To be honest, Deb has been trying not to overwhelm Jenny with offers to visit or babysit. She really likes holding a baby again."

"Amy has her moments, but she's been a little fussy lately. Are you sure you want us to come over?"

"As long as you take Amy home with you when you leave, we'll be happy to have her."

Jenny wasn't in her office, so I called her cell phone and asked her to meet me in my office. When she arrived, I gestured for her to sit in my guest chair, then I closed and locked the door.

"This looks ominous," she said.

I sat down, took her hands and leaned forward. "There's nothing bad going on." After that introduction, I told her about the meeting with Nancy, my expanded job, the raise, the disposition of Annika Banks' estate, and about Kerry's supper invitation.

"You're getting a twenty-five-thousand dollar raise?"

"Yes."

She leaned forward and kissed me. "That probably makes you the third highest paid person in Whistling Pines."

"After Nancy and Wendy?"

Jenny snorted. "After Nancy and the head cook. Food is *very* important."

"How do you feel about dinner with Kerry and Deb?"

"Buy a couple bottles of wine on your way home. We'll celebrate your promotion."

"I don't know if I should get white or red."

Jenny stood up and pecked my lips. "Get two bottles of each, dear. We can afford it." She opened the door, then peeked out to see if anyone was nearby. "Who knows, if you get a couple glasses of wine in me, we might have a private celebration after the children fall asleep."

The End

If you enjoyed this book, please leave a review.

Other Dean Hovey mysteries from BWL Publishing Inc.

Whistling Pines cozies
Whistling up a Ghost
Whistling Pirates
Whistling Bake Off
Whistling Artist

Doug Fletcher mysteries
Stolen Past
Washed Away
Devils Fall
Prairie Menace
Down River
Burnt Evidence
Gator Bait
Dead End Trail
The Last Rodeo (coming in 2023)

Pine County Mysteries
Killer Secrets
Deadly Mixture
Fatal Business
Taxed to Death (Coming in 2023)

Dean Hovey is the award-winning and best-selling author of three mystery series. He uses his scientific background, extensive research, and consultants to add reality and depth to his stories. One reader said his characters are like people he'd like to invite over for a beer and discussion.

Hovey's Doug Fletcher mysteries follow U.S. National Park Service investigators Doug and Jill Fletcher as their investigations take them to national parks from coast to coast. The Whistling Pines mysteries are humorous cozies set in a northern Minnesota senior residence, following Peter Rogers, the Whistling Pines recreation director, as he stumbles through the investigation of murders in his small town. The Pine County mystery series follows sheriff's deputies Pam Ryan, Floyd Swenson, and C.J. Jensen as they investigate murders in rural east-central Minnesota.

Dean and his wife split their year between northern Minnesota and Arizona.